Unfinished Business

BLUE FEATHER BOOKS, LTD.

Unfinished Business

A BLUE FEATHER BOOK

by

I. Christie

This is a work of fiction. All characters, locales and events are either products of the author's imagination or are used fictitiously.

UNFINISHED BUSINESS

Cover design by Ann Phillips

A Blue Feather Book
Published by Blue Feather Books, Ltd.
P.O. Box 5867
Atlanta, GA 31107-5967

www.bluefeatherbooks.com

ISBN: 978-1-935627-91-3

First edition: September, 2010

Printed in the United States of America and in the United Kingdom.

Acknowledgements

I would like to thank the dedicated and talented editing staff of Blue Feather Books for getting this story to market.

Chapter 1

Claire Hanson was having a streak of good luck that any veteran cop would suspect was a setup for something unpleasant. Even ordinary folks would expect something bad to end the streak, just to balance the scales of life. Her luck went like this: Monday, she won five hundred bucks in the office pool; Tuesday, a coworker asked to swap vacation time, which meant she would have two weeks off starting at the end of the week; Tuesday night, she was able to reserve her favorite campsite with a guarantee of no crowds and make arrangements for a cat-sitter on short notice; Friday morning, she checked the weather forecast for the coming week and no rain showed up; and to top it all off, she left work early to beat the Friday traffic. Wasn't that an unusual run of good luck for anyone?

As a general rule, she didn't do office pools, bet on the ponies, or attend late-night card games. However, her normal safe distance from the department's gambling group was breached by Officer Philip Mosley, her boss Jackson's weasel. His sales pitch was, "I got one square in the office pool with your name in it, so pay up, lackey." Officer Mosley, four times her size and all in bulk muscle, wore his uniform shirt so tight the pressed creases were like spider lines across his body.

Mosley was intimidating. His nickname could be "gorilla," but saying it could get you slammed, should you accidentally utter it. Shaking her head to forget the darker side of how she'd gotten involved in the office pool, she instead focused on the freeway off-ramp that would take her to Broadway Boulevard and then to her apartment.

Claire decided not to waste any time looking for a legal spot to park and claimed the red curb in front of her apartment building. She punched on her hazard lights and slid out of her vehicle. She gave a casual look for anyone likely to call parking enforcement. The curtains to John's apartment parted, and he peered out.

"Mr. Neighborhood Watch," she said. She glanced at her watch. "Twenty minutes to beat parking enforcement, and that's on his best days."

Taking the outside stairs two-at-a-time to her second-floor apartment, she paused at the landing to look over the neighborhood. Stopping served two purposes—she admired the view of the neighborhood through tree limbs, and she checked to see who was about. Many times, calling out loudly had discouraged taggers and drive-by thieves on bicycles from carrying out their intentions. That was her contribution to the Neighborhood Watch Program. Their weekly meetings told her way more than what she wanted to know about her neighbors who weren't there. She took a deep breath and reminded herself that she was starting her vacation. It was time to relax.

If there were room up here for more than a potted plant, I'd sit out here and pretend I was in a tree house. She chuckled at the impossibility of that ever happening. She jingled her keys to let the cats know it was her, unlocked the door, and stepped into the front room.

Both cats were on the four-tiered cat pole near the bay window. Cleopatra yawned and stood up on her perch, giving a slow, languid stretch. Ramses blinked at her as if to indicate her arrival was not a major event in his day. She spotted two flattened paper bags on the floor. It was a small pleasure to know the amusements she'd left behind were appreciated.

The previous night, she'd packed the trunk of her car with most of the supplies she'd need for her camping trip. The rest she'd left on the kitchen table so she could easily lift them without bending over. A pulled back muscle wasn't going to end her camping trip before she even got started. She tucked the box under her arm and hoisted the pack with her art equipment to her shoulder. As she thumped down the stairs, she gave a silent prayer that she wouldn't fall or drop anything. She dumped the box and backpack on the backseat and glanced down the street. Satisfied a parking enforcement vehicle wasn't rounding the corner, she ran back upstairs. She undressed in front of the washer and dryer in the utility room and tossed her clothes on top of the heap of clothes in the overflowing hamper. To her amazement, nothing toppled to the floor.

She entered her bedroom. Her camping clothes lay on her bed, and her hiking boots and thick socks sat ready on the floor. As she dressed, she did a mental recap for anything she might have forgotten. She didn't want to remember something later and have to stop on her way to the campsite. She needed to get her tent set up before it got dark. Last time, she'd had to put up her tent by the light of her car headlamps. When she'd crawled into her sleeping bag, the unmistakable smell told her she'd set up camp on top of dog poop left behind by the previous camper. Nope, she didn't need to relive that experience. If she forgot anything, she could get it at the camp store.

She checked the HK P7 pistol she wore off-duty and slid it into its holster resting on her hip. A baggy T-shirt that fell to her thighs covered it. As she left the bedroom, she stopped at the two flattened bags and reopened them. The apartment was cat-ready with boxes, paper bags without handles, and kitty toys spread around to keep them from being bored. She was still amazed that, at age thirty-eight, she was able to adapt to having two cats live with her.

"I want you two to behave nicely for the cat-sitter."

Claire glanced out the window at her car. No parking enforcement car and no ticket stuck under her windshield wiper yet.

"Bye, guys."

She closed the door and tested the lock before she ran down the stairs. She thought ahead to setting up camp in a choice spot near the river. She knew the camp area well, and visiting it during the off-season was a real plus.

Her luck was holding. She'd been there over ten minutes and still no parking officer. She started her car and pulled out. Next stop would be at Gail and Margie's to pick up Teddy, a Welsh Corgi mix dog who loved to go camping. Traffic was still light, and she reached her destination without having to use the freeway. She made a right onto Parker Avenue and saw official No Parking paper signs on both sides of the road. She parked near one of the signs and got out of her car.

Margie was standing on the porch, staring unhappily at a paper in her hand.

"Hey, Margie. How's it going?" Claire asked.

"Good." She looked up and smiled distractedly, then suddenly brightened up. "Can you do me a favor?"

"If it doesn't mean I have to give up my vacation, sure."

"I'd never do that to you. You're primed and ready, girlfriend." Margie waved her paper toward the posted No Parking signs. "The city waterworks is digging a trench along the street for pipe repair, meaning no parking day or night for about a week, or so they say."

"Yeah?"

Margie pointed at her custom-built Dodge Roadtrek motor home, dubbed the Molly Bree, parked in the driveway. "Molly Bree and our two SUVs don't fit in our driveway, but your compact car and the two SUVs will. Would you mind taking the Molly Bree camping? I can call Kelly and have you added to our van insurance coverage. Do you still have her as your agent?"

"I do. Are you sure you want me taking the Molly Bree?"

"Yes. The newness has worn off, and I can lend her out to people I trust without getting the shakes." Margie held her freckled hand out showing how steady it was. They both laughed.

"I'd love to help out."

"You're already helping us out by taking Teddy camping with you. If she doesn't get out at least once a month, she chews everything she can get her jaws wrapped around. She's eaten one of my slippers, and I know if she gets to Gail's, I'd better have another pair on hand, or Teddy's in trouble. Gail took her to the vet yesterday for her Lyme disease shot, and she's had her flea and tick treatment. Don't forget to put sunblock on her nose and ears if she's out in the sun. And don't leave her out alone on a leash. She'll tangle herself. We usually lock her in the motor home with the air conditioner on."

Claire nodded, making a mental note not to leave anything except Teddy's toys low enough to reach if she left her alone in the motor home.

Margie moved her SUV and the motor home out of the driveway, and Claire drove her car into the spot where the motor home had been. While Margie reparked her SUV behind Claire's car, Claire unloaded what she needed. She made two piles: "keepers" and "leave behind."

"We just restocked our emergency first-aid kit, so you don't have to take yours," Margie said. "We've got books you can exchange at the El Dorado Camp bookstore for something you haven't read."

Claire moved her books and first-aid kit into the "leave behind" stack.

"Can you call Ray and Sandy and cancel my tent space and get me an RV space instead?" Claire asked.

"Sure. Oh, hey. Why not take some DVDs in case you get tired of reading and can't sleep?" She leaned in to bump Claire. "We have some nice juicy ones."

"I'm not going out there to have a date with Rosy Palm and her five sisters."

"Of course not. You can do that at home with plug-and-play toys, but isn't this all about getting in touch with yourself? Here are the keys to Molly Bree." Margie tossed them to Claire.

"No, its taking advantage of someone wanting to switch vacation days."

"What DVDs do you want?"

"*Alien* series. A vacation with Sigourney Weaver." Claire sighed dramatically and placed her hands across her heart.

"There you go. Group therapy with Rosy and her sisters, you, and Sigourney."

Claire made a face at her. "That would come under the heading of sex therapy. I do believe she's married to the father of their child, so we'll just be friends."

"Before I met Gail, I heard a lot of 'Let's just be friends,'" Margie said melodramatically. She laughed at Claire's funny face. "I'll get the DVDs. I put Teddy's stuff on the porch."

Claire picked up a plastic lock-top container filled with Teddy's food and a bag with her bowls and toys. She stored them with other articles already in the motor home. She dropped her box of clothes and supplies in the back between the two beds. Extra water bottles were stored in the sink for easy access. One more check of her car confirmed she hadn't left something useful behind.

She strapped her pack into the passenger seat, removed her holster, and locked her weapon in the glove compartment. Margie returned with a small overnight bag stuffed with DVDs. She put the bag in the back closet.

"I'll ask Ray to give you our usual site by the river," Margie said. "That would be a very romantic spot to hang out with Sigourney." She pointed to one of the cabinets. "There are clean linens and towels in the storage drawer, and there are some staples you can use up, otherwise they'll go stale, if they haven't already. Oh, and in case you get your two pairs of shoes wet and need an extra pair, look in the storage space. We also keep extra warm clothing there." She stepped out of the van. "Get going before I forget that I need my job and that I dearly love my spouse and would lose them both if I took off with you and Teddy without prior notification."

Teddy settled in her portable bed and looked up expectantly at Claire.

"Doesn't Gail have a location device on you?" Claire joked. "Teddy, say bye-bye to Mommy number one."

"Don't forget to fill the propane tank. It's low. We refill at the station on Gilmore and Monroe. Ask for Bill. He's an old-timer. He'll check the lines and make sure everything's working. He'll recognize the Molly Bree. We tip him a ten for the extra care. Bye, Teddy. Remember your table manners, and you, too, Claire. Don't feed her your leftovers, or you're going to have a beggar on your hands."

"She doesn't need a bib, does she?"

"You behave, lady." Margie pointed a warning finger at Claire.

"And three pointing back atcha." Claire pointed her fingers at Margie and then spread them into a farewell wave. "Bye."

"Seriously, Claire. Be careful."

"It's not like I'm going into a strange land alone. There's always someone we know there besides Sandy and Ray. I'll be stopping at the store daily. Is all this worry because you aren't going along?"

Margie stared at her for a moment and then sighed. "That's probably it."

Claire watched her walk back to the house. She cranked the engine and pulled away from the curb. At last, sweet freedom.

Traffic was building with the end-of-day crowd. The slow progress gave her time to get a feel for the motor home and a chance to spot the gas station Margie had mentioned.

With every valve or tube he checked, Bill asked if she knew what it was for and how it functioned. She didn't know about all of them, and he readily filled her in—in great detail. She was ready to throttle him before he finished his inspection. At long last, he was done and Claire pulled the van onto the entrance ramp to the freeway.

"Well, Teddy, finally we're on the road."

Her merge into the bumper-to-bumper traffic on the freeway took a while since only the truckers were willing to make a space for her. After twenty minutes on the freeway at forty-five miles an hour, traffic came to a total stop.

"What's going on?" She found a radio station that was giving freeway news. "Great. An oil spill."

Using the GPS, she found an alternate route.

"This is real luxury. My van didn't have as many conveniences as this one. Oh, better call and let Margie know there's been a change to our route." She pressed the earbud in firmly, then leaned over to turn her cell on.

"Call Margie. Home." The call went to voice mail. "Hey, Margie, this is Claire. Course change update. I'm leaving the freeway traffic jam and taking an alternate route stored in your Magellan. Talk to you later. Oh, and Teddy Bear says, 'Hi, Moms! Miss you.' Bye." She pressed the Off button.

After an hour of unsynchronized traffic lights, she moved out of suburbia and into undeveloped land. She replaced the radio music with a CD of saxophone jazz.

Blinking her eyes to refocus them, she saw a figure walking along the side of the road far ahead. She lowered the radio volume as her eyes swept the empty land. Only a few trees broke the monotony. It was dusk, and no abandoned vehicles were in sight, nor had she passed any.

"Wonder what she's doing out here alone. No purse strap. No fanny pack. Not wearing walking shoes, though they aren't high heels. She looks tired." Claire rolled past the woman and parked the van a few yards ahead of her. She opened her window and leaned out as the woman drew even.

Claire studied her warily. She looked familiar. "Do you need a ride?"

The woman's lips pressed tight, and she looked at the motor home, then back at Claire. A puzzled look wrinkled her brows as she stared at Claire a bit longer.

"Have we met somewhere before?" The woman snapped her fingers. "Police department? Petima Police Department."

"Yes," Claire said. Since her danger antenna wasn't shaking, she didn't perceive the woman as a threat.

"I'm MaryLyn Smith. You were behind the information desk. I almost didn't recognize you out of uniform."

Now Claire remembered. She was with a muscle guy. Officer Mosley started preening like it was some kind of competition. Claire thought for sure he was going to rip some seams. She couldn't remember their business, though. That was just before she was promoted to detective.

"Claire Hanson." Claire stuck her hand out the window.

"Claire, I appreciate your offer for a ride."

MaryLyn shook Claire's hand, then walked around the front of the van.

Claire unlocked the passenger door and moved her pack to behind her seat. "Teddy's in the back. She'll need to sniff you so she knows you."

MaryLyn peered into the van's interior, presumably to see who Teddy was. "Hi, Teddy." She extended her hand slowly toward the dog.

"Where would you like to be dropped off?"

"Where there's a phone. Where are you headed?" MaryLyn clipped her seatbelt on.

"Up north." Claire undid her seatbelt. She leaned back, grabbed a bottle of water from the sink, and handed it to MaryLyn.

"Thanks."

"I have a cell, if you'd like to use it." Claire reached into the sink for another bottle of water and dropped it in the cup holder next to MaryLyn. "Just in case you're still thirsty after finishing that one off."

"Thanks. I am thirsty. I'd rather call from a phone where I can have someone pick me up."

"Okay. There's a gas station maybe twenty minutes from here." Claire refastened her seatbelt. "What are you doing in the middle of nowhere?"

"I was carjacked," MaryLyn said.

"Around here? Someone you knew?"

"I didn't know him personally," she answered calmly between taking large gulps of water.

"You want to use my cell to call it in?"

"No. Bo—that's my partner—is on his tail. Or he better be."

"Partner?"

"We hunt down bail fugitives."

"You're a bounty hunter?" Claire had met a handful of bounty hunters and occasionally watched a series about them on cable television. Besides not looking like any of the ones she saw at the station, MaryLyn didn't look anything like the family on the TV program, either.

"If I had my purse, I'd present you with a card." MaryLyn sounded more amused than insulted.

"Just what role do you play?"

"Whatever's necessary."

"It's hard to imagine you chasing down fugitives when you don't have the usual accessories."

"That's the idea. Like in this case, sometimes no matter how careful we are, when the unexpected happens, we end up holding an empty bag. I'm happy for getting away with what I have."

"Sounds like you were lucky. How much is on your bail jumper?"

"Three hundred thousand dollars. No bond hold. His record says he's assaulted bartenders and girlfriends, been charged with possession of a controlled substance, and all the rest of the usual stuff that goes with dealing drugs."

"What judge made that decision, and who put up the bail?"

"Didn't get that info, but there you have it. Two places the risk should have been evaluated differently, and it wasn't."

Claire glanced at her passenger and back at the road. Given the MO of the bail jumper, she was lucky. He must have been in an awful hurry to not spend more time neutralizing her.

Claire merged onto the freeway and picked up speed. Twenty minutes later, they neared the off-ramp to get gas and coffee. "This is where I usually stop. They have payphones, restrooms, and food."

"Could I borrow some coins?" MaryLyn's voice sounded apologetic.

"Sure."

Claire rolled the van up to a diesel pump. She pulled out her change purse and picked out two dollars' worth of change to drop in MaryLyn's palm.

"Do you think that's enough?" Claire asked.

"Yes, thanks. They don't ask for money to use the restrooms do they?"

"No. The restrooms are on the left side of the building. Come on, Teddy. This is your chance to leave your calling card." After they'd all stepped out, Claire locked the motor home. Looking around the station, she realized it wasn't a safe place to just leave someone.

"MaryLyn?"

MaryLyn turned to look at her.

"Let me know what you're going to do after the phone call, okay? This isn't a good place to be alone."

"I will, and thanks."

Claire ran her card through the reader and put the nozzle into the tank. While it pumped, she walked Teddy a few feet away to do her business. When Teddy finished, Claire deposited her on the passenger seat and lowered the window so Teddy could stick her nose out. She replaced the nozzle on the pump and, with thermos in hand, went into the mini-market to get her traditional coffee fill-up and flavored coffee creamers. She added two bags of trail mix to her purchase.

When she went outside, MaryLyn was standing by the motor home. Teddy's nose still poked out the window. They were both watching an old couple walking their miniature Pinscher. The dog was wearing a fuzzy pink coat with a glittery collar.

"Hi," Claire said.

"Hi. Here's your coins back."

"Thanks. Anyone answer your call?"

"No. Would you mind if I continued on with you? Without any funds or ID, I don't want to hang around here."

"No, I don't mind. My next stop is the El Dorado Campground I'll be staying at. There's a phone there."

"Thank you."

"How about a cup of coffee? The stuff they make is pretty decent. It tastes like the same brew as McDonald's, if you like theirs."

"As long as it doesn't taste like it's been around awhile, I can drink it, thanks. Black."

"I also have some trail mix." She handed one of the bags to MaryLyn. Claire poured two cups of coffee and resettled in her seat. She glanced back at Teddy who was sitting up as though waiting for the motor home to start.

Back on the highway, Claire switched on the headlights and checked her side mirrors before squeezing between a double trailer rig and an RV bus. She glanced at the dish on top, bikes strapped to the back, and the Canadian license plate. Must be nice to have fresh-perked coffee and a washer and dryer, as well as a bathroom with a tub instead of a closet for a shower. Still, Margie's van was better than the tent she normally camped in.

Her cell phone rang. She put in her earbud before picking up the call.

"Answer. Yes? Hey, Gail, did you just get home? Yeah, can you believe it? I didn't think Margie would let anyone sit in the driver's seat, at least until she permanently imprinted her fanny in it. I'm about a half hour from the campground. I'll call you when I get there. Yes, traffic is a real bear. Your GPS is great. I picked up a stranded motorist, MaryLyn Smith. You're kidding. You know her? Yeah, she said she does that." Small world. "Her bail jumper carjacked her and left her walking. Okay. You want to tell her that? Okay, then, I will. You'll get my daily hellos just so that you know Teddy is still alive and hasn't been eaten by a raccoon or carried off by Big Bird." Claire waited for Gail's reply. "You guys take care. Bye."

Claire glanced at MaryLyn who was sipping her coffee.

"Do you know Gail Quimby?"

"Quimby? She flew rescue missions with helicopters in the army, now she's a captain with law enforcement, and she does presentations at law enforcement conventions. That Quimby?"

"That's her. She said hi and how's your jaw?"

MaryLyn smiled, but didn't offer to enlighten Claire about the jaw comment.

"Have you thought about what you're going to do if you can't reach anyone tonight?" Thanks to Gail's familiarity with MaryLyn, she was no longer a total stranger.

"I was hoping you wouldn't mind too much if I spent the night. I left a message that I was all right. Since it's a Friday, I doubt anyone is hanging around the office. When we get to your campsite, I'll give them the location and phone number for a Saturday pickup."

"I don't mind. I have extra clothes, or you can check out what they have in the store."

Forty minutes later, Claire slowed at the off-ramp. The road went from a smooth highway to a poorly-maintained surface street. To the left, on the other side of the freeway overpass, was the public beach with a booth to pay for overnight camping and a few hook-up spots for those who wished to have electricity for their motor homes. To the right was a flat dirt parking lot that was also the entrance to a private campsite.

It was pitch dark. She had to use the neon markers embedded in the pavement to guide her into the campsite and not into the ditches that ran on both sides. If Claire had been alone, she would have pulled out her night vision goggles just for giggles. For now, the reflectors would have to do. She parked in front of the campsite's rental office and pulled the key from the ignition. "The phone's inside. The one outside hasn't worked for ages."

Streaks of light leaked out through curtains from the residence. Her booted feet made loud thumps on the wooden stairs, sufficient to warn the occupants of her arrival. She rang a bell beneath the CLOSED sign.

MaryLyn joined her at the door.

Ray opened the door wide and waved them in. He was clad in his usual open plaid shirt with an outrageous social comment painted across his T-shirt underneath. He used a paper napkin to wipe his whiskered chin that had captured bits of his meal. Claire could smell something overcooked and hear the sound of an adventure movie coming from the other side of the residence door.

She recognized John Wayne's voice in the "Howdy" coming from the audio.

"Hi, Ray."

"How're you doing, Claire? Margie called to change your spot. I didn't think she would be loaning out her rig to anyone for at least a couple of years yet."

"I'm doing fine, thanks. You're starting to look like a decent wilderness man with that beard. MaryLyn, this is Ray. Ray, this is MaryLyn. Can you let her use the phone? Put any charges on my bill."

"How are you, Ray?" MaryLyn said.

"I'm fine, and you? MaryLyn Smith, right?"

"You're right on about the name. I'm doing fine. Chief Hershey, isn't it?"

"The Hershey part is right. I retired. Looking for someone?"

Claire noted the change in his voice. It was just enough to reinforce that MaryLyn had history with him.

"Just looking for a ride back home. I'm off the clock, Chief," she said.

Yet another person in her life knew more about MaryLyn than she did. What were the odds that she'd find a stranded stranger that her friends knew but she didn't?

Ray led the way to the business office, a space the size of two closets. He gestured to the phone next to the corkboard that was used for campers who had information to post. Next to that was a bookcase overflowing with paperbacks. Claire scanned the easy-to-read titles, noting that her favorite science fiction hadn't been swapped back.

"Not like your old Dodge camping van, eh?" Ray said as he pulled out a contract from one of the slots above the desk.

"I miss that van. Next one I get is going to be loaded with gadgets and amenities. I'm even going to have a satellite dish on top, like Setgo."

"What are you going to do with a satellite dish—watch outdoor adventure movies?"

They both chuckled.

"It's good you could come up, Claire. Quite a few of the gang are here. Someone must have sent out a smoke signal that Sandy and I missed. It's her turn to visit her mother."

"How's her mother doing?"

"She doesn't recognize any of the family anymore. Sandy says there's no conversation between them, so she plays her flute. Her mother likes that."

"It's good that she has someone who looks in on her."

Ray nodded. "Something we all hope for when our time comes."

Claire paid the fee, plus extra for a guest, and then signed the contract. It was obviously too dark for someone to drive to the campsite to pick up MaryLyn. Ray closed the gates at 8 p.m. unless a customer called in advance that they'd be late. Until he opened the gates in the morning, they'd have to wait in the parking lot or use the public campground on the other side of the freeway. Knowing the manager of the place gave Claire the advantage of not having to do either.

"How long has it been since you've set up a rig?" Ray asked.

"It hasn't been so long that I don't know which hose goes where."

MaryLyn finished her call and joined them.

"Ray, I noticed you take messages," MaryLyn said. "I left your number with my office."

"We turn on voice mail from seven at night 'til nine in the morning. Each camp spot has a slot back here. C4 is yours."

"Thanks. I'll check with you tomorrow," MaryLyn said.

"Enjoy your stay. Good night, you two."

"Good night, Ray," Claire said.

Claire glanced at MaryLyn as she settled in her seat. "We'll be setting up alongside the river. It's nice waking up in the mornings to hear a different type of wildlife."

"Just what kind of wildlife are you anticipating?"

"Nothing bigger than Teddy."

Teddy stood beside her bed, her tail sticking straight up. Hearing her name, she wagged her tail a few times, then she scrambled to keep her balance as the motor home swayed and rolled to their site.

"We're far enough from the restrooms and showers to not feel like we're sharing our neighbors' private moments, but close enough not to work up a sweat to get there. Unless it's late at night or too cold, I use the public facilities—shower, toilet, washer and dryer. Ray and Sandy keep the place shipshape."

The rain-rutted road rocked the motor home as the tires labored to find a solid grip on the uneven surface. Claire hoped the cupboards wouldn't pop open.

"Shipshape if you don't count the roads," MaryLyn said. She was bracing herself with one hand on the dashboard and the other on the handgrip above the passenger door.

"They probably had heavy rains recently. This is the off-season. Just before the busy time, Ray and Sandy have a big party for their regulars to come up. If you help with the repair work on the trails and roads, you just pay for your electricity if you use the hookups."

The vehicle's lights flashed on a reflector with C4 written on it.

"This is it. Can you shine the spotlight on the side there? There's a way up to that flattened area."

"You know how to get this baby up there?" MaryLyn shined the light on a slope.

"Not a problem." Effortlessly, Claire rolled the vehicle onto the platform. Using the side mirror, she aligned the motor home to the hookups.

"Want to help set up?" Claire asked.

"Show me what you need done, and I'll do my best."

They connected the water and outtake hoses and made the electrical connection. Then they got the awning set up and unfurled. They moved the picnic table under the awning and covered it with a tablecloth. Claire filled Teddy's traveling water dish, heavy and deep, and placed it under the table. The final preparation was setting the outside motion detector that turned on security lights. Nothing taller than Teddy could approach the van without a bright light coming on. Claire turned on the gas that would heat the water in the tank and give her fuel for her stove and oven.

She and MaryLyn sat at the picnic table and drank deeply from water bottles, their breath puffs of vapor in the cold air. Something moved in the underbrush, and Teddy stared at it, her body quivering. Claire looked in the direction of the riverbed. She hoped nothing that they couldn't handle would challenge Teddy. It would ruin her trust that this was a safe place. Was that naïve or stupid, considering what she did for a living? She gave herself a shake. Take nothing for granted.

The canvas awning shook with the wind from the ocean. Claire shivered in the sweat-dampened clothes that clung to her. Her body heat was no longer enough to offset the cold.

She stood. "Let's see what we have for dinner."

"That sounds like a good idea."

Claire stepped into the motor home, and MaryLyn followed. Teddy raced by and settled in her customary safe place. Her bed was on the floorboard in front of the passenger's seat. Teddy circled the bed and threw herself down, letting out little groans of contentment.

Claire searched the cupboards for a pan in which to boil some water then unpacked her supplies.

"Can you help me store this stuff in the cupboards? If you see something you'd like for dinner, leave it out." She moved the box of staples in front of the stove.

Claire transferred her clothing from a duffle bag to the storage space below one of the two beds in the back of the van. MaryLyn was neatly storing the food in the cupboards, reading the labels as she went. By her expression, it was evident she wasn't acquainted with freeze-dried camp dinners.

"Here's something interesting, Piragis Northwoods Company's Jamaican BBQ chicken. It says for two. This stuff is palatable?" MaryLyn held up the packet.

"It's an acquired taste. Not being the cooking type, aside from the microwave, I can't say I've got a sensitive palate."

"Well, you're not too fat and not too skinny, so I'd say your eating habits aren't doing you an injustice. You have a lot of different brands and variety. Organic Garlic Pesto Fry Bread, Organic Focaccia Bread with Parmesan, and AlpineAire Blueberry Pancakes. Have you tasted them before, or are these tests?"

"I'm not saying. In the morning, we can go to the store and buy something that looks more familiar, but where's the adventure in that?"

"If it were just me, I'd rather choose to be adventurous in a roadside diner with medical facilities close by. By the way, the water's boiling."

"Turn off the burner, dump in the dinner packet you're willing to try, and cover it. While it's heating, we can clean up. If I'm here alone, I usually take Teddy and lock both of us in the building."

"Okay. So, are we all heading up to the showers, or would you rather shower alone?"

"Teddy can stay and protect the rig."

Claire pulled out sweatpants, a T-shirt, and a towel for MaryLyn. To her own shower kit, she added the same selection of clothing.

"All right, Teddy, this is your shift. Guard the castle, but not with your life."

Claire waited for MaryLyn to join her outside the van. The security light came on, giving them a good view of a shortcut up the slope to the road.

Claire shined her SureFire light before them as they picked their way up the slope. She took a deep breath, enjoying the chilly air with a heavy brine smell from the nearby ocean. As they climbed past the platform where RVs emptied their waste tanks and dumped their gray water, she wrinkled her nose. Closer to the showers and restroom facilities, the breeze shifted, bringing the smell of fresh paint from the shadowed buildings. The men's area was on the right and the women's on the left. The doors were dimly lit with the intention to not disturb the environment's natural atmosphere.

Claire shined her light carefully around the door frame. Whoever had painted had removed all cobwebs and all traces of other bugs that lived in the shelter of the overhang. Bugs. The natural kind, but she couldn't say for sure about the recording type left behind by sneaky people.

"Doesn't look dangerous," MaryLyn said.

Claire held the light longer at a dark spot on the door frame. "Can't be too careful. Some of the neighborhood bugs get pretty aggressive about being disturbed."

"Ah. The dropping-in type."

While MaryLyn stood by the entrance, Claire went through the toilet stalls and then the showers, making sure that nothing that shouldn't be there was in the building.

"All clear." Claire glanced at the door where she heard the lock click into place. "If we take adjoining stalls, I can slide the soap, shampoo, and conditioner over to you."

They took their showers and then finished up at the sink, towel-drying their hair before heading back down to the van.

Teddy was dancing around for her meal when they returned.

"I'll feed her. Dry dog food doesn't look too difficult," MaryLyn offered.

"One scoop. It's in the container."

Claire gripped the steaming dinner bag firmly in her hot mitt, lest it slip from her pinch and end up fit only for Teddy. MaryLyn set the table with plastic plates and silverware wrapped in paper napkins. She set a water bottle next to each plate.

She was quiet as they ate their meal.

"Are you all right?" Claire asked.

"I was just thinking it takes a hearty person with a firm resolve to pass up eating at a roadside diner in deference to eating trail food."

"It tastes better when you're tired and just want to fix dinner, clean up, and crawl into your sleeping bag."

"I suspect a lot of practice is needed to get to that point. You probably started this when you were young."

"Nope. I started in the military."

"What branch were you in?"

"Army. I left it about six years ago. Decided I liked civilian life better." Claire smiled at MaryLyn. "So, do you want to wash or dry?"

"Wash, since you boiled the water and dished it out."

With a lot of bumping into each other in the small space, they worked out a rhythm to clean up.

"You said two people usually camp in this thing?" MaryLyn asked, handing Claire a fork to dry.

"A few times when bad weather hit, we've had five of us in here, plus Teddy, and we did a lot of bumping and pinching for giggles. Since I got rid of my van, I've been camping in a tent, but if it's raining or really cold and someone I know offers a space in their motor home, I'll take it."

"What changed for this trip?"

"An opportunity I wasn't about to turn down." Claire pointed up at the ceiling where the heater was. "See that? The heater in my old Dodge van was the oven, and I could only use that if I left a window open and stayed awake to make sure I didn't gas myself to death. And believe me, my tent is even worse. Would you have taken me up on my offer if I only had a tent and one small dog for heat?"

"Since it didn't happen, I'd rather not think about it. Do you go to bed early?"

"If I was sleeping in a tent, yes. But I'm still wound up from the drive, and I have the luxury of HDTV and some DVDs. Would you like to watch a movie?"

"I don't mind at all. Can I take the bed on the left side?"

"Sure. I don't have a preference." Claire opened the drawer and removed a pair of heavier socks for herself and held a pair up for MaryLyn. "Need something warmer for your feet?"

"I won't turn down warm socks on a cold night."

Claire reached into the bag of movies. Holding her choice, she stared at it, surprised. Uh-oh. Margie packed more than the Alien series. Claire hoped she didn't put in any of her R-rated movies.

"Something wrong?"

Claire looked at her guest, comfortably propped up on her share of pillows.

"I told Margie I'd like to borrow the *Alien* series. She added a bunch of others."

MaryLyn plucked the DVD from her fingers. "*Rosemary and Thyme,*" she read. "Shall I put it in?"

"Yeah. It's a good show. British. Have you seen the series on Channel 28?" Claire asked.

"No."

"It only went for three seasons. It's too bad. I really liked it."

When the show ended, Claire ejected the DVD and put it away. Teddy was dancing near the door, reminding Claire to take her out. "I'm going to take Teddy out for her potty break."

She peered out the open door. As if she could see anything moving in the dark. She momentarily considered wearing her night vision goggles but put the idea aside. MaryLyn would probably wonder why she carried NV goggles, but then again, maybe not. Claire chuckled to herself. The entire gang always brought their NV goggles just in case a game of hunt was called, or if they had unpleasant neighbors and they wanted a nighttime advantage.

Cold air blew into the motor home.

"What do you think, Teddy? Is it clear?"

Teddy hurried past. Claire grabbed her coat and reluctantly followed. She pulled up the collar on her coat and huddled in it, grateful she wasn't in her tent. Now that she was reexperiencing the luxury of a motor home, she was wondering why she ever chose to camp out in a tent in cold weather. Maybe she should just break down and buy a used motor home and get back into sensible camping. Was this a sign of aging or just good sense? She could always rent motor homes of different sizes to find out which one she really liked. The image of her in a Type A motor home like the one from Canada she'd passed on the freeway had her laughing.

"For something that size, I might as well give up my apartment and live in it." It certainly would be one way to handle the cats' dislike for their cat carriers. The carriers always represented an unpleasant journey to the vet, and both cats made it clear that was not what they considered a good time. The idea of rolling up to the veterinarian's office in a motor home had her chuckling even harder.

Claire pulled her cell phone from her pocket. There was a tower on the top of the hill, and sometimes she could get a signal up here. She hated a full mailbox. While giving Teddy time to prowl around, she deleted mail she wasn't interested in and typed a few hurried answers to others.

The wind from the ocean shook the awning, causing Teddy to growl. She finished her business and waited for Claire to let her back into the motor home. Claire tucked her cell away, opened the door for Teddy, and set about cleaning up what Teddy had left behind. She splashed water from a bucket over places Teddy urinated and used a garden trowel to scoop and bag her solid wastes. With that done, she stepped back into the comfort of the motor home. She hung up her coat, refastened the locks, made sure Teddy was safe in her bed, washed her hands, and suddenly felt ready for a bodily meltdown. The overhead heater was whirling out heat.

"Night," Claire whispered after she slid between the sheets.

"G'night," was MaryLyn's muffled return.

Chapter 2

Claire's thoughts made no sense at all to her, but that halfway state between dreams and reality seldom did. She took a deep breath, identifying the smell of coffee along with crisp morning air in her nonsensical dreamscape. She opened her eyes to early morning darkness. In the bed across the narrow space from her, she saw no lumps that could pass for a body. A voice from close by startled her.

"Coffee's ready," MaryLyn said.

Her shadow appeared in the small space that separated the sleeping area from the rest of the motor home.

"What time is it?"

"Early morning sometime." MaryLyn moved out of sight. The motor home shifted as she exited and closed the door.

Claire stretched languidly then flipped the covers back. Teddy wasn't there, so she must be with MaryLyn.

"This is cold," she said, huffing, "but not as cold as it would be in a tent. Happiness is not having to face starting a campfire for coffee and warmth. I think Margie has convinced me that tents are only in my past." As Claire dressed, she wondered what to do with MaryLyn. She poured herself a cup of coffee and took a few sips, savoring the flavor. She opened the door and looked out. MaryLyn was sitting at the picnic table. She was wearing Margie's coat and had her hands wrapped around a cup of coffee. Each exhale left a vapor cloud. She had rolled up the privacy tarp, letting in the chilly breeze. Teddy sniffed around the edge of the tarp.

"You want a toasted bagel or something?" Claire asked.

"No, I'm fine with coffee. Thanks for the offer."

"Not a good way to start the day," Claire said. She left the door open for space and fresh air. She put a sliced bagel in a special wire-rack and laid it over a burner on the stove. While it crisped, she put on her coat.

She spread each half of the bagel with a thick layer of cream cheese. With coffee and bagel in hand, she stepped outside. Claire stood for a moment, absorbing nature's energy, filling her lungs with it in a steady inhale, and then exhaled the stress and weariness she'd been feeling of late.

"You look like you needed this vacation," MaryLyn said.

"I sure did. Did you see any wildlife bigger than Teddy?"

"I haven't seen anything. Maybe when it gets lighter." MaryLyn took a gulp of coffee. "Should I worry about something big and mean?"

"No. I don't think I've ever seen anything other than birds and Alvin's cousins, oh, and lizards, bees—just the usual small stuff."

"Alvin? You mean chipmunks or squirrels?"

"The ones with the bushy tails," Claire said. "They make these really cute noises while they're running around the branches, and their tails are always twitching." Claire took a bite of her bagel. "You sure you don't want a bagel? Just half..." Before MaryLyn could say no, she added, "It'll make me feel better. Coffee on an empty stomach isn't a kind way to treat your body."

"All right. If I share your bagel, will I be making you go hungry?"

"Not a chance. I have plenty of trail mix and fruit bars. I usually have Bear Mush or Maple Bulgur in the morning, but I wasn't in the mood to tackle anything more complicated than a bagel over a burner."

"Bear Mush?"

"Hot cereal. Couscous, blueberries, raisins, and poppy seeds." Claire smiled at MaryLyn's expression. "I'll pick up some fresh fruit at the camp store. They carry locally grown produce—the good stuff without the pesticides."

"You aren't doing that on my account are you?"

"No. I always buy my produce from them when I'm here. It's tasty. Especially their corn. Sometimes they have blue corn. Have you ever tried that?"

"No. Is blue corn healthy? Aren't you afraid the dye is bad for you?"

"It's not dyed. It's natural. Hopi Blue Corn. It's real corn that the Hopi have been growing for centuries."

"Really?"

Claire heard the doubt in her voice. "That's what Sandy says. She's Ray's wife, and they manage this campground."

The dawning sky caught their attention, and they watched the colors change through the tree branches. Dark lumps barely discernable from one another began to separate, taking on definition and detail. Claire burrowed deeper in her coat and blew out vapor trails. The breeze blew her breath back at her. It smelled of coffee. She saw birds hop from branch to branch then drop to the ground. They looked like leaves that had a life of their own, falling to the ground and then flying back up.

"What do you plan to do today?" Claire asked.

"I'll walk to the store to make another phone call. And you?"

"I usually go hiking or just kick back with a book. Teddy's not into blazing any trails, thank the gods. She watches over the place while I do whatever strikes my fancy."

"Aren't you afraid she might get eaten if you leave her here alone?"

"She stays in the motor home. If it gets warm, the air conditioner comes on. Teddy's a veteran of RV camping." She looked down at the dog lying under the picnic bench, obviously content to sniff the air.

"Where will you hike?"

"I don't know. Do you want to come along? I have an extra pair of shoes that are better than loafers, if they fit you."

MaryLyn shook her head. "Again, thanks for the offer, but I've had my share of hikes that exceed twenty minutes. No more workouts in these clothes. Do you know when the store opens?"

"Sometimes nine, sometimes ten. It depends. Just knock on the door, and if anyone's there, they'll answer. Until then, help yourself to the books and the DVDs."

Claire went inside to get ready for her hike. She prepared a sandwich, filled up her canteen with bottled water, and paused when she thought about her P7 semi-automatic in the glove compartment. She unlocked the glove compartment and slipped the pistol into her pack.

Through the window, she saw MaryLyn tossing a toy for Teddy to fetch. Some arm she had there. She relocked the glove compartment. What should she do if MaryLyn couldn't reach her office? Should she offer to drive her home or to the nearest bus depot and pay for her ticket? For that matter, was there any reason to hurry her off?

Claire walked back outside. "If you want to change into clean clothes, I have some extra jeans, shorts, tops, and socks. If they don't fit, Sandy and Ray keep emergency clothing for people who lose their rig or camping supplies for one reason or another. It's used clothing, but it's clean and in decent condition. They charge less than a second-hand store."

"Are you saying my clothes smell?" She pinched her shirt and sniffed it.

"I haven't smelled anything yet, but I've been wisely staying upwind of you."

"Thanks, but I don't think I'll be here much longer. I'll probably be gone by lunch. I'll leave a note if you're not back."

"I'll be back in about two hours, maybe less." Claire pointed to her naked wrist. "I don't do things by the clock out here."

"That's what a vacation is about, right?"

Claire hefted her pack onto her back, patted Teddy's head, and waved to MaryLyn before starting down the slope. She hopped over the nearly dry riverbed and scrambled up the river bank on the other side to a trail she'd hiked many times.

Unhurried and taking frequent breaks, she eventually found a place to sit and sketch by the dry riverbed. It took heavy rains to make it more than a trickle. Flooding had changed the area since her last visit, which gave her new scenes to draw. She plumped her pack into an acceptable cushion, then leaned against it to begin her work. She finished one and began another, swapping pencils whenever one became too soft.

"Hey, Hanson!"

Claire jerked her head up and saw Bob Black waving at her from across the riverbed.

"Hi, Bob." She waved back. "What are you doing here?"

"Camping, of course." Bob explained that he and Bobbie Reynolds—the B's, as they were nicknamed—were higher up the hill in their motor home. Claire had known them for years. They were retired ATF drug enforcement officers. Their motor home had been custom-made for a race-car driver who had either gotten out of the race-car business or upgraded to a new custom-built motor home, depending on who told the story. The interior was decorated in heavy, dark colors with enough shiny chrome to blind you when the lights were turned on. As the B's would say, "We got it for a steal, so we don't complain."

Before Claire could contemplate the option of finding a female race-car driver who might want to sell her custom-made motor home, Bob wobbled off the boulder he'd been standing on and slid off, banging his shin on a low-hanging branch.

"Ooh, I bet that hurt," she said.

"Nah, not much." He scrambled up the slope and dropped next to her.

"Nice morning. How's it going, Hanson?" He reached for her sketch pad. "May I?"

"Go ahead."

He began flipping through the pages. "Nice. You must've taken some art classes since you were last here. No more stick figures."

"I still have plenty of sticks in there. They're just attached to trunks and stuff." She rolled her pencil between her fingers. "I told you if I kept drawing sticks, someday I'd be able to do something with them."

"Oh, yeah. If I turn it this way it does look like a tree. Darn, you're good, a real Picasso." He jabbed her ribs in case she missed that it was a joke. He continued to flip through the pad, looking at sketches she'd made months ago.

Claire pulled out a penknife and sharpened her pencils while Bob chuckled over the comic characters she'd drawn, like the Easter Bunny in the middle of a busy intersection.

"Dear Diary," Bob said mockingly, "I saw a bunny rabbit with an empty Easter basket directing traffic. Why's the basket empty?" He looked more closely at the drawing. "Oh, the egg's on the driver's face. Road rage, Easter bunny style. What have you got against the Easter bunny? Not enough chocolate eggs last year?"

Claire ignored his commentary. "You're breathing pretty hard for that little climb."

"I'd like to see you cross that rocky riverbed and not feel winded." He turned a few more pages. "Is this the wolf and Little Red Riding Hood at a disco bar? What kind of kick were you on?"

She took the pad back. "How's retirement?"

"Good. I heard you have one of the Smiths staying with you."

"What about the Smiths?" Claire tried to sound as neutral as possible, annoyed that yet another person knew MaryLyn. Her curiosity about the bounty hunter Smiths went up another couple of notches.

"Are you bringing her over on gaming night?" Bob asked.

"You must be getting forgetful in your old age. I swore off your gaming nights, remember? If she's still around, she can decide for herself."

"Why's she here?"

"It's her story. If she wants it told, she can tell it herself. Why all the questions? Just how long have you known her?"

"I've never met her. Let her know a couple of retirees wouldn't mind swapping stories, playing cards, and taking her money."

"I'll tell her you threw down the gauntlet."

He grunted, staring at his clasped hands as if lost in thought. Claire was silent. He said, "Well then, I don't want to keep you from your art. See you around the trails." He rose from the ground, brushed off the seat of his jeans, and started back across the riverbed.

"That's it?" she asked before he was out of earshot.

"If you'd come to the card games, you'd know more," he yelled back.

"I hate card games, and you know it," she shouted. In a lower voice, she said, "What was that all about? How come I've never heard about the Smiths?" She stared at his retreating form. The card socials were always boring. All they did was drink, recount war stories, and play cards. More importantly, because of her job, it could be a potential death trap for her or for someone she might inadvertently expose by a slip of the tongue, even in an offhand remark. For that reason, she chose her friends carefully and avoided most social gatherings that required drinking alcohol.

Thirty minutes later, her growling stomach reminded her to take a break. She dragged the pack from behind her and pulled out the sandwich and trail mix from the side pocket. While she ate, she gazed over the view before her. A piece of trash flapped on one of the tree branches a few yards away, detracting from the romantic isolation of the area.

The idea of being isolated made her think of Vanessa Slaughter. She was a Deputy Marshal with the U.S. Marshals Service, whose most recent assignment had been working undercover in the Petima Police Department on a possible jury tampering case. But Vanessa had reported signs of other illegal activities in PPD, and her investigation had been broadened. Before she could send further information, something had gone horribly wrong and Vanessa's team couldn't get to her in time to save her life. Claire, also a U.S. Deputy Marshal, had volunteered to complete Vanessa's undercover investigations. She joined the Petima PD and was provided with a Fed contact to report her findings to: Deputy Marshal Charles Stiller.

Was she making the same mistakes? She hoped not. It was impossible to know, since Vanessa didn't keep notes. Carefully rehearsed hand signals and messages left at the cafés and restaurants where she ate were her only contact with her team. Despite distancing herself from everything that would link her with an investigative arm of the law, she had been killed.

Claire's trail mix lost its appeal. She picked up her pad and began another drawing, focusing on a fallen log and a bush that was under part of it. In her drawing, the log crushed a rose bush. She paid a lot of attention to the thorns.

"There you are." MaryLyn's voice broke her concentration.

Claire studied her intruder. MaryLyn's hair was mussed, and she was wearing a hooded coat, blue jeans, and hiking boots. They weren't Claire's or from Gail and Margie's stash of extra clothes.

"Is something wrong?" Claire asked. It had grown chilly. The winter sun would soon fall behind the trees. She laid her pad aside and put her sweatshirt on.

"It's getting dark. I was worried about you." MaryLyn pressed her hands into the small of her back and stretched. Her breathing was easy, not labored in the least. "I tried calling my office and home several times, but I couldn't find anyone, so I picked up some clothes from the store. I hope you don't mind me staying awhile longer. By the way, Ray said he has a message for you."

"No problem. Stay as long as you want." Claire handed MaryLyn the canteen. "You look like you need some water." Claire put her equipment in her pack and shouldered it. They headed back down the trail.

"The right shoes make it much easier to hike." MaryLyn handed the canteen back to Claire.

"Yes, it—" A flash of gray and a sudden noise cut her short. Instinctively, Claire jumped sideways. Her foot hit a loose rock, and she tumbled to the ground, knocking MaryLyn over. They crashed down the slope. MaryLyn bounced out of sight and careened into the underbrush.

Claire grabbed a fallen tree to stop her slide. She rested for a moment and let the stinging in her hands subside. She got to her feet and gingerly moved body parts to check for injuries.

"MaryLyn, where are you? Are you all right?" she called.

"I feel like I've been eaten by a wolf and shit over a cliff." MaryLyn's voice was faint, like she was far away.

Moving slowly, Claire tried to distribute her weight more equally on the uneven ground. Her left foot slid from under her, sending her headfirst down the rocky incline. Her backpack caught on a branch and left her hanging awkwardly over the leading edge of a drop off.

She struggled to get out of the straps, a task made more difficult by her lack of balance and the helplessness of being all but upside down over the ravine. Painstakingly, she freed herself and clawed her way to a more secure spot. She clung to a tree for security. Sweat beaded her forehead, and she panted for air. Leaning heavily against the tree, she pulled bits of the forest out of her hair and fought to regain her composure.

She called out again to MaryLyn but got no reply. She held fast to one of the tree's limbs and eased out to look over the drop. With a loud snap the branch gave way, and Claire plummeted down the rest of the embankment, her pack toppling down right beside her.

She wrapped her arms around her head and uttered silent prayers that whatever broke her fall would be soft. What felt to be a hundred years later, she stopped. On something soft. She waited a few minutes before attempting to get to her feet.

MaryLyn clapped her hands twice. "Nice dismount. Thank goodness there isn't enough light to see what we've landed in. I hope it isn't someone's poop pile."

Claire glowered at MaryLyn and wrinkled her nose at the thought. "It's not something I'd willingly inspect. Couldn't you have suggested something less disgusting?"

Overhead, a half-dozen squirrels resumed their noisy chatter. "I can't believe we were bushwhacked by squirrels." Claire glared at them.

"Is that the story you're going to tell?" MaryLyn straightened up stiffly, then brushed dirt off her clothing.

"No one likes long, complicated vacation stories except the person telling them." Claire spotted the canteen a few yards away and went to retrieve it.

MaryLyn made a couple of attempts to scale the first part of the slope but failed.

"We'll never be able to haul ourselves back up that way," Claire said. "Gail and I tried it one time when we were out here, and we had to give up and follow the riverbed back."

MaryLyn surrendered her efforts and leaned over to catch her breath. Her hair looked like a battered bird's nest with leaves, twigs, moss, and who knew what else poking out in every direction.

"Come on," Claire said. "The riverbed will lead us to our campsite." She watched MaryLyn slowly straighten up. "Are you all right?"

"No, but I'll live. My biggest worry is what might be sharing my clothes with me." MaryLyn looked at Claire and laughed. "I bet you look as bad as I feel."

"Good thing we're not expecting company."

Darkness descended quickly. Claire pulled her light from her pack to help them make slow progress over dead roots, branches, and rocks. In the pitch dark, finding the campsite wouldn't be easy. Claire knew the riverbed spilled into the ocean. If nothing else, from there, she'd be able to backtrack to their motor home.

Half an hour later, Teddy's muffled bark to their left gave them a reference point.

"Man's best friend. I've never heard a more welcome voice," MaryLyn said as they limped into the campsite.

Claire opened the door and Teddy leaped out.

"You're a lifesaver, Teddy." MaryLyn petted Teddy briefly before entering the motor home.

Claire stopped at the picnic table to discreetly remove her weapon from her pack. She tucked it into her waistband, then dropped the pack on the table.

Inside, she saw MaryLyn had collapsed in a chair and was sucking down water from a bottle.

"Gods, what a mess we are," Claire said.

"I feel about as sociable as a skunk at a lawn party."

"Hot showers will do us both a world of good." Claire picked up a bowl from the floor. "I'll feed Teddy before we go, and I'll grab the first-aid kit. After I clean the floor of the forest off me, I might find something worth putting a bandage on."

"Help yourself. My pride is too big for a small Band-Aid. I wouldn't say no to a nice stiff drink, though."

"That I don't have," Claire said, "and I regret it."

They labored up the hill, the reward of a shower giving them incentive to make the climb. While Claire was washing her hair a third time in hopes of ridding it of all the real and imaginary bugs, she heard MaryLyn's shower go off. That was a fast shower, considering how dirty they were.

"I hear a dog barking," MaryLyn said.

Claire turned off her shower and listened. "It doesn't sound like she's frantic." Just the same, she finished quickly and then hurried through drying and dressing.

She noted MaryLyn likewise dressing in a rush. "Teddy's safe in the motor home," she said, "but I left my pack on the table outside, and someone might think it's worth something."

On their way back to the campsite, Teddy occasionally yapped, as if reminding everyone she was on duty. Claire had camped with Teddy often enough to know she wouldn't continue to bark if the danger had passed. Either she'd been frightened, or someone was hanging around. She slipped her hand under her T-shirt and rested it on her gun.

"We're here, Teddy," Claire called as they reached the site. Claire looked at her pack. The zipper was facing up. She knew she'd left it face down. She picked it up and brought it into the motor home, where she dropped it on the passenger seat. She grabbed a flashlight from a storage bin and, keeping her P7 handy, went outside to inspect. She limited her movement around the exterior to checking the hookups for tampering. If someone had been there, she didn't want to risk destroying evidence she'd be better able to see in daylight. Lying on her stomach, she flashed her light along the undercarriage. Nothing appeared to have been added. Probably some nocturnal animal prowling in Teddy's realm, she mused.

A truck came up the road and slowed as it neared the entrance to their site.

"Claire?"

She recognized Ray's voice and replaced her gun in her waistband.

"Everything okay?" he asked.

Claire walked to the truck, shining the light on the ground in front of her as she went.

"Hey, Ray. We're okay. MaryLyn and I were up at the facilities and heard Teddy start to bark."

"I heard her. She was barking earlier, too. It's not like Teddy to bark without a cause. I asked Bob to take a look, and he didn't see anyone around. You're not hiking at night, are you?"

"I lost track of time and missed the trail on my way back." Claire was grateful Ray didn't comment on something so amateurish as losing track of time or how you can't lose the trail if you stay on it. But she knew if it happened again, her name would become synonymous with *Lost in Space* among the group.

"I know all the campers registered here. Were you expecting someone else, Claire?"

"Not me. MaryLyn said you have a message for me."

"I got a telephone call, but they didn't leave a name. Said they just wanted to know if you were up here."

"Who'd be checking up on me?"

Claire pointed to the seat beside Ray. His NV goggles and a large bunch of bananas rested there. "Are you going up the hill for a visit?" she asked.

"Bob's in a baking mood. The smell of baking banana nut bread will be a nice change from pine trees and outhouses. It's for the get-together. Maybe this will entice you to come."

Claire made a face and shook her head.

"Well, make sure you've got those security lights set right," Ray said.

"I will. Thanks for checking on us."

"Alrighty. G'night."

Claire picked her way through the darkness back to the motor home.

"Anything with big paw prints out there?" MaryLyn asked.

"If there was I'd be pulling up stakes, but by the time I finished, Teddy would've been eaten." She looked down at Teddy. "Sorry, Teddy Bear. Bad joke. I'm glad you didn't drive off without us, kiddo." She scratched Teddy's head and was rewarded with a lick on her wrist. Teddy yawned, stepped into her bed, circled three times, and dropped into a ball.

Claire prepared their meal while MaryLyn napped, although Claire thought it was likely MaryLyn was just listening for noises outside of the motor home with her eyes closed.

"Did you leave a message with anyone that you were here with me?" Claire asked.

"Not by name. My office knows the phone number here and to leave a message about when they plan to pick me up. Why?"

"Ray said someone called to ask if I was here, but they didn't leave a name."

"Maybe it's a friend who wants to surprise you with a visit."

Jackson, my asshole boss, would be the only one who'd do something like that. "No," she said aloud to MaryLyn.

"Think it has something to do with your job?" MaryLyn asked.

Of course she did, but she wasn't about to admit it to this relative stranger, and she couldn't be sure how much was healthy paranoia and how much was a real threat. The people who vacationed at the campsite, thanks to their years in various branches of law enforcement, were sensitive enough to pick up on people who'd be trouble to the peace and quiet of the place. They all had their own ghosts and bad memories.

MaryLyn offered a wry observation. "In my business, when someone calls and asks about my whereabouts and doesn't want to leave a name, I take a lot more interest in my surroundings."

"MaryLyn, for months now, I've sat behind a desk. I file other officers' reports and answer phones."

"A cop behind a desk," MaryLyn said. "Not ticketing or arresting anyone? What's the point of being a cop with a gun if that's all you do?"

"Nowhere else I'd rather be." Claire heard the cynicism in her own voice. She winced inwardly at her revelation.

"Must be the results of a shooting."

"What makes you say that?" Claire hoped she didn't sound too defensive.

"Because that's what puts most cops behind a desk."

"Well, I didn't shoot anyone. My partner was stupid and got shot... dead."

MaryLyn formed a silent "Oh" with her lips.

"He was an ass and should have been drummed out of the force a long time ago, but he wasn't. A snitch my partner thought he'd cut the balls off of found another pair and blew him away." Dammit. She needed to watch her mouth. MaryLyn had found the right button to push for her to vent about a topic she thought she had totally under control.

"Ah, the brotherhood of the ill-begotten," MaryLyn said softly.

Claire savored the empathy. It felt good to be understood for a change—until the alarms went off in her head. The sixth sense that warned her of lurking danger kicked in. She tried to drop the subject gracefully.

"He was a dirty cop," she said with less heat. "He got what was due. Subject closed." Claire wondered how much MaryLyn knew about the PPD since she wasn't aware that Ray was no longer police chief. Did bounty hunters make a habit of getting to know a city's police chief?

"Okay." MaryLyn drew the word out.

Claire studied her closer, hoping for a clue about what she was thinking.

After they ate, MaryLyn did the dishes while Claire took Teddy out for her potty break. Teddy didn't do any suspicious barking. Once Teddy was settled in her bed, MaryLyn asked, "So, what's tonight's movie?"

"It's your turn to choose."

MaryLyn reached in the bag and pulled out a DVD.

"What's the pick?" Claire asked.

"Alien Resurrection."

No further conversation passed between them that night. Claire's thoughts kept returning to puzzling over who was looking for her. She couldn't shake the feeling that MaryLyn was somehow involved, but that didn't make any sense at all.

That night she dreamed of the last time she had seen Vanessa at the airport. They took basic training for U.S. Deputy Marshal at the same time. At the end of training, Claire was assigned to New York, and Vanessa was off to Florida. They both were excited and promised to keep in touch. Neither was good at calling or sending letters, but it didn't mean their friendship went to the wayside.

Chapter 3

The next morning, Claire woke stiff and achy from the previous day's tumble. She could tell from the brighter light in the motor home that she'd slept in longer than she had the previous day. MaryLyn's bed was empty. The smell of coffee greeted her, which, come to think of it, was what had awakened her.

"Oh, gods... oh." She moaned as she sat up. "A dip in a hot tub would be so nice. Maybe I should reconsider and get a fancy motor home with a hot tub. I'm sure there's some celebrity who wants to give me a real bargain on their used mansion on wheels."

She dressed and stopped in the galley for coffee. She was pleased to find a bowl of Blue Mountain Bear Mush, still warm. Claire took the bowl and coffee out to the picnic table where MaryLyn was carrying on a conversation, but no one except Teddy was there.

"Morning, MaryLyn. Are you talking to yourself this early in the day?"

"Your bodyguard took issue with a squirrel that was interested in her territory. I was giving her some advice on the futility of chasing it from tree to tree."

"If it's the one that bushwhacked us on the trail, I hope she scares it half to death."

"*You* were bushwhacked by a squirrel. I was bushwhacked by a squirrely hiker."

"Witnesses always have to put a kink in the story. This could have been a Disney version of a vacation with Roger the Squirrel, I'll give you that." It would take a long time to outlive that story if word got around to Ray and the others.

"I tasted your Bear Mush," MaryLyn said flatly. "Doesn't mistreating yourself first thing in the morning set you up for a bad day?"

"It takes some getting used to, especially if you don't usually eat breakfast. How do you feel?"

"That nursery rhyme about Humpty Dumpty has new meaning."

"You do know that Humpty Dumpty was a cannon, right?"

"You're undermining my happy childhood images. I'm sticking to the pictures in my book of a fat egg knocked off the wall."

"Speaking of which, I'm sorry about knocking you down yesterday. That squirrel took me by surprise."

"I'll remember you're dangerous to stand next to." With effort, MaryLyn rose from the bench. "I'm going to the store to see if I have any messages. I'm hoping I get a ride out of here today. No offense meant, but your type of vacation isn't what I'd plan for myself."

"What do you do for vacation?" Claire asked.

"I haven't had one for quite a while, so I haven't thought about it."

"How do you know Ray?"

"I know a lot of cops, detectives, police chiefs, attorneys, judges, and political heads, as well as other people. It's part of my business to know who's who on the cop scene."

"Knew," Claire said. "You didn't know he'd retired."

MaryLyn looked like something important occurred to her. "You knew Detective Sam Thompson?"

"He was my partner—the one who got shot by his street snitch. Let's say it was a short partnership."

"Given how he treated women, you're better off without him. Thank whoever your God is that your time with him was short."

"He was intimidating," Claire said, "and so are his friends who're still there."

"I was in law enforcement for a while. I decided to take my experience and do something a lot healthier with it."

"Where was that?"

"Not important anymore. It's a closed chapter. I'm sorry about your partner getting killed. Even if you did everything by the book, it still puts a stigma on you that can follow you for years. Brotherhoods can be positive, but all it takes is one manipulative psycho in the ranks and things turn abusive and intolerant in a snap." She snapped her fingers for emphasis. "Too much testosterone is as bad as too much estrogen. They both cause irrational behavior."

"Amen to that." The more time she spent with MaryLyn, the higher her curiosity rose. Next time she saw Ray, she was going to get some background from him on MaryLyn and the rest of the Smiths.

"Who's your chief now?" MaryLyn asked.

"William Dobbs."

"Will Dobbs from Arizona?"

"You know him, too? Where do you meet all these people?"

"I told you, because of my business, I cross paths with all sorts of people." After a pause she asked, "How are you getting along with him?"

"You first. Tell me how you know him."

"Probably ran across him at some cop gathering. Don't you go to law enforcement conventions or police bars?"

"No. I see enough of them while I'm on the clock. Dobbs told me I'll be done being a desk clerk in a month or two. Having me in a uniform behind a desk is a waste of the department's resources. But he also made it pretty clear I shouldn't plan on going back to my detective slot, so I'll be out pounding the pavement like other uniforms."

"Sounds like he gave you fair warning."

Claire snorted. "Clerking can be outsourced pretty easily." She wondered what—or more precisely who—else she and MaryLyn knew in common. "Do you know Ron Jackson?"

"Bad News Jackson?"

"That's what he likes to be called on the streets. He's a lieutenant, acting captain of the detectives. I was hoping with a new chief, the bad apples would be removed. Mr. Bad News made it clear to me that things aren't going to change. It's still a boys-only club, and if I make a squeak, one day sooner rather than later, I'll be coming home in a body bag like another female who didn't know her place. I'm pretty sure he was talking about Detective Vanessa Slaughter. She was shot and left in an alley. It all happened before I was hired."

"And there was Julie Hutton before her," MaryLyn said. "With that group, you never know what's truth and what they lie about to cover each other's asses. But good gods, lady, if they've openly threatened you, what are you still doing there?"

"Because it galls me that..." Claire stopped, realizing how naïve what she was about to say would sound.

"Oh, I get it." MaryLyn's mockery was clear. "You're figuring out how to slay the dragon without getting eaten. Noble, but make sure you leave more than bread crumbs to get you back to your safe hole, and don't depend on just one source for protection or weapons.

Hutton and Slaughter were ambitious for promotion in the wrong environment. Ray Hershey is—make that was—a great manager and Dobbs is okay, too, but with Jackson's infection of the department, it will take more than good management to remove such an entrenched disease."

"How do you know so much?"

"You have a classic case of bad guys infiltrating an organization and corrupting everyone around them. How many books and movies have come out with that very plot?"

Claire frowned. "This isn't some game or story to me. And I'm not some hero rushing to slay the dragon."

"I'm not questioning your motives, Claire. I'm an outsider who's seen with her own eyes what you're facing from both within and without. I'm just saying you need to do more than watch your back. You said you file reports. Unless I miss my guess, you're collecting data... evidence against a group that's using your police department to run their illegal activities. Right?"

Claire didn't answer. MaryLyn shot her a look and continued. "Working with files gives you knowledge, and therefore, you're not any safer than you'd be out on the street in uniform or as a detective. If someone thinks you're a threat, you're history."

Claire sat mute. She saw MaryLyn's eyes turn dark before she spoke again. "Jackson and his crowd are no better than a gang in the streets and just as mean and nasty. I heard about both women's deaths and all the rumors that went with why they died."

"I'm only doing my job. I'm not a hero, brave or stupid," Claire said.

"There's no such thing as a neutral party, and if you think that... well, never mind. The investigation into Thompson's shooting must still be going on. That's why Jackson is *acting* captain. Why did Chief Hershey leave?"

"The case hasn't been closed, and the investigating team will have something in two months." Claire had often wondered why the files covering the investigation were kept in the chief's office. No one had told her who was working on the investigation.

Her musings were interrupted by MaryLyn asking about Ray Hershey again.

"It was common knowledge," Claire said, "that the mayor wasn't going to renew Ray's contract. For someone who knows so much, how come you didn't know that?"

"I want to live a long life, so I don't visit police departments that kill their own. Did Ray partner you up with Sam?"

"There was a position open for detective, and I qualified. I passed the tests. And I took the job with my eyes wide open."

"And you come up here for vacations... a place where your old chief happens to live? Is there something going down here that I should know about?"

"No!" Claire was outraged. Enough! Everyone else knew MaryLyn. Why didn't she? And MaryLyn had more information on things she should know about than Claire herself had. Damn it. Enough.

Claire studied MaryLyn and got the distinct impression MaryLyn was doing the same.

"Why did you go into bounty hunter work?" Claire asked.

"I run a diversified business enterprise with one of the ventures being chasing down bail jumpers. In my other businesses, I know a lot of civilians, many of whom aren't involved in criminal activity."

"I see." Claire rose and collected her dishes. "You know what? I'm going for my hike now."

Inside the motor home, she fixed a tuna sandwich, added a bag of trail mix to her pack, and filled her canteen. MaryLyn came in to refill her coffee cup and get her book.

"Be careful on the trail. I heard there are dangerous critters out there," MaryLyn said.

"I'm packing, so if there's another attempted attack, I'll fire my water pistol at them." She looked at the book in MaryLyn's hand. "The store won't open for another two hours. There are some comfortable camp chairs in storage under the beds. I'll unlock the back so you can get to them if you'd like."

"Thanks. My back could use some support when I sit out outside."

Claire helped MaryLyn get her chair set up and then headed up a trail she hadn't previously taken. Her body complained in the early going, making her regret she hadn't brought her walking stick.

Given the overcast sky, she decided noon would be a good time to start back if the clouds didn't clear. She found a spot well-cushioned with leaves and not easily seen from the path. She left her drawing supplies in her pack and settled in for some serious thinking about the investigation into her partner's shooting.

Since being put on desk duty, she was always second-guessing herself, worried that someone would realize she was keeping track of specific people and the cases they became involved in. It was bound to happen that an officer or detective in Jackson's cabal would be shot by someone they were shaking down, but Sam Thompson's murder was too close for comfort.

Carefully, she recalled every detail of what had happened the night Sam was shot. Without a doubt, her biggest slipup had been not realizing her iced soft drink was drugged. Concerns about what other details she'd missed plagued her, especially at times like this when—thanks to MaryLyn stirring up all the memories she'd tried to wipe from her mind—she reflected on what could have happened, but for a twist or two of fate. It was incredible luck that it was Sam who died and not her. And if the plan was for her to take the fall for his death, no one had planted evidence on her—at least not yet.

Three groups were independently looking into the whole deal, and that included Sam's shooting, the assassination of the boy who shot him, and why she'd been drugged and left unharmed in the car. As best she could tell, none of the groups was any closer to an answer on any front yet.

Sam was the only one who'd had access to her drink that night. That meant he'd drugged her, probably because he had something nasty planned for her that required she be unconscious.

Thoughts of what had happened to her brought up thoughts of Vanessa. What went wrong in Vanessa's assignment? Why hadn't her team recognized the danger and stepped in?

Would her team be too late, too? She had no evidence that she couldn't trust her team. She wasn't going to sit there and undermine her confidence in them.

But what about Vanessa's PPD partner, Detective Andy Yorke? Where was he the night Vanessa was killed? They were both on duty that night but not together. Yorke reported he was unaware of any reason for her to be where she was found. A month later, Yorke transferred to another police department and then quit that job and moved out of the area. Claire had seen what happened in similar situations and figured it was the same for Yorke. If other detectives felt he hung his partner out to dry, no one would want to partner with him. The Petima Police Department didn't have a good reputation with neighboring cities. That's what stunk about this. If cops in other cities knew how dirty the cops in Petima were, why didn't they do anything about it? Instead the U.S. Marshals got involved, but only because one of their cases crossed paths—jury tampering.

She thought about her acting boss, Jackson. His threat about her being hauled off in a body bag hadn't been subtle in the least. Why? What was his game? And why was she pressured to participate in an office pool she normally shunned? There was something wrong with the money, was her guess. She'd handed it over to one of her undercover team members to check out.

She went over the lottery scene again, focusing on the red flags the delivery of the winnings had raised for her. As always, she'd been at her desk, and she'd recognized Officer Mosley's heavy footsteps on the stairs, and his cheap cologne as he entered the room.

Every time he crossed her path, something unpleasant ensued.

"Hey, dickless Hanson, you won some money." Mosley sneered as he tossed a brown bag onto her desk. "Go ahead and count it, just so you know we're not stealing from your purse. Oh, that's right, you don't carry a purse. A mugger stole your last one." Then he laughed, too loudly, and Claire's internal radar went off.

"Count it yourself, Mosley, so I know it's not just a bag of shit." She used a pen to push the bag to the corner of her desk.

Filing cabinets lined the walls on three sides of her desk, which sat in the center of the barely-bigger-than-a-closet space. Two normal-sized people could fit without feeling too cramped, but someone of Mosley's proportions shrank it down so much they'd need a shoehorn just to get them both in.

"Just count it, Hanson. Surely you know how to count up to five hundred by twenties."

"Like I said, if anyone is going to stick their hand in there, it'll be you, not me. If you want it counted, do it yourself."

"Count the fucking money, Hanson, or I'll shake you by your chicken neck."

"For God's sake, if you're so attached to the money, take it back."

He'd stared at her, but didn't move into the room. Why had it been so important for her to open the bag and count the money? A nasty prank? Or something a lot more serious? She'd kept her eye on Mosley, but she made it clear she wasn't going to touch the bag. At length, he'd turned and stomped back up the stairs.

"Bitch. Lackey. Loser." He snarled with each word as he went up the stairs.

She'd pulled on a pair of latex gloves from the box she kept in the bottom drawer of her desk, and then using a mirror, with the bag facing away from her, she'd gingerly opened the sack and looked at the reflection to see what was in the sack. A stack of bills were rubber-banded together. They looked harmless, but Mosley's insistence that she count it—that she touch the bills—raised her suspicions.

Come to think of it, the swap of vacation weeks didn't feel right, either. But hell, she was at a campsite she knew well, and she felt safe because Ray and others she trusted were there to watch her back. It was no secret that this was where she hung out on her vacations. It was a favorite hangout for law enforcement types and campers who either fancied themselves as like-minded souls or who needed to feel really protected when they were away from the city.

"If Jackson wants to get rid of me, it would take a lot of balls to do it here in Ray's backyard," she said aloud. *And who the hell is MaryLyn Smith that everyone but me has heard of her? Is she a plant? How would anyone know I was going to take an alternative route up here and what that route would be? Nah, it was just a coincidence that she was on the road I took, and besides, if MaryLyn was dangerous, Gail or Ray or Bob would have said something to me.*

The purpose of her being moved up to detective in the first place—for her undercover work—was something only a few people were aware of, one of whom was Ray. The timing of his retirement was part of the larger plan. She was sure no one in Jackson's group had a clue, otherwise she would be dead. They were so confident of their position in the department that they flaunted their tyrannical rule over everyone.

Just thinking of their condescending arrogance made her blood pressure rise. She wouldn't let Vanessa's death be for naught. Andy Yorke? He was just another scared cop who ran from something he knew was too big to face on his own. He had a family, and that made him vulnerable.

Enough thinking. It was time to head back to the store. As she thumped down the path, she chastised herself for discussing her job with a stranger. As a rule, she was tight-lipped about everything that went on in the department. And now she'd proved to herself why that was the best plan, seeing how she'd inadvertently shared far too much information with MaryLyn.

"I'm an idiot," she muttered. "I was a damn Chatty Cathy doll." In response to the bell that clanged when Claire opened the store's door, Sandy stepped out of the office.

"Hi, Claire. How're you doing?"

"Hi, Sandy. I'm fine. Nice seeing you. How's your day?" They exchanged heartfelt hugs.

"Busy. I was only gone for a few days, but I have a week's worth of catch-up to do. How's your camping spot?"

"Sweet. Even better now that I'm not in a tent. What have you got for fresh produce today?"

"The corn is good—tender and tasty," Sandy said. "With so much of the gang up here, I brought a box back with me. I've got strawberries and apples, too."

"How's your mother doing?"

Sandy bagged some ears of corn, a package of strawberries, and half a dozen apples Claire handed her. Claire dug in her pocket and gave Sandy some folded bills.

"She's going steadily downhill. She's oblivious to it, which makes it easier to bear."

Claire did her best to hold a neutral look on her face while she tried to think of something comforting to say. She drew a blank.

"It's okay. You don't have to say anything."

After an awkward pause, Claire asked, "Where's Ray?"

"He's out stocking supplies in the toilets. He said he was going to swing by your campsite to drop off a message he had for MaryLyn. Is she a new friend of yours?"

"No. She was carjacked by a bail jumper she was bringing in. I found her walking along a deserted side road. It's amazing what using a GPS for alternate routes will find for you."

"Hmm." She handed Claire her change. "Did Ray invite you two to the weekly dinner with banana nut bread as dessert?"

"Yes, he did. Thanks. So how do you know MaryLyn?"

"I don't, except by reputation. But if you came to some of the socials, you'd have heard about her and some of the characters she and her cousin have pulled in. You know how everyone likes to tell stories. We have a new rule that you pay a fine for any story you retell."

"Everyone seems to have heard of her but me."

"You picked up a stranger? That's nice of you, but how safe was that?"

"A deserted two-lane road with no buildings in sight wasn't a safe place to leave her. She didn't have a purse or jacket to hide anything like a weapon." Claire snapped her fingers. "Crap, I didn't check her ankle."

"All right, you," Sandy said. "Make fun of me if you want to, but remember, with or without your superwoman outfit, you can't stop every bullet."

"She wasn't a total stranger, Sandy, and I couldn't leave her or anyone who didn't look dangerous out in the middle of nowhere."

"Wasn't a total stranger? You just said you didn't know her."

Damn it. Now Sandy was grilling her about MaryLyn. Claire tried to backpedal. "Gail knows her," she said.

"And you know this because?"

"I called Gail on the cell phone to let her know I was taking a different route."

"Oh," Sandy said. "So why didn't you drop her off at a bus station and give her bus fare back into town?" Now she was teasing Claire, knowing how to trick more information from her than Ray could.

"On a Friday night, look for a bus station? The GPS lists gas stations, eating joints, and banks, but not bus stations. It's impossible to find a pay phone that still has a phone book intact. If I thought she was dangerous, I wouldn't have let her stay in the motor home with me. I'd have figured out a way to safely drop her off somewhere. I'm careful, Sandy. I even left a voicemail for Gail telling her I'd left the freeway and changed course."

"I'm glad to hear you don't take big chances needlessly. Being around cops so much, I hear stories that make me wonder about the intelligence of some people, and that includes the people telling the stories."

"Given that you're a therapist, I'd think your clients have stranger than strange stories to tell."

"Yeah, but in my line of work, you'd expect them to."

"At least your ethical code keeps you from repeating what you hear, unless it's potentially physically harmful to someone else."

"We shrinks do have our rules."

"See you later." Claire took a step, but then turned back. "And Sandy, thanks for worrying about me. I really do appreciate it."

"Your appreciation is accepted. Have a nice day."

Claire drank in the scenery and enjoyed the bird calls she never heard in the city, which reminded her how much she liked being at the campground. She inhaled deeply, hoping to pick up the smell of the ocean brine. She couldn't, but she did smell the pine trees, and either brine or pine was preferable to vehicle exhaust and bird songs were better than the roaring background noise of street traffic. She shifted her pack to her back and began her walk up the slope to take a roundabout trail to the campsite.

She caught the sound of someone stumbling on the trail behind her. She wheeled around to look, but no one was there and there was no further sound. A few paces ahead, she came to a fork in the trail. The left trail would take her to a turnout which hikers often used for rest breaks. From there, she'd be able to look down at the trail she was currently on. She broke into a jog. At the turnout, she crouched beside some bushes and surveyed the path she's just left.

Nothing. She waited and watched, but birds and squirrels were the only signs of life.

She retraced her steps, once again jogging to cover the ground more quickly. As she rounded a curve, she barely missed a pile of rock and branch debris in the middle of the path. Her sudden movement threw her off balance. She grabbed a tree trunk to prevent herself from sliding down the steep embankment. As she clung to the tree, her brain kicked into overdrive. The heap of stones and sticks had not been there when she passed by a few minutes ago. Whoever set the trap must have figured she'd be hurrying to get back and that she'd trip over the camouflaged snare.

Claire was more careful along the trail as she headed back to the campsite. Darkness was falling and shadows hid everything but what was in the direct beam of her flashlight. She hefted the light as though it were a billy club. Yeah, it was heavy enough to be a weapon, if she needed one besides her gun. She trained her eyes on the ground and strained to hear anything other than the crunch of her boots on the path. She stepped across the invisible line around the motor home, and the motion-activated lights came on.

MaryLyn hastened out of the motor home. "I was getting worried about you."

"Sorry, time got away from me again. I'd have thought you would have left by now."

"I'd have thought so, too. Ray dropped off a note from my office. Bo is still tracking the bail jumper, and everyone else is busy. I'm not in any danger up here, so business goes on as usual until someone has time to fetch me. I hope you won't mind if I hang around awhile longer."

"No, not at all." Claire stepped into the motor home. She unzipped her pack and pulled out the container of strawberries. Holding them under her nose, she breathed deeply. "Ah, the smell of real strawberries." She offered the container to MaryLyn and then pulled out the apples. "Did anyone else come by?" Claire asked.

"No."

Claire stripped the husks from the corn and tossed the remains into the paper bag they'd come from. "Sandy didn't have any blue corn, just the traditional yellow."

"As hungry as I am, it won't matter." MaryLyn put water in a pan and put it on the stove to boil. Claire grabbed a two-person package of lasagna and placed it in another pan with water. They sat at the small dinette table while they waited for the water to cook their meal.

"How are you at cards?" MaryLyn asked. She extracted a pack from the back pocket of the driver's seat. "I found some back here."

"So-so. I hate cards."

"Too bad. We're going to play anyway. What'll it be? How about a hand or two of poker?" MaryLyn tapped the cards, expertly cut them, and shuffled them like she was at a blackjack table in Vegas.

"Where did you learn to shuffle like that?" Claire asked. As she watched, she noticed that MaryLyn's hands were stronger than most women's. Mindful not to stare too long, she focused on the cards themselves. She leaned closer to get a better view. "What's on the back of those cards?"

MaryLyn stopped shuffling and pondered the back of one card. "Looks like someone's version of bedroom solitaire, don't you think?"

Claire looked closely. Yes indeed, Rosy Palm and her five lovely sisters were working their magic on some very private body parts. "How can anyone play cards with backs like that?"

MaryLyn dodged the question with one of her own. "So, how good are you?"

"You mean at cards, right?"

"Yes, cards. What else are we playing?"

"I suck at cards. Even at Go Fish."

MaryLyn dealt the cards "You're first. Bid, discard, or draw."

"Can you do me a favor?" Claire asked.

"What?"

"Don't clutch her like that."

MaryLyn said nothing but moved one finger over a fraction of an inch without looking at the card.

"Doesn't it bother you that your hands are holding a woman doing herself?" Claire tightened her lips and carefully put down a card.

"Just one card? No, it doesn't bother me. My boyfriend had cards you could only buy online." MaryLyn chuckled and then fanned a straight out on the table.

"Boyfriend?"

MaryLyn gathered up the cards, shuffled quickly, then dealt another hand. "Does 'boyfriend' sound like I'm robbing the cradle? You cops take some things too literally. He was old enough to hire hookers, and old enough to know that when he played with fire, he'd get burned sooner or later. You're right. Boyfriend isn't the right term. How about 'lover'? Is that a better word?"

"Was he in your business, too?"

"In my business?"

Claire felt her face turn red. "You know what I mean. Was he a bounty hunter?"

"More like a booty hunter. On occasion, I watched him run his game. It was very informational. My grandmother would have said, 'That boy is just big hat, no cattle.'" She laid down a full house of three kings and two jacks.

Claire held two fives and a worthless mess. "You weren't jealous?"

"No. As long as he didn't bring anything home, including little critters that would leap from him to me, I was okay with it."

Claire rested her chin in her palm. "If I'm in a relationship, it's monogamous. I can't even tolerate flirting with someone else."

"Oh, you're a strict one."

"It's disrespectful to the person you're with to flirt with someone else."

"How's that?"

"It's telling everyone that the person you're with isn't enough."

"Flirting isn't serious. And in my experience, one person isn't always enough. Does that make me sound self-absorbed?"

Claire couldn't tell if MaryLyn was kidding or not. "Do you fool around when you're in a relationship?"

"As in having sexual relations with someone other than my partner? Sometimes. It depends."

"What kind of relationship is that?"

"Tailored to fit." MaryLyn collected the cards, and smiled at Claire. "It smells like the corn is ready."

"Do you have a boyfriend now?"

"Is this entrapment? By the way, you're not much of a card player," MaryLyn said.

"No, I'm not. I've tried, but never could get into them. I still want to know how you can concentrate on playing cards when the backside of the cards you're using has a woman masturbating."

MaryLyn offered a noncommittal shrug as her answer.

Claire served the lasagna onto two plates and put the ears of corn and pats of butter in special curved corn dishes and stuck corn holders in the ends. She took a container of moist towelettes from the cabinet and set it on the counter.

While the corn cooled, they ate their lasagna. Claire had never met a sober woman who admitted she preferred an open relationship. And she still had no idea how much of what MaryLyn said was fact and how much was just to yank her chain.

"The corn was palatable," MaryLyn said. "I'm still not sure about those dehydrated concoctions in the pouches, though." She reached for the pre-moistened wipes on the counter.

"You ate it, so it must not have been too bad."

"Are we doing the movie thing again tonight?" MaryLyn asked.

"Yes, unless you'd rather read."

"I've read enough for one day. A movie sounds good to me."

"Okay, a movie it is. I'm going to..." Claire hesitated, then decided it was her vacation and her motor home—make that her *borrowed* motor home—so she didn't need to explain her actions to MaryLyn. "I'm going to shower here, if you don't mind."

"What's up? Some reason we shouldn't climb the hill to the public showers?"

Claire noted MaryLyn's heightened awareness. Maybe she was worried about her bail jumper having followed her to the campground. That was absurd... or was it? And since MaryLyn was the one who'd recently been carjacked and relieved of her cash, purse, and other valuables, wouldn't it make sense that someone would be setting traps for her instead of for Claire?

Maybe it was time to lay some figurative cards on the table. "I'm pretty sure someone was following me earlier."

"Is that why you asked if anyone came by?"

"Uh-huh. I took a path up the hill that has a view of the trail and store. I thought I heard someone following me."

"Was that before or after you stopped at the store?"

"After. By the time I got back from the place where I could overlook the trail, whoever was following me was gone. I doubled back and found a boot print on top of mine, so I know someone had been behind me." Claire opted not to tell her about the trap left for her to stumble on.

"A woman should always trust her instincts."

Claire rolled her eyes, but gave a nod of acquiescence. "With that bit of advice, if it's all the same to you, I'd like to skip using the camp shower facilities and instead stay close to the motor home tonight."

"Until we find out who's following you, I'm all in favor of staying right here."

"Do you think there's any chance the person you were looking for followed you here?"

"No. He's more interested in making it over the border where he'll be safe from arrest by U.S. law enforcement. He may have had the dumb luck to get out on bail, but he knows by now his bail has been rescinded."

"Okay. I might have been wrong about being followed, but right or wrong, I don't want to take chances out there in the dark." Claire took a half-step toward the shower. "I'll be quick so I don't use all the lukewarm water. The doors to this dinky thing they dare call a shower stall cut off half the motor home. Do you want to be in the front half or the back?"

"I'll sit up front." MaryLyn dropped into the driver's seat. "Hey, do you happen to have a map of the area around here?"

"Margie has all sorts of maps in the glove box." Claire unlocked the cubby in the dash and laid the maps on the passenger seat. Then she relocked the glove compartment and took the key with her.

After their showers, they watched *The Bourne Identity.* Following the movie, Claire took Teddy out for her potty break. Both Claire and Teddy kept a keen eye out for threats, but the motor home appeared safe for another night.

MaryLyn was already asleep when Claire and Teddy returned. As quietly as she could, Claire slid into her bed, put her gun under the pillow, and lay on her back. She stared at the ceiling for a long time. Sighing, she turned on her side, then promptly rolled back onto her back. Sleep was nowhere near. She eased out of bed and shuffled to the front of the motor home. Teddy curled into a tighter ball, probably in hopes of avoiding an errant footfall.

Claire collapsed in the captain's chair behind the steering wheel and parted the curtains. She strained to make out whatever might be out there in the pitch black. Without her night goggles, she wasn't going to see anything. She smoothed the curtain back into place.

"Do you want to talk about it?"

The sound of MaryLyn's voice set Claire's heart to racing.

MaryLyn slid into the passenger seat.

"Talk about what?"

"Why you can't sleep."

"Too much coffee. How did you get up here so quietly in the dark?"

"I have good night vision."

"Good thing. Teddy wouldn't have been happy to get kicked or stepped on."

"You're avoiding the subject. Are you worried about the person following you?"

"No. I'm just… I just can't sleep."

"Want to play some cards?"

"No. I don't want to stare at you holding a porno queen peeking at me between your fingers. It's gross."

MaryLyn went to one of the cupboards and pulled out a small case filled with games. "What's your preference?" she asked. "I found this when I was looking for books yesterday."

"You don't have to stay up because I can't sleep." Claire leaned over and looked at what was offered. "Okay, how about checkers?"

"I can't sleep either. I keep wondering who was following you and why."

They played four games. Claire won one, but only because MaryLyn dozed off between Claire's moves.

"I'm ready to sleep now," Claire said as she folded the board.

And sleep they did.

Chapter 4

Claire woke to Teddy's whining. As had been the case each morning, MaryLyn's bed was made, but for a change, the smell of fresh coffee was absent. She let Teddy out and made coffee. While it sputtered, she washed up and dressed. She decided on blueberry pancakes for breakfast, and while she ate, she wondered where MaryLyn had gone. Maybe she should have pressed Ray for more information about the mysterious MaryLyn, but surely Ray would've told her anything she really needed to know about her. Just the same, would it have killed MaryLyn to leave a note saying where she was and when she'd be back?

Claire donned her hiking boots and a sweatshirt and slipped her P7 into her belt. She left her canteen behind and took a couple of bottles of water instead. She tucked a day's supply of food in the pockets of her backpack, then filled Teddy's water bowl and gave her a treat. With a pat on the dog's head, she left her curled in her bed with her favorite toys around her.

She followed the stream toward the ocean. As she passed by the parking lot, she saw only one vehicle and a small dome tent. A group on the far side of the parking lot let out enough whoops to give her an idea of what they were about. She continued on, walking under the freeway overpass.

Her destination was a rock that sat well above the waves. She regarded it as her personal thinking rock, and for sure, she had a lot of thinking to do. She hopped from stone to stone until she reached her favorite. It offered a good view of the cliffs, beach, and ocean. Depending on which direction she faced, she could close out her surroundings and feel like she was adrift in the ocean. It was a perfect spot for drawing, and for letting her mind float free to deal with thoughts that were too hard to hang onto in other places.

She rummaged in her pack for her drawing supplies. She jammed her finger against a jagged edge. Closer examination revealed that the hard plastic case that held her pencils had been shattered, probably during her fall after the ambush by the squirrels. "Damn, I should have checked this two days ago." She sucked the blood from her fingertip. "So much for my plan to use my thinking rock."

Disappointed, she made her way back to the shore and up along the stream. As she moved beneath the overpass, she kept the partygoers in sight. She studied the men from behind her dark glasses, and she knew they were watching her in return. With no tents or RVs in sight, she had to wonder what they were doing there and where they slept or kept their supplies.

"Great, a potential idiot mob." She lost sight of them as she neared the private campground. She turned to look behind her. The same uneasy feeling that she was being watched crept over her. This time, instead of trying to double back to catch whoever was tailing her, she headed to the store.

Ray was unloading supplies from his truck.

"Hey, Ray," Claire called.

"Morning, Claire."

"Need some help?"

He laughed as he lifted the last box out of the bed of the truck. "Your timing is perfect. Get my keys, will you?"

Claire grabbed them from the ignition and followed him into the store. "I think someone's following me around, Ray. Have you seen anyone who strikes you as someone I need to keep an eye on?"

"Nope. No one like that is registered in our park. Just the regulars are here." He gestured for her to follow him to the back of the store where no one could hear them, but he could keep sight of the front door. "Anything to do with your work?" he asked in a soft voice.

"Maybe. Jackson gave me a warning two weeks ago about not returning to the detective position unless I'm interested in wearing a body bag."

He whistled softly. "That's a strong message." His brow furrowed in thought. "Maybe someone's pushing his buttons, but I don't believe it's someone within the department. He's the head honcho there. Unless he knows for sure that you'd write your reports the way he wants them, you moving back to detective would interfere with his influence on the outcome of investigations."

Ray shifted gears. "What's Smith doing here? Did you hire her to watch your back?"

"No! I don't need a bodyguard. I gave her a ride and a place to stay until she gets a way out of here."

"So, you two aren't making up a story of convenience?" He tilted his head. "What were you doing in the middle of nowhere?"

"The GPS sent me on some side roads to avoid an oil spill and car wreck on the freeway. No one could have guessed I'd be on that road, Ray."

"The people you're dealing with have plenty of gangbangers who want to prove themselves by taking out a cop. Five police officers from the department have been killed in ways that can only be described as suspicious, and for my money, an awful lot of questions have gone unanswered."

Claire watched Ray unpack the fresh produce. "Sounds to me like you almost regret not being in the middle of this."

"Not for a minute. Sandy and I like entertaining our cop friends out here, and it suits me fine to be nothing more than an occasional consultant. I was glad they offered me an early retirement. You know as well as I do that I had no backing from the city council to eliminate the dirty cops and their cohorts and start fresh." He brushed some soil from the bottom of a head of lettuce. "When dirt is too deep in the cracks, it's better to change solvents to get it out."

He handed her an apple.

She chewed a bite before continuing the conversation. "Typically, if Jackson has something to say, his cronies echo the party line every chance they get. But no one came to me to make sure I got the message that he didn't want me back as a detective," Claire said. "I thought that was odd." She studied her apple as though it might reveal some clue she was missing. "But I got pushed into playing the office lottery—something you know I never do— and be damned if I didn't win. And right on the heels of that, I got the chance to switch my vacation time with Nimes. That struck me as too much of a good coincidence."

"In my opinion," Ray said, "Officer Nimes is harmless. He may be just a pawn, but I don't think he's part of what's really going on with you. The fact that you're being followed, though, is nothing to mess around with. I don't think Jackson is stupid enough to send out his troops to try something up here. If he does, he'll find out we're ready for him. I'll let the others know to keep their eyes and ears open. I hope nothing comes of it, but if it does, it could be more fun than staging a hunt."

"I'd rather not have to explain our hunts to MaryLyn."

"Why not? She can keep a secret, and she'd probably send her group up here for training. Our gear is more up-to-date than most police departments."

"I've been meaning to ask you about her. She doesn't strike me as the type to do dirty work."

Ray laughed heartily. "Why don't you two come by and have dinner with us tonight? We'll make her feel comfortable, and then we can pump her for stories of her exploits."

"I'll think about it. It's not that I don't enjoy spending an evening with you and Sandy, but—"

Ray cut her off. "But the others always drop by, and you don't like crowds. It can get to be a late night. I can drive you back to your campsite afterwards, so you won't have to worry about getting back safely."

"Like I said, I'll think about it. Right now, there's some barbecued Jamaican chicken with rice and fresh strawberries calling me to lunch."

Ray blanched. "I don't know how you single people live as long as you do. I tried microwaving some packaged meals the few days Sandy was away, and they almost made a widow of her."

Claire moved toward the door.

"Whatever you decide about tonight," Ray said, "keep me posted on any more sightings of your stalker."

"Will do."

Claire smiled sardonically as she walked the trail. Whoever was following her was in for a very big surprise. Ray and the rest of the bunch would eagerly grab their night vision goggles, body heat sensors, and every other gadget—whether purchased on the open market or from their less-well-regarded suppliers—and start a game of tag. She almost felt sorry for whoever was tailing her. He—or she—didn't stand a chance against Ray and the others.

But until that situation came to a head, her immediate job was to ferret out more information about the elusive MaryLyn Smith.

Teddy was happy to see her. Like Claire, Teddy probably wondered about MaryLyn's whereabouts, since she'd stuck close to camp on previous days. Claire dug out one of Teddy's throw toys, and they played until Teddy's interest lagged.

Claire was about to put the water on to boil for her Jamaican chicken when the door to the motor home opened and MaryLyn walked in.

"Hey, I hope you're fixing enough for two. I'm starving." MaryLyn flopped into a chair.

"Sure." Claire handed MaryLyn a bottle of water. "So tell me, how did your skulking about go?"

"Can't hide anything from you, can I?" MaryLyn laughed. "It went well. I found your stalker."

"Is it one of those rowdy guys I saw on the beach?"

"No. There's a rental car parked up the road. The name on the contract is a John R-e-g-a-n. Ever heard of him?"

Claire shook her head. "No. No Regans in my arrest files. What about you?"

"Nope, no one I know, either."

"Is he packing?" Claire asked.

"He's shooting plenty... with a camera."

Claire's jaw dropped. "He's taking pictures of me? I'm not on disability, I'm not dating a movie star, and I'm not fooling around with someone who's married. That doesn't make any sense at all."

She went back to fixing lunch. She put the lunch plates on the table. "I'm still not sure I've got a good idea as to why you were in the middle of nowhere when I picked you up."

"It seems to me that the fact this John Regan snapped a lot of shots of you this morning ought to be what you're paying attention to now. He had a digital camera with a 35 mm telephoto lens." She patted Claire's hand. "I think you're up to something with that bunch in your department, and it's making you jumpy."

Claire jerked her hand away. "I'm jumpy because there are crazy people out there and because some lunatic is following me."

"And don't forget someone called the store to ask if you were here but didn't leave his name," MaryLyn added. "My antenna is shaking like there's something nasty going on here."

"Thanks a lot. Now I have to worry about my own version of *ET*—or was it *My Favorite Martian?*" She gestured at MaryLyn. "So, you're feeling a rumble in the ethers? This was supposed to be my vacation."

They finished their meal in silence. After they'd cleaned up the dishes, Claire grabbed her pack and unzipped it.

"Going out to draw?" MaryLyn asked.

"No, I haven't cleaned out my pack from the tumble down the hill, and I found out this morning that I broke some stuff. When I reached in earlier, one of my pencils attacked me." Claire dropped a sketch pad on the table. "A hell of a vacation this has turned out to be."

"Do you want me to leave?"

"No, I don't want you to leave. I'm just..." She dumped the rest of the pack's contents onto the small table. Amidst the broken pencils and shattered plastic container was an unfamiliar object.

"What's this?" She picked up a small, oblong box. She shook it gingerly. No sound, not much weight.

"Well?" MaryLyn asked.

Claire set it on the kitchenette table and stared at it. "It looks like a cheap jewelry box, but those aren't cheap hinges, and the lock isn't cheap, either."

"I wish I had my lock-picking tools so I could open it," MaryLyn said.

Claire pulled a multifunctional-tool knife from one of the pack's side pockets. With a couple of deft twists, she pried the lid open. One quick look was enough. They both had sufficient experience on the streets to know exactly what was in the box.

"Rock cocaine," Claire said through suddenly parched lips

The box was stuffed. No rattle, no wiggle, no doubt about what was going on.

For a long moment neither woman spoke.

"Your antenna was right. This is nasty," Claire whispered.

"Well..."

"Oh, crap." Claire slapped her forehead with her open palm. "What a setup."

"You're always putting stuff in or taking stuff out of that bag. How come you only now noticed it?"

"It wasn't in there when we tumbled down the hill. I'd have felt it." Claire gathered a few pieces of her plastic pencil box. "Look at this. It's a lot flatter than that box of coke, and it cracked all apart. If I'd rolled over that"—she pointed at the box—"I know I'd have felt it."

"Maybe someone put it there when Teddy was barking that night. Remember, you left your pack on the table out front while we were showering."

"That's probably it." Claire ran possible scenarios in her head. Only a drug dealer would carry that much cocaine. Was the intention for her to be caught with it and shot as a drug dealer?

"MaryLyn, you have to leave. I don't know what's going on, but you need to get out of here. There's no point in your being collateral damage if this goes bad in a hurry."

Claire's mind raced a mile a minute. Where to hide the box? A drug dog would easily find it if she left it in the motor home. "It's got to be the Mexican Mafia," she said more to herself than to MaryLyn. Claire took a rag and wiped her prints from the box.

"How can you know that?"

"Who else in Southern California would have this amount of cocaine?"

"Lots of other gangs have businesses here. Besides the usual black, brown, and white, the Russian Mafia is going strong in a few neighborhoods in L.A. County. What are you going to do with it?"

"Damned if I know." Claire dropped the box into her pack and slung the pack over her shoulders. "I'll be back. Look, call a taxi. I'll pay for it. Go to the store and tell Ray I said to get a cab out here for you. He knows I'm good for it."

"Are you nuts? It's too late to try to keep me out of this. Just by being here, I'm already involved. Splitting up won't do a darn bit of good, and it'll probably get one or both of us killed."

"Fine. Stay here if you want to, but don't you dare follow me, understand?" Claire clipped her cell phone to her pocket, jumped out of the motor home, and headed up the trail. The amount of cocaine in the box made it clear a major player was involved. The evidence room at the Petima PD wouldn't have that much good stuff in a whole year, so it had to have come from the outside. Something big was going down, and she only hoped it wouldn't take her with it when it went. Tossing the box over a cliff would help her immediate problem, but it was evidence that could tell them if all the rocks were from the same source and where they came from. She had to stash it some place it wouldn't be found. How could she alert Ray and the others about this development? Her every move was being watched… and probably photographed.

Jackson had to be behind this. Who else could it be? He'd thrown down the gauntlet at work, and now he'd thrown the first punch in what he probably thought was a sure knockout round.

She flipped open her cell and got a good signal. Quickly, she sent a coded text message to Deputy Marshal Stiller with information about the box and what she planned to do with it. She had no intention of ending up like Vanessa.

She did what she could to lay a false trail, while she hid the box in what she could only hope was a safe spot. She took a roundabout way back to the motor home. Once inside, she plopped in the chair opposite MaryLyn.

"While you were gone, Ray came by to tell me my office called again."

Before Claire could reply, her cell phone vibrated on her hip. She pressed the button in her earbud. "Hello?"

"Hey, Miss Vacation. How are Teddy and Molly Bree?" Gail asked.

"We're all doing fine. Teddy Bear has had two occasions to bark at someone who came too close to the motor home. Bob and Ray came over to investigate."

"Trouble?"

"Trouble of sorts, but nothing we can't manage."

"The planets must be out of alignment and in a mood to cause trouble for all of us. A package came for you at our address."

"Who's it from? I didn't order anything, and I wouldn't use your address unless I asked first."

"No return address. That's what has me worried. Are you involved in any cases?"

"Not while I'm on vacation."

"Well, I asked Jeff to bring his pooch over for a test sniff. In the meantime, it's sitting out in the middle of the backyard."

"Who delivered it?"

"It came by regular mail."

"Did you run an electronic bug detector over it?"

"Of course I did. I'm not stupid, you know. I did all that stuff."

"It can't be the battery-powered French tickler I ordered. That came before I left." Claire heard the nervousness in her own voice.

"Can I open it after the dog is done running his nose over it?" Gail asked.

"Go ahead, but be careful. Maybe you should get one of those robots the bomb squad uses."

"That's an idea. Catch you later."

"Listen, stay safe, you hear? Bye."

Claire disconnected the call. The fact that Gail sounded calm even though trouble might be brewing in her neck of the woods was all the more upsetting. What if Jackson was going after her friends, too?

"What's the problem?" MaryLyn asked, distracting Claire from her worrisome thoughts.

"Tell me about your phone call first."

"Our bail fugitive was caught booking passage the opposite direction we expected him to go. They snagged him while he was making plans to travel to Alaska in a small Cessna. Supposedly, he'd be doing some hunting in the Alaskan wilderness."

"I guess that means someone will be coming to pick you up soon."

"Nope. I told my office I have some unfinished business here," MaryLyn said. "What was your call about?"

"Gail received a package in the mail. It had my name, her address, and no return address. First the box in my pack, and now Margie and Gail getting a box with my name on it. Damn, but I hate being blindsided."

"You think the photographer shooting pictures of you ties in with all this other stuff somehow?"

Claire laughed wearily. "I don't know. I sure wish I knew what was in the box at Gail's house. I hope it's not the cash that allegedly goes with what we found in my pack a little while ago. I should have asked her for more details about it—size, weight, postmark. She was waiting for a friend with his drug dog to check it out. I'll call her later and see what else she can tell me."

MaryLyn offered only silence for a long moment. At length she asked, "How about eating dinner and watching a movie? We can't do much about the whole mess right now anyway."

Claire looked out the window. Darkness had fallen. MaryLyn was right. The situation was out of her control. Nothing to do but wait. Leaving the motor home now would be stupid. She'd be setting them up to be shot, kidnapped, or something worse, which she'd rather not think about. She needed evidence, and the best way to get it was staying inside, where anyone who came visiting would be on her turf.

They ate and then settled in to watch *The Banger Sisters*. Claire's cell phone rang once but cut off before Claire could answer. Then it rang once again. Someone was trying to warn her. Ten minutes later, Teddy bristled, growled menacingly, and broke into frantic barking.

Claire heard something, but the security lights hadn't come on. She took a deep breath, drew her P7, and cautiously opened the door. It was wrenched out of her hand, and a hard knock to her wrist sent her gun flying. Someone yanked her out of the motor home and body-slammed her to the ground. Her assailant kicked and kneed her with brute force. The attacker all but tore her shoulders from her sockets as her hands were bound behind her. The nylon cord burned her skin and cut off her circulation. At least he—or was it they?— weren't beating her head. That left her mind reasonably clear.

She willed herself to tune in to what was happening. Two dogs were barking. One was deep and ferocious. She heard who she presumed was the dog's handler tell him to get ready for action. The other bark was Teddy, but suddenly, it was muffled. *Don't you dare hurt that dog, you bastard.*

The awning was ripped from the side of the motor home and flung on the ground. She'd have some explaining to do to Gail and Maggie—if she got out alive, that is. Deep male voices shouted orders over top of one another... too many to identify who was in charge or to readily discern how many men were present. It was too dark to make out any faces.

Someone jerked her to her feet and put her in a chokehold. She struggled for air. A rifle butt slammed into her stomach and knocked the wind out of her. Oddly, it affected her eyesight and made her head swim, disorienting her. She shook her head in an attempt to get her bearing. Just as her vision came into focus, she was blinded by several flashlights shining in her eyes. She wrenched her head to avoid the light, but someone slapped her in the face so hard she went weak in the knees.

A rough pair of hands lifted her off her feet and dropped her on the picnic table bench. Her spine slammed against the edge of the table. With the lights no longer blinding her, she saw rifle muzzles pointed at her head. She sagged against the table and wished she could meld with the bench and vanish. She struggled to breathe through her nose but had to settle for wheezing through her raw lips. She tasted something dripping in her mouth.

Blood.

Claire turned her head to look for MaryLyn. A bare-handed slap to her face rocked her head back.

She hadn't seen MaryLyn, but she did catch a glimpse of her badge on the table. Her semi-automatic wasn't with it.

"Where is it?" a deep voice asked.

"What?" Her ribs hurt, and uttering the single word made her cough uncontrollably.

"Don't play games with me!" The punch that accompanied the order all but flung her head off her neck. It lifted her off the seat, and she dropped back down with bone-rattling force. Several hands pulled her into a standing position. They hit her again. She fell to the ground. Rapid kicks from hard-toed shoes pummeled her sides and back.

She was barely conscious. The men grabbed her under her arms and dragged her into the motor home. Her shins hit the edge of each of the stairs, bringing pain to yet one more part of her body. She felt her pulse beat painfully against her jaw. Broken, was her best guess, and probably in more than one place. Her captors shoved her into one of the chairs, but she couldn't sit upright. Each breath was agony, and every passing second made it harder to see out of her rapidly swelling eyes.

One man shook Claire roughly by the shoulder. "I'm going to feed your borrowed pooch to my dog and then beat your girlfriend to a pulp if you don't give me some answers."

She didn't have the strength to mock his bullying or come up with a plan to save herself, MaryLyn, and Teddy.

Teddy.

Her terrified barking in the toilet closet made Claire want to hang on to consciousness. Something tracked down her cheeks. Blood or tears? She couldn't tell. *Not blood, I hope. I already owe Gail for the awning. I don't want to have to replace blood-stained carpet, too.* The fleeting inappropriate thought made her fear she was slipping into darkness.

The man shook her so hard her eyes rolled back in their sockets. The pain in her head was excruciating.

"Where is it?"

Don't give in to the fear. Fight the pain. If I give them what they want, we're all dead. Where are Ray and the gang? They've got to have enough evidence by now.

Off in the distance, she heard a droning noise. It grew louder and louder.

A voice boomed through a megaphone. "This is the sheriff. Drop your weapons, raise your hands, and come out where we can see you!"

Claire wavered between here and not here. She felt as though she were suspended in a bubble that distorted everything around her. Sounds were garbled, images out of focus, her body present, but distant.

Were her hands free?

Something cold was pressed against her face, and she raised her hand to touch it. She felt warm fingers.

"Hey, you back with us?" Sandy asked gently.

Claire blinked. Pain radiated across her face from the mere motion of opening and closing her eyes.

Sandy pressed the ice bag against Claire's jaw. "I don't think your jaw's broken, but I'm pretty sure it will hurt just as bad as if it were. And the rest of you won't feel so good, either. You should probably see your doctor and get some pictures taken of your brain to see if there's any serious damage."

"Whaaa haaaunn?" Claire swallowed and choked on a sob from the pain.

"Steady there. Their credentials identify them as DEA. They claim you're a courier for a Mexican drug cartel they've been watching. You were supposed to have drugs and money on you. But they didn't find anything."

"Gaa asssin?"

"Aspirin? That won't begin to help. I'll give you something stronger that will knock you out in less than ten minutes. The paramedics who came with the chopper checked you out and said you didn't need to be transported to a hospital, but that means you're stuck with me as your doctor for now. Ray is keeping Detective Rogers outside until I make sure you're all right to be questioned."

"Hmmm. Where's my unnn?"

"No gun." Sandy held up Claire's badge. "Any magazine?"

Claire pointed at the cupboard. Sandy checked where Claire indicated.

"Nothing here," Sandy said. "Guess they took them both. Let's get the interview over so you can pass out and sleep off some of the pain." Sandy took two steps toward the open door. "Detective, she's ready for some questions, but her jaw is so swollen that she'll have to write her answers."

Claire couldn't see through her swollen eyelids, but she heard the detective settle himself in the passenger seat across from her.

"Howz Mar lyn?"

"She's all right. In fact, she's right here." He cleared his throat. "In case you don't recognize my voice, I'm Detective Rogers. Since these guys didn't lay a hand on MaryLyn, it looks to me like you're the one they were after. Any reason you can think of for someone to knock you around like this?" He offered her a pad and pen.

She took them from him and awkwardly wrote "no." Nothing seemed to work right. The pad fell off her lap, and then the pen slipped from her stiff fingers. The detective picked them up. "Let's move to the galley table. It'll be easier for you to write on it instead of your lap." Detective Rogers helped Claire cover the short distance and get reseated.

"You're a cop, Claire. Is there anyone connected with any of your cases or any of your contacts that would finger you as a courier?"

She tapped the "no" on the pad.

"I talked with your chief a little while ago. Want to tell me why he's pissed at you?"

Shit. That's not how I wanted to come to the chief's attention.
She shook her head carefully.

"Okay. Did you recognize any of the guys who broke in here?"

Again, she pointed at the word she'd written on the pad.

"I've got to tell you, you're one very lucky person. If they'd had any more time to work you over, we'd have had to wait a few days from now to have this conversation in a hospital." He stood and retrieved his pad. "When you're able to speak, before you head home, I'll talk to you again. As soon as you can, write down what happened and bring it with you when we meet. And I guess I should remind you, a lot of folks will want a copy of your report." The detective left the motor home.

Claire leaned back and held the ice bag to her aching face.

"Ready for your medicine?" MaryLyn asked.

Nausea and fatigue washed over her. It took every remaining bit of energy to give her answer. "Yeah."

"Good. Drink this, and then let's get you to bed."

Chapter 5

Ray's voice droned above her and then suddenly became crystal clear. "...supervisors have a lot of explaining to do about how this operation was put together and why no one told the local Bureau or law enforcement what was going on. And they sure as hell should have verified who was in the van."

Claire struggled to sit up. She swung her legs over the bed and grabbed onto the small set of drawers between the two beds. She took a deep breath and focused on the person sitting across from her.

"Good afternoon, kiddo," Sandy said. "You've been sleeping off and on for two days. That's a good thing." Sandy handed her a glass of something. "Drink this. It'll take the edge off most of that rotten feeling you still have."

"Two days? Where's MaryLyn?"

"She's sniffing around," Ray said, "with some of the gang." He gently touched her swollen jaw in an almost fatherly gesture.

"Teddy? What about Teddy?"

Teddy poked her muzzle through Ray's legs at the mention of her name. Ray bent down and scratched her head. "I think that German Shepherd scared the hell out of her."

"I'm glad she's okay. I'll bet Margie and Gail won't let me borrow their motor home again or let me bring Teddy along with me, either."

"We cleaned up most of the mess," Sandy said. "We've talked to them a couple of times, and they're more worried about you than the Molly Bree. As for the damage, we took enough pictures to embarrass the Feds into making a reimbursement. Here." She offered a packet to Claire. "Eat a few crackers. It'll settle your stomach so you can take some pills."

"Sandy's right about the reimbursement. We've already got a lawyer working on it." Ray shook his head. "Wrongful bust to begin with, and the way they beat up on you while your hands were tied…" He shook his head again. "I don't care what the DEA says, that's not right. Nowhere is beating a suspect in custody okay."

"I'm glad they didn't have a taser." Claire's bruised jaw made every word a challenge.

"Thank God they didn't haul you off someplace to practice water-boarding interrogation," Ray said. "My guess is this doesn't go too high up in their organization. If it did, you'd have disappeared."

"It feels like parts of me are missing." Claire moved a hand over her face. "How bad do I look?"

"The pain pill's doing its job. You want some of you to be numb until it's farther along in healing." Sandy handed her a mirror.

She had shiners around both eyes. She turned her head to get a better view of the imprint left in her skin by a heavy blow from someone wearing a distinctive ring. She fingered it gingerly. "I got a look at the ring on the guy who was punching me."

"We got a picture of him." Ray handed a photo to her. "I recognized the ring, too. I wish we could have stopped this before it happened, but we couldn't get to you sooner. I knew if we came barging down here too soon, we'd only make things worse. The good news is we got plenty of film of their operation. At least I was able to light a bonfire under the local sheriff to swing over with his helicopter to break up the party."

"Which office are the agents from?"

"Texas. They made two strategic errors. They didn't notify the local Bureau office that they were dropping in for a bust, and they didn't bother to verify that you were who their snitch said you were. Their drug dog went over every inch of the motor home and found nothing. Otherwise, they'd have arrested you by now."

"Why do you think he has a ring like Sam Thompson's?"

"He's one ghost that won't go away," Ray said.

"Thompson's the sort of bad news you can't run away from," Sandy added.

"Well, I'm not running," Claire said as forcefully as her tender jaw permitted.

The door of the motor home opened, and MaryLyn squeezed into the small space. Claire caught sight of white gauze bandages around MaryLyn's wrists and a bruise on her jaw.

"MaryLyn, it's good to see you. I'm sorry you got caught in this mess. How are you?"

"Alive. But they weren't interested in me."

"If all that we went through was a legitimate bust, for sure those frat boys on the beach would have been the target," Claire mumbled. She touched her sore jaw.

"They were so open with their drugs," Ray said, "I thought they were one of three things—decoys for DEA, donkeys gone wild, or idiots who stumbled on someone's stash that they used for their own private party." He shook his head and looked perplexed. "The beach is Fed territory, and my leaving messages at the nearest FBI office didn't get any return calls."

"Decoys? Are they still there?" Claire asked.

"No, but they buried some of their stash under the trash bin," MaryLyn said. "The sheriff's drug dog found it."

"There's a feud going on," Ray said, "between the Feds who say the beach is theirs, and the locals. The locals claim it was a wrongful bust, which therefore makes it their business. They're not happy about being left out of the loop. If it wasn't such a stupid blunder and hadn't made the local news, the sheriff could have let it rest, but he's got a reelection to think about."

Ray looked at Sandy. "You about ready to go? We've got a card game to get ready for." He shifted his gaze to Claire. "Strip poker is out, so you want to join us?"

Claire slowly shook her head, regretting even that small movement. "The noise of the shuffling cards would probably kill me. Even the light hurts my eyes."

"That reminds me," Ray said. "We fixed your security lights. Those idiots damaged the motion sensors."

Sandy pulled on Ray's arm as she rose. "No more conversation. She needs to rest. She's still exhausted, and those pills will knock her out again." She pointed to a couple more pills next to a bottle of water on the small table. "Take those in a half hour or so. Believe me when I say you'll feel a lot better if you sleep for one more day."

Claire believed it.

Chapter 6

Claire's eyes fluttered open. Daylight. It took her a few moments to remember where she was, what had happened, and to assess how her battered body was feeling. Slowly she rose. A breeze blew through the open window, flapping a note clipped on the curtain.

Claire,
I've gone for a walk. I'll be back before dark. I left
you a whistle. If you need anything, use it. You have
friends hanging around if you need help.
MaryLyn

Claire got up. Teddy came to inspect her briefly before returning to her doggie bed. Claire used the toilet then prepared to take a shower. She struggled out of her clothes and limped into the cramped stall. She washed her hair and soaped the rest of her body. By the time she was finished, she was exhausted. She laughed ruefully at herself. "Woman, you should be happy this rough and tumble isn't your bag. You'd be a scary person to live with. Blame it on being forty. You didn't used to be such a wimp."

She opened the door to the sleeping area and hoped she had the strength to dress. She heard a sound behind her, covered herself with a towel, and turned.

"Need some clothes?" MaryLyn asked as she rolled the room divider back. She was carrying an armload of clean clothes.

"Yes, thanks. My old ones can almost walk by themselves." Securing the towel around her, Claire pulled out a pair of clean jeans, underwear, and a shirt. She held the T-shirt to her nose and took a deep breath. It was Sandy's soap.

"I've only got two sets of clothes, and they both needed washing, so I thought I'd help you out with yours," MaryLyn said.

They were standing very close, yet there was no tension between them. Straight or lesbian, one naked woman standing this close to another clothed woman should have produced tension, uneasiness. This was all wrong somehow, and Claire couldn't bear it.

"Who are you?" Claire asked softly.

MaryLyn raised her eyebrows. "Why do you ask that?"

Claire took the clothes and sat on the bed. "Because you don't feel right."

"Don't feel right? Oh, my. That's a twist to an old line. I used to hear that while someone was feeling me up."

Claire stared at her with uncertainty, "Are you a cross-dresser?"

"No. Been there, past that."

"A transgender?"

MaryLyn nodded.

Claire exhaled loudly. "I... usually..."

"Let me guess. You were going to say 'can tell.' You were expecting exaggerated feminine mannerisms or noticeable skeletal differences, like big hands, big feet, a masculine jaw."

"I've only known ones who act like flaming queens," Claire said before she could censor herself.

"Well, it's like this... heterosexual women express their femininity in different ways from each other, and some don't express much at all. And just like not all gay men are flaming queens, not all transgenders look like flawed effigies of effeminate women. You can think about that while you put your clothes on."

MaryLyn went to the front of the motor home while Claire dressed. Once clad, she followed MaryLyn to the captain's chairs. As far as Claire was concerned, their relationship wasn't based on sexual attraction—not in the least—but if that was the case, why was she so taken aback by MaryLyn's revelation? Did Ray and Sandy and the others know? Was that why they kept asking her about MaryLyn? About the Smiths? Come to think of it, who was the other Smith? Her husband?

MaryLyn fired a question before Claire could drop into her seat. "Don't you think it's time to admit that whatever is happening at your job has followed you here?" Claire didn't answer, so MaryLyn continued. "What are you going to do now? You sure as hell can't pretend nothing's going on."

"I need to think about that. There's no simple answer and no way to know what's the right thing to do." Claire moved to the kitchen and began preparing a pot of coffee. "I worry that the other shoe is going to drop. That raid the other night was an awfully big operation for a single box of cocaine."

"It seemed like overkill to me, although that was a lot of cocaine for a run-of-the-mill dealer," MaryLyn said. "Unless they were expecting you to sell it to the group on the beach."

"I didn't think of that. But from my brief look at that bunch, I wouldn't approach them for anything." Claire poured two cups of coffee. She joined MaryLyn in the chairs up front. As she sipped her coffee, she thought about how Jackson fit into the bust.

Jackson was behind Vanessa's death—she was sure of it. If Vanessa had experienced anything like the crap she'd just been through, Claire suspected Vanessa had been overwhelmed by the mix of players and complexity of the illegal dealings going on in the small city police station.

For Claire's part, the day Jackson threatened her, she had turned all the information she had accumulated about him and his cronies over to Deputy Marshal Stiller, her undercover contact. At least if something happened to her, her findings could still be put to good use. When she returned from vacation, her first order of business would be to continue her assignment to find out who in the court was working with Jackson to rig the juries to vote the way he wanted them to. Stiller hadn't told her whether the hidden surveillance equipment she'd installed in the courthouse had yielded anything yet. The fog was starting to lift. Maybe it wasn't the jury tampering that Vanessa was sent to investigate that got her done in. It was more likely to have been what one of the rocks she turned over in her broadened search had revealed. If Claire's hunch was right, Vanessa had discovered how the slimy stuff under the rock tied to Jackson.

She lifted her eyes and stared into MaryLyn's dark ones boring into her. Time passed slowly as the two regarded each other.

Teddy yapped, announcing someone she knew was approaching. They glanced out the window. The two Bobs were climbing up the riverbed and coming toward the motor home.

Claire opened the door.

Bobbie looked at her face. "Whoa, that must hurt like hell."

"Yeah, ouch," Bob said as he cringed.

"Thanks for the reminder, guys."

MaryLyn came and stood beside Claire. "Have you met MaryLyn?" Claire asked.

They nodded.

"We got some bad news, Claire. You maybe better sit down."

"Break it to me gently," Claire said as she took a seat at the picnic table.

Bob put a voice scrambler on the corner near his elbow. "Your cocaine box had a five-carat diamond in it."

"How did you find it?" Claire asked. Guess her text message to Stiller was useless.

Bob grinned. "We had you under surveillance to see who all was following you."

"Naturally, we were curious about what you were off the trail about," Bobbie said. "So we dug it up and checked it out."

"A diamond?" Claire whispered. "Five carat?" She tried to picture the size of it. "Isn't that huge? When I opened the box, I didn't see a diamond." She looked at MaryLyn, whose mouth was open in obvious surprise. "Did you see a diamond?"

"No. Was it a cut diamond?" MaryLyn asked.

"It was at the bottom of the box. For an average guy on the street, it's huge. One carat will break a newlywed's pocket. The stone is quality stuff and expertly cut," Bobbie said.

"What did you do with it?" Claire asked.

"We gave it to the local sheriff," Bob said. "He nearly fainted when the jeweler gave his appraisal."

"He was so damn nervous he had six armed deputies walk the jeweler over to his safe to lock it up. They'll put an advertisement out for it, and if no one claims it, his office keeps it," Bobbie said. "He's already making a mental shopping list of computers, radios, vehicles, and new CSI goodies."

"They'll keep it? No finder's fees?" Then the implication of her being the finder dawned on her. "You're right. If it turns out to be stolen—which it most likely is—I certainly don't want to get involved. Plus, I have no idea how—"

Bob held up his hands. "Say no more. We don't want to hear anything close to a confession."

"Confession? I don't have anything to confess. But I've got a feeling that diamond wasn't part of a typical purchase," Claire said. She'd have to pass this extra info on to Stiller.

"Could be," Bob agreed. "So, Bobbie and I are the John Doe One and John Doe Two who found it in the forest where you have not been."

"You think those agents who stormed in here knew the diamond was in the box?" MaryLyn asked.

Both Bobs shrugged.

"Still a box of cocaine and one diamond aren't enough to risk getting called out for making a bad bust and beating the crap out of someone in their custody," Claire said. "It's got to be part of something bigger. If these are rogue agents, I've never heard of them dealing in gems. Drugs, yes. They're easier to unload and harder to trace. Maybe this has some international link." She sighed. "We need more information."

They were all quiet.

"This doesn't make sense," Claire said. "The guys who staged the raid said they'd been following me as part of a Mexican drug cartel. I'd have known if I was being followed. I know how to check my rearview mirror on a regular basis. And my apartment building has a tenant who thinks of himself as Mr. Neighborhood Watch. He'd have noticed some stranger hanging around and commented on it at our meetings. What did you tell the local sheriff?"

"Ray knows him. He did Ray a favor and like we just said, he wrote it up as two John Does having turned it in," Bob said. "I don't want to draw attention to our group here. It's lots better without all sorts of wannabes making reservations just to rub elbows with us."

"You really think people will come up here just because retired law enforcement officers make this their private vacation spot? I doubt it," Claire said.

"Oh yeah? Then why are you up here all the time?"

Claire smiled to acknowledge his point.

"The sheriff will keep Ray abreast of what's happening. Your name didn't come up, but I'm sure he suspects this has to do with the DEA bust," Bobbie said. "The Feds didn't say exactly what they were looking for… just a large quantity of street drugs. What was in that box wasn't street ready."

"So that would mean they risked their jobs for a bust that wasn't properly coordinated with whoever was supposed to have been watching me. Like I said, it doesn't feel right. I don't think they're telling us the truth."

"Why do you think that?"

"If they were after drugs, they'd have said, 'Where's the drugs?' When they were knocking me around, they kept asking, 'Where is it?' Everything about this feels off. For a deal like this, they'd have planned it way in advance, because they'd want to know what they were roughing me up for."

MaryLyn chimed in. "She's right. Federal agents don't gamble unless they have high odds it will go right for them. If they hadn't said they'd been watching you for a year, I might have thought they somehow missed the guys on the beach and came here by mistake. Now I wonder if maybe the guys on the beach were undercover Narc agents."

"We'll never know," Bob said.

"Do you think this might be tied to Sam Thompson?" Bobbie said. "Everybody knows he was a dirty cop, and you being his partner puts you in the light, too."

"One of the agents who used my face as a punching bag wore a ring just like his." Claire traced the edges of the wound with her fingertip.

Both men sighed. "That guy is still haunting you," Bobbie said.

"You know the old saying—it isn't over until the fat lady sings," Bob said.

"I guess that explains everything. No fat ladies warbling around here." Claire looked toward the sky. She watched big fluffy white and gray clouds moving inland between the bare tree branches.

"What about that photographer?" she asked. "I'd almost forgotten about him."

"We found out he's a DEA agent. Doris Maxwell nearly broke his nose when she pushed his camera into his face. You don't wave a camera in her face when she's having writer's block on chapter five." Doris and Gil Maxwell's motor home was parked near the spot the Bobs always occupied.

"Now that you're feeling better, are you coming over tonight for cards?" Bobbie asked.

"You know better than to ask me that. I don't do the card games, and sitting around listening to war stories from all you guys bores me to death." She turned to look at MaryLyn. "You're the card shark. You want to join them?"

Bobbie smiled invitingly. "You'd be more than welcome, MaryLyn. We won't hold the fact you're a bounty hunter against you."

"Just remember, we take no prisoners," Bob said. "If you tell a story you've already told, you have to pay."

"You should be safe, though, since you've never been to one of our get-togethers," Bobbie added.

"Tell me when and where," MaryLyn said. "I could stand to win a few hands of poker."

"When they get you stupid drunk, you're bound to repeat some stories, you know," Claire said.

"Not a problem," MaryLyn replied. "I'm good at remembering what I've said, drunk or sober."

"Be at the store at five," Bob told her. "Doris and Sandy will do dinner, so come hungry. Oh, and we don't use real money. We don't want anyone thinking we're into illegal gambling and calling the sheriff on us."

"Got it," MaryLyn said.

The Bobs said their good-byes and left.

"I'll loan you a twenty." Claire dug in her wallet. "That's the most they'll let any one person lose per night."

MaryLyn tucked it in her bra. "Thanks. I'll pay you back."

Chapter 7

The shifting of the motor home woke Claire from her drugged sleep. Her heart beat rapidly as she struggled to become fully alert. She needed two tries to turn on the lamp beside her bed. Thank goodness she'd cut the sleeping pill in half, otherwise she might have slept right through whatever invasion was taking place. The small bulb barely threw enough light to illuminate the interior of the sleeping area. Claire was stunned to see MaryLyn leaning in the open doorway to the motor home.

"Don't panic. Iz jus' me." MaryLyn lurched a few steps nearer to Claire.

The garble in MaryLyn's voice told Claire she's succumbed to the drinking game. "How'd you manage to make it up here?" Claire grunted from the effort of moving her stiff body as she rose to help MaryLyn.

"The guys dropped me off," MaryLyn said. "They sure do drink, but I won all their matchsticks and never repeated the same story."

"That's why I don't gamble with them. They drink too much and always try to goad me into doing stupid things, like trying to keep up with them." She grabbed MaryLyn's arm as she stumbled. "Here, let me help you."

MaryLyn's head hit the panel at the head of the bed. "Ouch."

Claire pulled the covers back so MaryLyn could get in bed. "Did you have a good time?"

A soft snore was her only reply.

Claire started to undress MaryLyn. Bending even a little was a real pain. Her medication had obviously worn off. She cupped MaryLyn's calf as she pulled off one loafer and then the other. She dropped the shoes in the corner against the night table. She reached up under the loose pant legs and pulled down her socks, noting how smooth her legs were. Claire reached for MaryLyn's belt, but two hands clamped down firmly on her wrists.

"Thank you, but I can manage from here," MaryLyn said.

Claire sank back on her bed. "Good. I'm too tired to yank the rest of your clothes off anyway."

"Uh-huh."

More snores were the last she heard.

* * *

The next morning, Claire awoke to find MaryLyn gone, and she was certain she'd left the campsite. The sheets and the pillowcase were stuffed in the mesh laundry bag. A note was propped on the pillow. Claire tucked the unread note in her pocket, let Teddy out, and made some coffee. She fixed a bagel with cream cheese and a thin slice of purple onion. Her lingering pain forced her to move in slow motion. She set the bagel and a cup of coffee on the dinette table and eased onto the seat. Unfolding the note, she read:

> *Claire,*
> *It looks like you have a good group of friends here to keep an eye out for you, so I'm heading back to civilization.*
> *Thanks for the lift and for all the excitement.*
> *MLS*
> *P.S. Here's my cell phone number. Call when you're back in town, and we'll get together for coffee.*

Claire memorized the number, then folded the note carefully and put it back it in her pocket. After she ate, she pulled out her backpack and loaded it with bottled water and a variety of snacks. She got as far as the picnic table, where she stopped to take stock of the world she'd been missing out on for the past few days. She watched the breeze shake a branch hanging over the stream and listened to the birds, water trickling over rocks, and Teddy's scratching inside the door of the motor home. She let Teddy out and reclaimed her seat on the bench. Teddy hopped up next to her.

Claire studied the campsite. The awning that had been ripped down during the scuffle seemed to have escaped damage. Or maybe someone had repaired it while she'd hung out in halfway land on painkillers.

She gave Teddy a pat. Her body sure didn't feel up to a hike. Maybe she'd just sit here for a while and read a book.

Chapter 8

Claire drove slowly along Rose Avenue, looking for a parking space. She couldn't park in the red zone—she'd be there too long. She was hoping for a spot close to her apartment building, but at three in the morning, what were the odds? Hot damn. Right next to her building. She pulled in and cut the engine.

"How about that? Maybe my lucky streak is back." The sign on the post warned that Thursday was street-sweeping day. She'd have to get up and move her car before nine. She grabbed the duffel bag filled with her dirty laundry and her backpack of art equipment. The rest could stay in the car until daylight. As she exited the car, she almost gagged on cigarette smoke hanging heavy in the morning air. In the bushes that ran along the building, a lit cigarette butt was smoldering in the damp leaves right under one of her apartment windows. She slid her toe under the bush and put it out. The heavy duffle almost tipped her off balance.

That was just what she needed—a neighbor who smoked under her window at all hours of the night.

Quietly, she climbed the stairs. Resting the duffel bag on the railing, she shook her keys to let the cats know she was back. She struggled to fit the right key in the lock. The motion detector on the porch light should have turned on with her arrival. Damn bulb was probably burned out again. Or maybe not.

Cautiously, she pushed the door open with her foot. She peered into the dark room, waiting for a cat or two to come to the door to greet her. No cats. She reached inside and flipped on the light. Neither feline stirred on the cat tree. She closed the door, set the duffel bag down, and hurried over to make sure they were all right. They were breathing. "Okay, you're pissed that I was gone. I get it."

She rubbed Cleopatra's ears and Ramses's back. "Hey, guys. Did you miss me?" Nary a reaction. "Did Amy wear you two out?" She sniffed the air and caught the faint smell of cigarette smoke in the apartment. Her windows were open.

Claire picked up the duffel bag and dropped it in the service porch. The heap of dirty garments she'd left there was gone. Had Amy washed her clothes? She peered in the dryer. Empty. She'd have to call Amy later and thank her. Nonetheless, the idea of someone going through her things, even if it was to help out, had her twitching. She'd never known Amy to do anything more than the bare minimum when she was cat-sitting. Maybe she was bucking for some bonus pay.

She knew she should sleep, but she was too wound up for that. She went back to the front room and booted up her PC. When she'd returned the Molly Bree, Gail and Margie had pried every detail about the drug bust from her. They'd discussed the situation at length. Gail offered some information about the Smiths, and it wasn't all relative to their bounty-hunting activities. She'd seen MaryLyn at electronic surveillance conventions, demonstrating the effectiveness of that sort of equipment for law enforcement operations.

After hours of conversation, they'd all dozed off after one too many glasses of wine. That had been just enough sleep to take the edge off Claire's exhaustion.

While waiting for the computer to come to life, she reflected on Gail and Margie's comments on the drug bust. They'd been pretty harsh about beating a person in custody while they were bound. They both felt very strongly about law enforcement personnel who betrayed their badges. The Feds should have confirmed they were hitting the right target, and they'd failed to do so. Neither Gail nor Margie believed the DEA had been investigating Claire for any length of time. The three of them had gone places together lots of times, and none of them had felt they were being watched.

The mysterious box that was mailed to Claire at Gail and Margie's house contained nothing but ink pens embossed with the name of a local mortuary. Every one of the pens was intentionally damaged in some way: no ink, broken clicker, spring removed, whatever. Who in Jackson's club would have the intelligence to send a message like that? Margie had had the box dusted for fingerprints. There were none on the inside of the box or the pens, just on the outside, and those were probably from the postal workers who handled the parcel.

They speculated about the drugs and had spent much of the night trying to come up with reasons to explain why Claire had been set up with the drugs in the first place. They concurred that Jackson wouldn't waste planting that much cocaine on her for a simple sting.

Likewise, they didn't think he was important enough in the drug dealing business to have that much on him. And for sure hiding a real diamond in the box wasn't something Jackson would do. Jackson was into influencing juries and who knew what else. Claire had heard rumors, but nothing concrete, about his being involved in buying and selling flesh, and she was keeping her eyes and ears open about that. She'd never heard anything connecting him to stolen diamonds.

Claire, Gail, and Margie brainstormed every possibility they could think of as to why and by whom the drugs and diamond had been planted on Claire. She was pretty sure that whoever lost the dope was dead by now.

Before settling in to work on the computer, Claire stepped out to the service porch, turned on the washer, and tossed in her camping clothes. On her way back through the front room, she glanced at the cats. They'd shifted positions but still showed no delight at her return. She dropped into her office chair and typed in her password.

Her leg pressed against the computer tower. It was warm.

Something screwy was going on here.

She accessed her account on an Internet service called *I Spy* to review activities taken while she was gone. Someone had logged on four times during her absence. Amy was the only one who should have been in her apartment. Was she savvy enough to wipe out evidence of her access? Then again, why would she want to disguise the fact that she'd been on Claire's computer—unless she was doing something she wouldn't want Claire to know about? The log-on script was wiped clean except for one access on the day she left on vacation. But Claire hadn't been on the computer that day. It was definitely time to bring in an expert to check for sabotage.

She went to her bedroom closet and got her counter-surveillance device. She kept it in the pocket of a snow coat she seldom wore. If anyone with any competence had searched her apartment, they should have found it.

She ran it through her bedroom first. Her phone lit up the LED light for level 3. She was about to open the drawer where she kept her latex gloves, but she noticed the drawer wasn't closed with the telltale tiny opening she always left as her test for intruders. Okay, now she knew she needed to be extra careful. She made sure the gloves hadn't been tampered with. She looked at each glove closely for something left inside them, then pulled them on. Working around the Jackson crew had made her more careful about spotting nasty pranks.

The evidence envelopes she stored with the gloves had also been disturbed. She held one up to the light to see if something had been added to contaminate whatever she might put in the envelope. Nothing, at least, not that she could see.

She disassembled the phone and found the bug. She dropped it into the envelope and wrote identifying information on the exterior. She resumed her scan and found a camera in the overhead light. Great. Someone with a recording device was watching her every move. The rest of the bedroom yielded nothing more. The bathroom was clean. She pawed through the trashcan in the washroom. She'd dumped the trash the night before she left, so it should be empty, but it wasn't. She found a plastic container from a health food drink she didn't recognize. Would a smoker drink health food beverages?

She found another camera in the kitchen wall clock. Someone had been very busy while she was gone. As a rule, she didn't spend much time in the kitchen, but the clock faced the front room, and she spent nearly every waking moment she was at home in that room. She looked behind her favorite chair; her phone tap detector was detached. What were they hoping to gain? More importantly, who was doing this?

Without a doubt, her apartment wasn't safe for her. Someone had planned and executed this infiltration of her place while she was gone. And they'd staged the raid on her in the motor home right in Ray's backyard, too. Claire stopped cold. It wasn't likely anyone, no matter how well connected, could have done all this in a short time. It had been in the works well before she left on vacation. Was winning the office lottery and getting her vacation time switched all part of a more elaborate scheme? But how could whoever was behind all this know she'd go camping?

Claire's mind raced. What about the trap on the trail? If she'd stepped in it, she'd have taken a serious tumble down the cliff. And if that had happened, would there have been an opportunity to plant the box of drugs and the diamond on her? Come to think of it, who'd have found her if she'd plunged into the ravine? Would anyone think to look in her backpack? Who knew she carried her art equipment in it? Too damn many complications and contingencies. Whoever was out to get her had plans, fallback plans, and probably an army of trusted foot soldiers who'd make sure that one way or another, Claire would be caught in the web being spun around her.

Amy, the cat-sitter, was the only person who should have been in her apartment over the last two weeks. Maybe the health food beverage had been hers. Gail and Margie had recommended her, so Claire had assumed she was trustworthy. From the looks of things, that may have been a bad assumption. Claire prided herself on meticulous attention to detail. This time, she slipped up. She should have researched Amy's background herself. She looked around the room. Everything felt off-kilter. Even the cats were too calm. They should be mewing for food or begging to be let outside for a quick inspection of the neighborhood. Their food dishes were empty, but they had plenty of water. She checked their dry food dispenser— empty. She tossed a handful of dry food in the bowls and replaced the water in the water dish.

She hurried to her bedroom closet and dug out a new wiretap detector. She kept all her spy gear in a shoe box. It didn't look like it had been opened. Whoever had gone through her apartment hadn't been very thorough. Or maybe they didn't care if she knew they were bugging her. Was it Jackson and his too cocky Boys' Club? Or was it the Feds who had supposedly been watching her for a while? Yeah, right. Like she wouldn't notice she was being watched. Then again, sometimes the obvious was really the red herring.

After attaching the device to the phone, she dialed a friend's number.

"Good morning, Richard. Hey, I just got home from vacation, and I need your help. I know you usually get up about this time, so I hope it's okay that I'm calling so early. Someone's been on my PC and bugged my apartment. The computer tower was warm to the touch when I booted up. I've been gone for two weeks, so that tells me someone else was on it shortly before I got here. Yes, I did a check, and the log is showing the last log-on was the day I left for vacation. The thing is, I didn't log on that day, so whoever was on it tried to cover their tracks but screwed up." She listened to his comments. "I'd appreciate that. I've got to be up before nine to move my car, so call me as soon as you've got some news for me. Thanks, Richard. Bye."

Richard would log remotely onto her PC and inspect every detail of recent use. She roamed restlessly through the apartment, unsure of what to do. Uncharacteristically, she turned on the television and stretched out on the couch. In minutes, the droning background noise lulled her into a light sleep.

She sensed more than heard the familiar thump of a cat jumping onto the back of the couch. Soon, a pair of paws kneaded her stomach and a purr vibrated through her chest. At least that part of her life was still predictable. She relaxed and gave in to deep slumber.

Claire bolted upright, disoriented. Cleo walked along the couch back and jumped to the floor. She scurried to the front door and waited.

Claire shook the cobwebs from her brain. *I'm home.*

Someone was ringing her doorbell. She heaved herself to her feet and went to the door. She looked through the peephole. Richard. Using her foot to prevent Cleo from running outside, Claire opened the door.

"Hey, girlfriend. Forgive me for saying so, but you look like crap." He gave her a one-armed hug. "Looks like you had a run-in with a tree."

"I did, and then some. What did you find?"

"I logged onto your PC and found someone's tracks. I'm going to pull your hard drive."

Cleo, mewing all the way, followed Richard to Claire's computer.

"I'll make us some coffee." As Claire headed for the kitchen, she noticed Ramses join Richard and Cleo. Both of them obviously expected Richard to favor them with some kitty treats.

"Better move your car first," he said. "I'll feed them their breakfast while you're gone."

"Oh, that's right. Thanks for reminding me. Canned cat food is in the cabinet. I'll be back as soon as I can find a legal parking place."

Claire circled the block twice without success, so she ventured five blocks out and finally found a spot. As she jogged back to her apartment, she reminded herself the next apartment she rented was going to have tenant parking.

"Have you found anything more?" she asked. Richard clicked away on the computer.

"Don't know yet. I've removed your hard drive and put in a mirror of what you had a month ago." Richard pointed to the table by the couch. "What's with the evidence bags?"

"I found bugs in a couple of places in my apartment. I can't imagine who'd be interested in what I'm doing. I think I lead a boring life. I'll take them to Matthew to check for fingerprints and chemicals. Maybe he can trace where they came from."

"Now there's a good man wasting his time with the wrong woman," Richard said.

"He does seem to have a habit of picking the controlling types who clean him out and then disappear."

"Too bad my adorable Kelly is only interested in matchmaking for the boys. You could use some help in that department."

"No, it's a good thing Kelly sticks with what he knows. Once he's focused on matchmaking, he's relentless. I'd rather not be one of the people he thinks he needs to get married off, but thank you very much for the thought."

"He hasn't made a bad match yet." Richard resumed his inspection of Claire's computer.

She let a few silent moments go by. As he reassembled the computer tower, she posed a question. "Richard, do you know anything about transgenders?"

Richard looked at her over his glasses. "Okay, spill it. Did you meet someone of interest in the woods?"

"I'm just curious."

"I don't know much about those sisters and brothers." He smiled ruefully. "Kelly would have a fit if I ever spoke to one of 'those' people. He feels threatened for some reason."

"Kelly's not alone. Others besides straights feel threatened." She took a step toward the kitchen. "Do you want some coffee? I can put a pot on."

"Don't bother on my account. I need to run. I'm going in early to tend to as many private customers as I can before noon. Then I'm out to the college. They want forty hard drives reimaged with the new operating system they bought." He tucked his tools into their carrying case. "When do you go back to work?"

"Day after tomorrow. First I have to get a doctor's clearance." And check on the surveillance she had set up at the courthouse. She had gotten the equipment from Richard, but he wasn't aware of its purpose.

"Why?"

"Because I got beat up on my vacation. The chief wants a licensed doctor—which of course means the department's medico—to pass me before I go back on duty."

"But all you do is sit at a desk," Richard said. "Are you going to tell me how you got the bruises on your face?"

"I had a misadventure. A scrambled brain can misfile things, you know?"

Richard gathered his things. "Did you meet up with a trannie who worked you over?"

"Way off the mark with that guess, buddy." The image of MaryLyn beating her up struck her as funny, but she covered it up rather than have to explain it to Richard. He pushed the tower under the table and rebooted the PC.

"Your vacations are rougher than your workdays. After your last one, you were limping like a horse kicked you. Maybe you should go on a vacation with us from now on. Kelly plans out every minute of the day so that there's no room for shenanigans—or in your case, mishaps hazardous to your health."

"I went to a jujitsu tourney on my last vacation and did get kicked by what felt like a horse." Claire punched Richard lightly on the arm. "How many potty breaks does Kelly allow? Does he do campouts? Tents only, or are RVs allowed?"

"Don't go asking for trouble. Hand the planning over to Kelly and be entertained with his list of what places are allowed and which aren't. And you'll never want to sleep in another bed until you sanitize it." Richard checked to make sure he'd gotten all his tools. "I'll talk to you later." He scratched each of the cats on his way to the door. "See ya later, Cleo, Ramses." They acknowledged him with flips of their tails.

After he left, Claire stared at her pets. She couldn't prove it, but given the way they'd acted when she got home in the wee hours of the morning, she was sure they'd been given something to sedate them. Why would anyone want to drug her cats? Sure, if they were dogs and someone wanted free access to her apartment, that would make sense, but cats weren't known for their property-protecting instincts. Maybe they didn't want them to sneak out while they were opening the door? A foot in their face would take care of that. A stranger in her apartment would send them behind furniture or under.

Was it just another of Jackson's tactics to let her know that she was vulnerable? No. He was the type who'd kill an enemy's pet to get a point across, not give them knockout drops that might or might not be detected.

She had double locks on her front and back doors in hopes that her neighbors would notice if someone was trying to pick them and would call the police. Maybe she should get Matthew to set up a camera system so she could watch whoever was watching her. Obviously, the locks weren't working as well as she intended.

She stood on the front porch and surveyed every inch—which reminded her to replace the bulb in the motion sensor fixture. She dragged her stepladder out and reached up to untwist the old bulb. It had been unscrewed just enough to break the contact. When she tightened it, the light came on.

"I wonder if Matt can fix it so that the next person who unscrews this gets a nasty shock." She put the ladder away and made a list of things to ask Matt.

She'd met Matt at a city marathon for some charity fundraiser—she couldn't remember which charity. She only participated because she was given an either/or ultimatum. She could either be paired with one of Jackson's gang to hand out water to the runners along the course, or she could slap her feet along the pavement and run the distance. No way was she was going to suffer through standing next to some idiot for the duration of the race.

Since she ran regularly, she figured she could make it to the finish line before the sun set that day. As luck would have it, Matt settled in next to her and paced her. He probably could have won the race, but he was using the marathon as a warm-up for a triathlon, or so he told her. By the end of the race, they'd become friends, and to her amusement, Matt also became her trainer for running. To her delight, as her running time improved, so did her jujitsu skills.

She gathered the evidence she'd found in her apartment and put it in a brown bag. She had time to do some warm-up exercises, katas, and take a run around the school track before she needed to leave for her doctor's appointment. She hadn't gone six blocks before she noticed a car following her. She studied the driver via her rearview mirror. She was convinced her eyes locked with the driver's for a moment and then the car turned down the next side street. Too obvious. She was meant to notice the tail. But why was Jackson stepping up his harassment? Was it Jackson?

Isn't that the way it goes? I work on one assignment and end up uncovering other messes that are giving me issues. Damn, but I love my job.

Doctor Williams kept her waiting for over an hour and then spent a grand total of five minutes with her. He asked two questions, looked at her eyes, and signed a piece of paper, which he handed off to the woman behind the desk. She dated it, made a copy, and handed the original to Claire. So much for Sandy's recommendation about X-rays and an MRI. Doctor Williams didn't think they were necessary.

As Claire drove out of the parking structure, she pulled out her cell phone and dialed MaryLyn's number. The call went to her voice mail.

"Hi, MaryLyn. This is Claire. I'm back in the land of freeways and endless streets. Any chance you're available for coffee one evening soon? I'll catch up with you later."

Her next destination was Matt's condo. She paused at the security gate to press the access code for his unit and identified herself when he answered.

"Come on up."

Claire thought he sounded more than happy to see her.

His condo was at the very back of the three-plex. His balcony overlooked a small backyard that he shared with other residents. Since her last visit, someone had set out potted plants along the stairway and balcony. Whoever had done it had a good eye for color and a green thumb... and knew how to plant electronic eyes in the pots to monitor comings and goings on the stairs. Was Matt paranoid? More likely he had given in to his nerdy nature and was just playing with his toys.

Matt's door stood wide open. As she stepped inside, she saw him dressed in his running clothes. He was gulping the last of his energy drink. He pointed at the sack Claire was holding. "What did you bring me?"

"A mystery." Claire handed him the bag filled with the collection of electronic bugs and trash from her apartment.

He peered in the bag. "How soon do you need to hear what I find out about these?"

"I don't want you to work 24/7, but the sooner the better."

Matt motioned for Claire to follow him. "Step into my office."

What was once a second bedroom was now a miniature science lab. He shook the sack. "I'll start on this right away. I'll have something for you in a few days. Any idea who's bugging you?"

"I've got some hunches, but I'll wait to see what you discover in your analysis. And I'm open to suggestions, so don't be shy in letting me know what you find."

"Is your apartment safe? Have you set up some security so this won't happen again?"

"Not yet. I was hoping you could help me with that, too."

From the look on his face, Claire could tell Matt was already mentally going through her apartment and deciding on the perfect hiding places for security cameras.

"You need to work on your poker face, Matt. The gleam in your eye tells me this is a turn-on for you. Are you willing to do it for me? If it doesn't cost too much, that is."

"Tell me what you want to accomplish, and I'll get it done in your price range."

"I want to know who's visiting my place when I'm not there, and I don't want them to know I'm keeping an eye on them."

"All right. Do you leave your computer on all the time?"

"Not anymore. I've learned my lesson."

"How many network drops do you have for plugging in a cable?"

"I have one DSL in the front room, and three landlines in the kitchen, front room, and bedroom."

"You need to monitor all your rooms. I'll do what I can to be sure you don't have any blind spots."

"Let me know where you put the cameras, their range, and how to disable them. And I need to be able to tell if someone else has disabled them. For sure I don't want someone to be able to tap into what you set up."

"No problem. I can handle that."

"I knew I could count on you." She drew a breath. "I'm sure I'm being tailed, too. None of this was going on before I went on vacation. I'm positive I'd have noticed it."

"What about hooking up a camera on the back of your car?"

"How big is it? I don't want it to be obvious."

"You and I would be the only ones who know it's there."

"How long would it take to hook up?"

"A day."

"I'll have to wait on that. I need my car today."

"You could borrow mine while I'm working on yours."

"The last time I borrowed someone's vehicle, the DEA dropped in on me with guns and dog and left me with this." She pointed to her still-bruised face.

"Claire, it's time to start protecting yourself. For sure you need to wire up for protection. Take my car and let me get started on putting the camera in yours this afternoon. I'll do the same at your apartment just as soon as I can."

She exchanged car keys with him and gave him the extra apartment key she brought along just in case he had said yes.

As she left Matt's place, she tried MaryLyn again. Maybe she was free to have lunch. A quick conversation left that option closed.

MaryLyn had been hired to keep order at a teenagers' pool party. Keeping them away from the alcohol, out of the bedrooms upstairs, and from pulling dangerous pranks had her more than busy. MaryLyn suggested they get together the next day.

"No can do," Claire told her. "It's my first day back at work."

Claire and MaryLyn wished each other the best of luck with their respective obligations and promised to get together one day soon.

Chapter 9

Claire had disguised herself as a frumpy cleaning woman to permit her freer access to the rooms in the courthouse. She was dressed in tight jeans that puckered over her thighs, which were padded with fake cellulite. Her loose-fitting top failed to camouflage the rolls of pseudo-fat around her upper body. She pushed a cleaning cart laden with the tools of the trade. She wanted to see if the monitoring equipment she'd put in the judge's chambers with Matt's help was still installed, but a light shone from beneath the door of the chambers and she could hear muffled voices coming from inside, so she rolled her cart by without pausing.

Around the corner, she stopped in front of a maintenance closet and unlocked it with a key from her jangling ring of keys. She kept her back to the new security camera pointed at the closet door. Once inside, she saw that various items had been moved around, as if someone had made a quick search of the closet since her last visit, a week ago. She was relieved to find her surveillance equipment still taped beneath the lowest shelf. She yanked it free and looked at it for evidence of tampering. Finding none, she replaced the eight AA batteries, removed the SD card, and retaped the recorder in its original location. She dropped the SD card into a padded pocket that made her thighs four times their usual size. Claire emptied and refilled her mop bucket before backing the cart out of the closet.

She relocked the door and headed to the restrooms. She put "Caution Wet Floor" signs in front of the doors and propped them open with rubber stoppers. She did the men's room first, then the women's room. While she mopped the floors, she searched for hidden surveillance equipment but found none. She gathered her cleaning supplies and moved on.

In the first jurors' room, she only found two trash cans. There should have been four. As she leaned down to pick up one of the trash cans, the door behind her opened. The rush of air from the force of the door opening carried the odor of two distinct colognes—one masculine and one feminine. Much as she wanted to, she didn't look to see who was watching her. The door closed hastily. She pretended to dust a picture on the wall, but with her back to the rest of the room, she removed the motion-activated camera concealed behind it. She slipped out the SD Card, renewed the batteries, and replaced the camera. She finished the room and continued to the next jurors' room, again replenishing the equipment and removing the SD card. Afterward, she did the same with the rest of the rooms on the floor. When she finished the last room, she listened at the judge's chamber, but it was still occupied, so she headed back to the elevator. She noticed that the door to one of the rooms that she'd cleaned was partially open. The doors were hinged to automatically close, and she was sure she hadn't left that door ajar. Once again, she forced herself to stay in character. She reminded herself that giving in to her curiosity to look in the room could well lead to her undoing. Grudgingly, she pushed her cart into the elevator and went to the maintenance room in the basement.

Claire moved slowly to stow her cart so that the rest of the cleaning staff could vacate the room ahead of her. She kept her head low as she passed by Jorge, the cleaning crew supervisor, and muttered a barely audible "G'night."

She left the building and ducked around the corner. She carefully watched everyone leaving the building and parking lot across the street. Three silhouettes she didn't recognize walked to the parking lot. They got into separate cars, but only two of them left.

Claire took a long angle across the street and let herself into the backseat of Matt's hybrid. She eased out of her cleaning lady clothes and fat packs and then pulled a curly wig over her matted hair and slipped on a pair of non-correcting eyeglasses. She stuffed the cleaning lady clothes under the seat and climbed over the seat to sit behind the steering wheel. She started the engine. No sound. It made her smile. Quiet was exactly what she needed right now. Unlike her own vehicle, this car required the driver to turn on the headlamps, and in this situation, darkness was her ally.

Claire used her night vision goggles to look across the darkness at the shadowy figure in the driver's seat of the other vehicle that remained in the lot. He was talking to a passenger she couldn't see. She dropped her NV goggles in her lap and tried to figure a way to maneuver herself, unobserved, to get a clear view of the license plate. Before she could take action, the headlights came on and the car exited the parking lot and made a right on Main Street.

Claire followed. He quickly picked up speed. She presumed the driver would head to the freeway on-ramp, but the vehicle took a left at the first light and headed to Condo City.

She tried to calm her jumpy nerves. Condo City was a mess of sprawling buildings the city had struck a construction deal on in hopes of cutting down on gang violence. The idea was to replace the dilapidated houses that had been there with affordable high-rise units. But the bust in the housing market had left the place worse off than before the rebuilding effort. After a year of not filling the units, desperate to end the vandalism and break-ins, the manager of the sales team gave up on selling the units and instead offered them for rent. What was most amazing was that some genius was building more condos even though the others were still largely unfilled.

No time to think about economic blunders in real estate now, though. The car she was following turned into a parking structure next to one of the buildings under construction. Claire parked two blocks away and put up a disability parking permit on the dash of the hybrid so she could park illegally. It didn't always work, but sometimes it did.

She limped slowly around the block, checked to see if anyone was watching her, then sprinted the next block and down the hill to the construction site. She tried to keep a mental tally of the cars parked along the streets as she went. She climbed over the fence at the site and moved around scattered construction trash and building supplies under tarps. A sound on her left caused her to pause behind a stack of lumber. She concentrated on the sounds and smells around her. What she'd heard was the humming from night vision goggles, and it was very close to her.

"Where the fuck is she?" The voice was familiar. It sounded as though it came from the other side of the lumber Claire was crouching behind. She held her breath and tried to hear something more than her pounding heart.

"Shut your piehole, you ass," another voice whispered. That voice was someone she ought to know, too. Before she could place it, she identified the aftershave—the same scent she'd smelled in the jurors' room earlier that night. That cinched it. One of these goons was Officer Philip Mosley from Petima PD.

Claire decided to wait them out and see who the "she" was. Mosley was not known to be a patient man.

"What the fuck is she doing?" Mosley's companion whispered. "Call Jorge." Claire still couldn't put a name on him.

"Hey, Jorge. Can you see her? You said she was following us." Mosley sounded pissed. "Well then, where the fuck is she? Screw you, Jorge!" Claire heard the cell phone snap shut.

"Well?" the companion demanded.

"He lost her. Let's get back to the car. I want to get this over with and just put a bullet through her fucking brain. That way we won't have to worry about her anymore."

"Killing any kind of cop, even if you're a cop, puts a price tag on your head," the other man said. "Besides, we need that information from her."

Claire's eyes opened wide. Holy crap. Were they talking about her? What information? How would they know she was following them? She'd been so careful. If it wasn't her, who else could it be? Her mind sped from one possibility to the next. Who else did she know of that was interested in their business? What other woman tailed people?

MaryLyn.

Claire knew she was jumping to conclusions, but MaryLyn was the only other woman she knew who hunted people. She wasn't a cop, but she said she used to be in law enforcement. Did it make a difference to these men?

"We killed that fucking Deputy Marshal bitch, and there's no price tag on our heads, so that's fucking not true."

"They just ain't got the right stuff. They keep sending bitches when it's a man's job, eh?"

They both laughed.

Anger rushed over Claire as she heard them leave. She struggled with her urge to follow them, but losing control now wouldn't help anything. She needed to get these SD cards to Stiller ASAP.

She surreptitiously looked around the construction site. Staring hard, she finally made out a man and a dog a couple of hundred yards away. Were Mosley and his accomplice planning on killing a woman and letting the night guard and his dog find her? But they said they needed information. Her mind was working double-time, looking for possible answers.

Once she was sure no one could see her, she climbed back over the fence and hurried to the car. She counted the cars parked on each block, comparing it with how many had been there when she had passed by earlier. She checked every bush and alley, too. Before opening the car door, she checked under the chassis and hood for anything that could explode or track her.

Satisfied that the car was safe, she turned on the lights and pulled out. Before going back to her apartment, she stopped to check the 24-hour-access mailbox she rented. There was one envelope waiting for her. Quickly, she glanced over the information.

Claire chuckled. A team member contact told her the judge whose chamber was bugged had requested a jury tampering investigation in three of the jurors' rooms and also in his chambers.

Well, well. The U.S. Marshals Service would be called in officially now. She could hand over the SD cards and hope they held evidence that would even further incriminate the jury tamperers. Stiller had been very pleased with the earlier results of her evidence gathering. Now maybe she could get his okay to focus on this drug and diamond mess that had suddenly cropped up.

Claire made her way home via a circuitous route. She texted Stiller to set up a pickup of the SD cards. By two a.m., she was in bed. If she could convince sleep to come quickly, she could get four hours of much-needed rest.

Claire rolled onto her side. The remnants of another weird dream evaporated as she awoke. "Ramses," she whispered to the orange tabby perched on the foot of the bed. He hated the sound of the alarm clock and once again had awakened Claire before it buzzed. She moved to shut off the alarm, but was too late. Ramses scurried from the room.

Claire thumped the top of the alarm and turned it off.

Cleo meowed from the doorway.

"I know. I didn't give you your dinner last night, and I forgot to clean your cat box."

Cleo meowed more loudly.

"You're right. I'm neglecting you."

She tossed off her bed covers. She put wet food in the cats' bowls and reminded herself to get some dry food for them. While they ate, she cleaned out the litter boxes. She checked her text messages. Stiller had given her the go-ahead for the moment to pursue the drug and diamond trail. He told her he would send a team member to the track Claire usually ran on. She was to fasten a baggie holding the SD cards to the inside-left of the front-opening trash can at the entrance to the track. Each time she had evidence to turn in, Stiller chose a different method for her to do that. The methods usually coincided with her daily routine.

After that, she did an hour of katas and dressed in her running gear. She put the SD cards in a baggie, popped some spearmint gum into her mouth, and headed to the high school track. She pretended to toss the wad of chewing gum into the trash receptacle, but instead, she used it to fasten the baggie in the designated place. Joining the runners already on the track, she settled into her pace. The runners limited their interactions to polite nods, choosing to focus on counting laps and monitoring pulse rate instead of chatter.

Claire used the run to clear her head. She pushed her nervous flutters over returning to work and having to explain to the chief how she got involved in a drug bust at the campground to the back of her mind.

When she finished her laps, she had to force herself not to check on the trash receptacle.

Pleased to find she was only one lap short of what she had been able to do before her vacation, she used her walk back to the apartment to cool down.

She showered quickly and dressed in pressed jeans, a starched tan cotton blouse, and a brocade vest. Her police shoes with steel-reinforced toes and heels weren't freshly polished, but they weren't scuffed.

Her laundered uniform should be waiting for her at the office. Her handgun was in the safe inside her locker. She looked at herself in the mirror. If for some reason her uniform hadn't been delivered, she'd be okay in what she was wearing. She grabbed a brown leather jacket from the closet, collected her keys and wallet and the keys to Matt's car, and went out the door.

She left her parking spot and headed to the freeway, making note of the vehicles she passed.

One lane over, she noticed a car that had been parked half a block from her apartment. As she entered the police station parking lot, that same car drove by, just a little too slowly, she thought. She strained to see the driver but couldn't make an ID. A number of unfamiliar cars were parked in the employee slots. She hadn't been gone that long, had she? Maybe it was a public lot now. She looked around and spied a sign that said the lot was for PD employees only. Just in case, she wrote a note and laid it on the dashboard. The last thing she needed was to have Matt's car towed for illegal parking. She would have to gamble that Jackson's crew wouldn't mess with the car. She glanced at the camera that had a view of the employee parking lot. That was new, but would it do any good with catching any of Jackson's cohorts?

She steeled herself for her walk through the hallways that were sure to have more than a handful of Jackson's posse hanging around. Her face still had traces from the worst bruises, and Jackson's thugs wouldn't miss a chance to make snide remarks.

An unfamiliar officer sat at the front desk behind a bulletproof shield that hadn't been there when Claire left for vacation. Claire flashed her badge, which the officer inspected.

"I'm Officer Gloria Malone. Welcome back from vacation, Hanson." She came around the desk and shook Claire's hand. She pointed to the marks on Claire's face. "You must have had an exciting vacation."

"Hiking has it hazards."

Malone handed Claire a piece of paper. "It's the new code to open the door. Only commit it to short-term memory. In a month it'll be something else." Malone smiled and gestured toward the cipher pad.

Claire accepted the paper with the number code. "Thanks. Nice to meet you, Officer Malone."

She tapped in the code. This whole security setup was new. Jackson must be expecting unwanted visitors. Maybe he was afraid some of the gangs he consorted with would come looking for him. Other changes had been made, too. There was a new door to the chief's office, the walls were freshly painted, and the floor was new, too.

She knocked on the chief's door but got no answer. She slid her clearance form from the doctor through the mail slot.

Downstairs in the file room, she unlocked her desk drawer and examined the contents to see if anything had been disturbed. Nothing looked out of place. That was surprising. Wouldn't that be the first place to look for incriminating evidence with which to trap her? New files were neatly stacked in the inbox, but other than that, it was exactly as she'd left it the day she went on vacation. She relocked the drawer and went to the women's locker room to change. Her uniform was not hanging from her locker door.

It was hard not to jump to conclusions and suspect that Jackson and his lot were responsible for its absence. Her anxiety began to rise. She'd thought she was prepared for her return to the war zone, but every little change had her on full alert.

"Hey, Hanson!"

It was a friendly, happy voice calling her name from the doorway.

Claire turned to look at Monica, who was dressed in civvies with a detective's badge looped over her belt. In uniform, Monica had always looked bulky, thanks to the bulletproof vest all uniformed police officers wore. She looked trim and surprisingly attractive in street clothes. Her makeup was lighter, more subdued, and she was wearing new glasses. If she and Claire had been casual friends and not sister officers, Claire would have asked her if she had a new boyfriend.

"Hi, Monica. How're you doing?" Claire's eyes lingered on the badge.

"Great! You like?" Monica fingered her badge and swaggered over to her. "I passed the detective test and finally got promoted. It's about time all those degrees I have in criminology paid off."

"Detective?" Claire hoped she hid her disbelief. Something really strange was going on at this station, and it was leaving her off balance.

"Yep. And you've been transferred back to homicide. I put your uniform in the detectives' office." Monica gestured for Claire to follow her.

Claire removed her utility holster and Glock from her locker. She checked it and then slammed the door, locked it, and followed Monica.

Instead of going to the detectives' room, Monica pushed open the door to the women's restroom. The walls still gave off a hint of fresh paint. The floor sported new tiles, the stalls all had new doors, and a shower stood where a supply closet used to be.

"Are you sure this is a good place to talk?" Claire asked suspiciously. She pulled out a pen that detected hidden cameras and telephone bugs.

"I checked it a few moments ago," Monica said. "No spy equipment. What do you think of what happened while you were gone?"

"It's nice that they finally painted the place. Having a shower with hot water will help a lot. The place looks good."

"I'm not talking about interior decorating, Hanson."

"Well, other than the cipher code on the door and some new paint and floor coverings, I haven't seen much else that's different."

"Damn." Monica gave Claire a look of disbelief. "But we all thought everything was tied to you going on vacation early and being away for two weeks."

"What the hell are you talking about?"

"You really don't know, do you?"

Claire shook her head.

"The FBI and Internal Affairs cleaned house with arrest warrants and subpoenas. They arrested Jackson and his pals.

They're locked up in some undisclosed place. The Feds removed all the PCs from the detectives' department."

"What's the deal? Is Jackson some kind of Mafia king, the devil, or what?"

"Close to the devil, I'd say. Apparently he and his Boys' Club are part of an international human trafficking ring that brings in women and girls from other countries and sells them in the sex trade. Rumor is he's not above snatching young kids from their neighborhoods if he thinks it's worth his time. I can't wait until he's on the other end of the bend-over in the men's club."

"I had no idea," Claire said. Why was she assigned here to investigate jury tampering when human trafficking was suspected? Maybe the trafficking investigation was close to wrapping up before she was sent here. "What else?"

"Judge Mendoza denied them bail. No bond hold because they're a flight risk."

Monica leaned forward and pushed Claire's open mouth closed with a nicely-manicured finger. "If you leave that hanging loose like that, you're gonna catch flies, as my dad would say."

Claire caught the curious look on Monica's face. "I swear I didn't have a clue."

"A few minutes after you left the building, the cleanup crew came in. It was impressive. All the detectives that were here, a dozen uniforms including Mr. Muscle, and one of the coroners were arrested. Some of them were just handed their walking papers but told not to leave town because they'd be contacted again to answer more questions. This is by far the biggest investigation I've ever seen." Monica scrutinized Claire's face. "Have they questioned you yet?"

Claire was shell-shocked. She shook her head slowly.

"You'll get your turn. You can about imagine all the jobs that opened up." Monica fingered her new badge again. "A lot of hopefuls from other cities came knocking on the chief's door hoping to get a shot at a better position."

Monica's voice dropped a decibel or two. "And here's a real shocker. Word is that Sam Thompson isn't dead."

Claire felt the blood drain from her face.

Monica patted Claire's shoulder clumsily. "Since you didn't know about the other stuff, I thought I'd better tell you before you heard it from some unfriendly source."

"Unfriendly? Who's still around?" Claire asked.

"I don't know, but someone has been vandalizing the building, inside and out. The chief ordered cameras put up at all the doors, and he's told us he doesn't want to believe that someone within the ranks would pull that sort of crap." She laughed ruefully. "Like cameras will stop someone with an axe to grind."

Claire leaned against the sink for support. She convinced herself to breathe slowly and tried to regain her equilibrium. Had all this come about because she'd turned in the results of her own investigation on Jackson? She took Jackson's threat on her life seriously. Could it be that Deputy Marshal Stiller, or whoever was looking out for her, knew what Jackson was planning to do to her and arranged for her to be away on a hurry-up vacation?

Mosley obviously had been one of those given their walking papers, but not held. That was why he had time on his hands to track down some woman at night. If someone at Petima PD had got wind of her collecting evidence on jury tampering, there could still be a lot more trouble to come.

Monica's voice brought her back to the moment. "The first time they broke in, they trashed the detectives' room, but there wasn't much left after the FBI took the PCs, desk contents, and files. The intruders spray painted everything they could find."

"It's happened more than once?" Claire asked.

"The second time, they vandalized the halls. This building is open for business all the time, so they had to arrange for it to be empty. What do you think got the place emptied enough for someone to get in and punch holes in the walls and scribble graffiti all over the place?"

"Had to be a bomb scare. While everyone's outside waiting for LAPD to send over their team, the perps get in and wreck the place."

"Right."

"Was it tied to any of the gangs? Any familiar tags?"

"Nope, not that anyone can find anyway. The next time, they messed up the workout room, broke the fixtures in the restrooms, and left a major leak after flushing paper towels down the toilets. They were interrupted trying to get into the chief's office. Somebody saw three guys in hooded sweatshirts running out the back exit. That was the last episode."

"But the place looks great now."

"Chief Dobbs told us that if we pitched in to fix up the mess, the city would foot the budget for new office equipment. So we had a remodeling day. All the new people who wanted to make a good impression showed up, but so did the rest of us. One of the uniform's brothers owns a carpet and tile store, and he gave us a deal on flooring. Some of the guys are good handymen. And get this, the guys didn't complain when some of us women asked them to show us how to roll out carpet and put down tile. We have private showers with locks now, just off the workout room. Boys on the right and girls on the left. You might not believe it, but we had a good time fixing this place up." Monica smiled wistfully. "It's like our second home, you know?"

"That's great," was all Claire could say. She needed time alone to reflect on all the changes around the department and especially to consider what Monica had said about Sam Thomson. He wasn't dead? What was that about? Her eyes narrowed as she thought about Judge Mendoza.

"Monica, you said Judge Mendoza put the bad apples in jail without bond. I thought he was in traffic court."

"Not that Mendoza. You know there's a lot of Mendozas around here."

Claire detected an undercurrent of irritation from Monica. Odd, on a point that ought to be inconsequential.

Monica went on. "Judge Mendoza is a Federal judge who replaced Judge Hertzog, who died of cancer."

Why was Monica keeping up with Federal judges? Maybe it was something they were requiring of new detectives now. What the hell?

"You know the FBI uses Federal judges for their warrants," Monica continued. "Anyway, for now, there's six detectives, counting you and me, Linda Chandler from NYPD, Harrison Harvard from Colorado, Rob Dankest and Kennie Reynolds from L.A. I'm training with Linda, or Linnie as she likes to be called, and then I'll be partnered with either Dankest or Reynolds. You're partnered with Harvard. It's a kick getting used to Linnie. She's so New York, you know? I'm learning to talk like her, like saying 'I'm jelly' for 'I'm jealous,' you know?"

"So who from the old crowd is still around?"

"You mean Jackson's boot lickers? Hard to say for sure. You know how he twisted people's souls with blackmail. All of third shift's uniformed officers are still around. On second shift, only Junior, Moody, Marciano, Wells, and Hall survived. On dayshift, you and me, Marcos, Sanchez, Boyce, and Treitler."

She paused and looked around. It was a habit they'd all developed. You never knew who was listening to your conversations. "Anyone who was reviewed by Jackson or his pals is being reevaluated. That's a good thing. Only Jackson's friends did well on their reviews. All those classes I took were never included in my records, and now they are. I feel like my history is up-to-date finally."

"I'm glad it's working out for you. You have a lot to be proud of. Where's the chief? Usually he's in early."

"He stops at the prosecutor's office every morning. Roll call in five minutes. It's so great not to have to wear a uniform. Hey, Hanson, can I ask you a question?"

"What?"

"What happened to your face?"

"I fell off a cliff."

They heard the chief's voice in the hallway asking who was going to make the coffee.

"Monica, I'll catch up with you. I need to check in with the chief." Claire left the room and hurried to the chief's office.

Chief Dobbs was sitting at his desk reading the report from Claire's doctor. Claire knocked and he waved her in.

"Hi, Chief. I heard you had some excitement while I was gone." She wished she hadn't blurted that out. She wasn't on friendly terms with him, and pretending she was wouldn't ever put her there.

"Close the door and sit down, Hanson."

Claire did as he directed and noticed new padded fold-up chairs leaning against the wall. She noted a number of other changes as well. She hadn't been in the office since Chief Dobbs took over from Chief Hershey.

A new duty board filled with names and badge numbers nearly covered one entire wall. She was pleased to see her name there. On the opposite wall, a second board identified the department's open cases. The badge numbers of the detectives assigned to them were written next to each case. A large flat-screen monitor, phone, and an all-in-one printer/scanner/fax sat on a separate table. The chief's desk looked bigger than she remembered, but it could have been because there weren't the old mounds of paperwork on it.

"I want to know what happened on your vacation," Dobbs said.

Claire had anticipated his request. She reached into her back pocket for a copy of what she had given to the detective up north. Dobbs laid it on his desk without so much as a glance.

"Tell me in your own words."

She recited her story to the chief and answered all his questions. He seemed oblivious to the fact that he kept her well beyond the time she should have left for roll call. She waited for him to say something about the changes in the department or to offer some comments or reactions to what she'd told him. He hadn't even raised an eyebrow when Claire mentioned MaryLyn Smith. She really thought he should have had some follow-up questions since MaryLyn was a witness to what had happened up at the campsite. Instead, he acted like she was recounting old news.

"You're back to working as a detective in homicide. You'll be teamed with Captain Harrison Harvard. He's a veteran in the investigative end of the business and has worked with different law enforcement agencies, so he can give you a good foundation in homicide and how to network with other organizations. He's working on a stack of cases now. He'll show you where your desk is." He extended his hand. "Welcome back, Detective Hanson."

Claire shook his hand and thanked him. Before entering the detectives' area, she paused to gather herself. She stepped over the threshold into a strikingly different environment from what she had known before vacation. For starters, the room was brighter. Handwritten name cards were posted chest high on the six new cubicles in the room. She spotted Captain Harvard's name and headed to his workspace. Sticky notes were plastered on almost every surface of two nearby desks. Files were piled high on a third desk. One desk was painfully clean. The name card said it belonged to Detective Robert Dankest.

All of the desks had new, large, flat-screen monitors atop them, and the chairs looked a lot more comfortable than the old ones. The air smelled a lot cleaner, too. As Monica had told her, the room was newly carpeted and painted, and better lighting made it feel like a room Claire had never seen before. A uniform, which she assumed must be hers, hung in the drycleaner's bag on a real coatrack. To the left where they had three interrogation rooms that the uniformed officers shared, the one door she could see was new with a double-glassed viewer. Filing cabinets minus the dents from kicks and punches from the previous occupants were standing taller in their familiar place. Two all-in-one printer/fax/copiers, and two large posting boards—one a duplicate of what was in the chief's office—were in another corner. The boards showed assigned cases with names.

A white-haired, broad-shouldered man with a short marine-style haircut was watching her. He had two bottles of water and an uneaten apple on his desk. A handwritten name card identified him as Captain Harrison Harvard.

"Captain Harvard?" She held out her hand. "I'm Claire Hanson, your new partner."

He reached over to grasp her hand. She wondered how she measured up in his eyes.

"I go by Harrison in the field and in the office. How are you? Is Hanson all right, or Claire?"

"Hanson in the field and Claire in the office. I'm feeling great and ready to get to work."

"Good. We have morning shift and start work at 7 a.m. unless we're on call, and then you know how it goes." He gestured to the desk next to his. "I'm four cases ahead of you. Dig in. My aim is to get through a dozen before lunch. We've been given every homicide case that was handled by the previous group of detectives to verify the credibility of the witnesses, the evidence, and make sure there aren't any discrepancies that will be challenged in court. I understand you filed most of these. Did you read any of them?" Claire nodded. "Good. How are you with remembering names?"

"Good enough on some. Thai and Indian, not so good." She hung her coat over the back of her chair with one hand and turned on her new computer with the other.

"I haven't run across any of those yet. Your name and password for first time sign-on is your first initial and last name, no space."

Her name card was sitting in the center of the desk. Detective Claire Hanson. She placed it on the rim of the cubicle wall as the others were. She was open for business.

Claire selected the first case on top of her stack. She remembered it. When she read it originally before filing it, she didn't take notes because it didn't concern any of the people she was interested in. Now she regretted it.

She tugged open the desk drawer and noticed the key to the desk was taped to the inside. She peeled that off and added it to her key ring. There were steno pads, a box of pens, pencils, paper clips, and other odds and ends needed for keeping a neat desk. In another drawer, she found a box of gloves and a small black case for evidence gathering. She unzipped the case and found tweezers, small pliers, four cotton swabs in plastic cases, and small evidence packets. She pulled out three pairs of gloves from the box, stuffed them in one of her coat pockets, and added the case to her other coat pocket. In yet another drawer, she found empty files and evidence envelopes larger than those in the small case. She fit those in the inner pocket of her coat. Always be prepared, her first mentor had told her.

"Did I forget anything?" Harrison asked.

"Camera."

"Do you have a digital camera that can take close-ups?" Harrison asked. "The department has maxed out the budget with the repairs and replacements. I go by the rule 'never go anywhere without a camera.'"

"I have a digital at home that fits in my pocket. I'll carry it from now on."

"Good idea."

"And you?"

"Mine's somewhere." He waved a hand. "In all the packing and some unpacking, I haven't run across it yet."

Claire got busy on the open file. One by one, she worked her way through them.

She finished a call, made notations in file seven, then tossed it in her Out basket. She looked over at Harrison to see how he was doing. By the sounds her stomach was making, she knew it was lunchtime. She liked Harrison already because he had come over several times to see what she was taking notes on from her phone calls to names connected to the cases.

"I can hear your stomach from over here," Harrison said. "Why don't we get lunch? After lunch we'll compare notes for what we've gone over and see where we are. Do you have any contacts on the street?"

"No. Do you mind walking? There's a sandwich place two blocks up and two more blocks from the furniture store that was in two of these reports. I was thinking we can take a look at the back to get a real view of it."

"Okay. Walking sounds like a good idea after eating."

The two headed out of the building with Claire lengthening her strides to keep up with Harrison.

"I spoke with the Petima CSI group," he said, turning slightly to look at her. "We're going to get together and discuss evidence-handling and crime scene investigation so we're all on the same page. We'll be doing the same with the uniforms since they're first on the scene. It'll be a refresher course for everyone. We're in need of some bonding within this police department."

Claire nodded. Detectives ask the questions, she remembered a friend had told her, they don't do CSI work unless needed, and they don't do police work unless needed.

"What else has you interested about this furniture warehouse?" Harrison asked.

"Some of the pictures of it aren't in the file. I want to see what we're missing. The owners can't say we're harassing them because we have authorization by the judge to spot-check to see that they're keeping their space clean of drug paraphernalia. They're supposed to call us to clean it up if they see anything."

"I saw the report on the drug bust. Everyone arrested got off on a technicality. The only thing that stuck was that spot-check," Harrison said.

"Another great move by the Boys' Club. I suspect they did it purposely so their friends could get off."

"Everyone calls them the Boys' Club. I've been meaning to ask why."

"They called themselves that. It was an inside joke they didn't share with anyone outside of their group. I called them Jackson's posse."

"It must have been difficult for some of you who just wanted to be good cops."

"Yeah, it was."

Harrison followed her down the block into the sandwich shop where uniformed cops were getting their orders filled. Everyone nodded politely, but Claire recognized only a few of them. She wondered how Angel, the shop owner, felt with the change of attitude in his clientele. He looked the same to her. As polite and attentive as ever while he and his staff rushed to put together ordered sandwiches. Everyone was on a clock.

They found a table outside. After Claire finished half her sandwich, she was ready to talk.

"There were two drug busts at the furniture warehouse. Both were based on tips from 'Booker B.' He's got a drug record longer than most, and he's past the three strikes. The same judge and the same deputy prosecutor are involved, and he's always sent to the local jail then released due to overcrowding."

Harrison stared at her, his grey-blue eyes penetrating hers. "You suggesting the judge and deputy prosecutor are part of a conspiracy?"

"Those two cases regarding the furniture warehouse, regardless of Booker's information, were failures in prosecution. The defense attorney, the same one in all cases, challenged the method of collection and handling of evidence and rightly so. There was no real evidence the Deputy DA was willing to bring up so... no trial."

"Yes. And?"

"You know how overlapping pictures are taken of the crime scene, unless you have a camera that takes panoramic pictures? When used in court, they aren't smoothly fitted like a Photoshop image so the defense attorney can't say they were doctored by the PD. Just from looking at the pictures in the files, I can tell some are missing.

"You said we were going through the cases to see if anyone who was found guilty wasn't framed or could claim they were, but what about cases purposely mishandled? Shouldn't we look into who was involved?" She was thinking jury tampering could have been involved, too.

"Okay." He smiled amiably. "You can do the follow-up on those cases."

"No problem."

After dumping their trash, they walked to the furniture store.

"Too bad we don't have a drug dog or a camera," Claire said. Trash littered the parking lot that two warehouse buildings shared. A few vehicles were parked in it. "It looks like someone is still using this place for selling drugs. I see a needle there and a ripped bag with a broken pipe. Looks like it could be from last night. A fight must have broken out, and everyone split in a hurry. It's noontime and we haven't received a call to come out and collect evidence."

"I guess the owners don't take a judge's warning seriously." Harrison pulled out his cell. He spoke into it for a short time, giving the address of the store.

"Making a date?" Claire asked.

"Yep, and I have one for you, too."

"She doesn't look like a dog, does she?"

"Spitting image. It's a he though. No kissing on the first date."

Claire laughed, delighted with his humor.

He called another number and asked for a CSI team to be dispatched to where they were. Flipping the cell phone closed, he turned to Claire. "CSI won't be free for another hour. If you find something that can fit in your envelopes, take a picture with your cell phone and collect it. I asked for some uniforms to be sent over to protect the scene, but I was told since it's not an emergency, and they're on patrol or working at another crime scene, we'll have to wait. Lt. Bostitch, the new dayshift manager of the street cops, doesn't want to spread his team thin."

Claire thought she heard irritation in Harrison's voice. It sounded like the new department heads were having territory issues.

While they waited for someone to arrive, they took photos of the area with their cell phone cameras and picked up two more broken needles and a dozen small baggies.

"The photos in the department files don't match up with this scene," Claire said. "The building structures are different. Maybe someone doctored the pictures to eliminate something from the scene that they couldn't remove any other way."

"I'll ask CSI to check their files for photos. They keep separate files from the other departments so we'll see just what we're missing."

Harrison continued to walk around, snapping photos with his cell. Claire leaned close to look at a cigarette butt. Something looked familiar about it. After taking a shot of it, she tweezed it into a small envelope and wrote the relevant information on the outside.

An SUV drove up and a woman who looked to be about fifty slid out, followed closely by a Heinz dog. His short tail was fully engaged as he sniffed at Harrison's pocket. Harrison pulled out a cookie and signaled the dog to sit before giving it to him.

"Claire, this is my wife, Ellen. Ellen, this is Claire Hanson, my new partner."

"Hi, Ellen. Nice buddy you have there. Is he registered?"

"Hi, Claire. Nice to meet you. Blueblood's registered with the Feds." Ellen leaned down and stroked the dog's head. "So, where's the target?"

"This area here," Harrison said.

Ellen immediately got Blueblood into work mode. Harrison looked closely and took a picture everywhere the dog stopped and sniffed. He had his own tweezers and cotton swabs.

"What do you think?" Claire asked.

"I think we need CSI to go over this place. My cell's drained with all those pictures. How's yours?"

"Dead. I keep two spares in my locker. Always be prepared," she said in a mocking tone.

"Ellen, can you give us a lift back to the office?"

"Sure, but I can do better than that. I have that camera you got for your birthday. It's in the glove compartment."

"Is that where it is? I thought I lost it."

"You did. It was on the floorboard under the seat. It must have dropped from your coat pocket."

He went to retrieve it and found the batteries were dead. Ellen gave them a ride to the office. Harrison replaced the camera batteries and picked up a car charger for his cell phone. Claire grabbed the extra phone batteries from her locker, inserted one into her cell phone, and slipped the other into her pocket while Harrison got hold of a CSI team.

When they returned thirty minutes later with the team, the entire place had been washed down and smelled of bleach.

"Looks like you've got something going on here, Harrison," Sanborne, the CSI agent, said. "Regarding your request for pictures of this place in our files, the chief has us auditing our files and so far I haven't gotten to any of the recent cases. The previous CSI team wasn't into details when saving information. If you want anything sooner, you can send over one of your detectives to help out."

"I might just do that."

"Well, at least the bleach takes care of the urine stink." Claire wrinkled her nose at the strong bleach smell.

Harrison studied the two businesses. Heavy metal screen doors secured the backdoors against illegal entry. "Someone's nervous," he said.

Claire thought she caught movement from behind one of the screen doors. Squinting, she could barely make out a large shadow of a person who was watching them.

Sanborne and his partner went around the area with bottles of Luminol and portable fluorescent lights. The evidence they gathered was logged in with the CSI lab.

Claire realized suddenly that the butt she found was like those her supposedly dead ex-partner, Sam Thompson, smoked. What a coincidence. That was not welcome news.

Sanborne pulled out his cell phone and read the display.

"Anything I need to know?" Harrison asked.

"We're done here, unless you have something else." Sanborne showed Harrison what was on his cell.

"No. Between what we picked up and what you haven't found, that does it. I'll talk to you later, Sanborne." Harrison turned to Claire. "Let's start questioning the employees of this furniture store. You can—"

"Watch schoolmaster Harrison at work."

"Schoolmaster Harrison? Sounds like a porno flick, Hanson."

Harrison knocked on the door to the furniture store's screened in area. The dark shadow morphed into a silhouette of something large, backlit by the store's interior light. Harrison introduced himself and Claire to the worker and showed his badge. The man, not bothering to disguise the contempt in his voice, said he didn't speak English.

Harrison turned to Claire and told her in a low voice, "Go around to the front and see if you can get a manager."

"Backup?"

"Yeah. Give another call and put a rush on it."

Claire glanced at the shadow. "Are you going to wait for them to get here?"

"No."

"Okay." Claire hurried around to the front of the building, scanning the street for any suspicious activity. She made a call to the PD front desk and requested backup. She was impressed that the new dispatcher was professional and took the call without comment. She quickly slipped in the front door and heard a buzz from behind a desk that became silent when the door closed. A dozen workers from south of the border were huddled around the doorway, looking into the back room and then looking at her. Business must be good to have this many workers standing around, she thought.

"All right! Let me have your attention!" She remembered not to say "police." That would be like yelling "fire" in a theater. She held up her badge so they all could see she wasn't a Fed. They moved to where she gestured for them to stand. Harrison came into the store, motioning to the giant who had been blocking his entrance to join the others.

"Anyone speak English?" he asked.

No one volunteered to speak for the group.

"If none of you can speak English," Claire said, "we can take you all down to police headquarters and arrange for a translator."

"Maria," the big man said and pushed a young woman forward. Claire studied the man closely, noticing the gang tattoos across his forehead, neck, arms, and fingers. She and Harrison might have stepped into big trouble.

"Maria, can you understand English?" Harrison asked.

"I speak a little," she said softly.

"Is the owner or manager of this place here?" Harrison asked.

Maria looked at the tattooed man and hesitantly asked him the question. The answer was longer than a simple no.

"The owner is on vacations, and the manager is taking break," she translated.

"I want to know the name of each person here, what time they get here for work, and when they leave. I also want to know how long each person has been working here." Harrison kept looking at the lined-up workers and around the shop as if expecting someone else to appear.

"Who gave the order to clean the back alley with bleach?" Harrison stared at the tattooed leader.

Maria asked and everyone looked at the leader. Two of the men were slowly inching their way to the sides of the group.

"Get back in line and put your hands in plain sight," Claire ordered. She walked along the line of men, careful to keep a respectful distance. None of them smelled of bleach. Someone was missing. How did he sneak away?

"Where's the guy that was standing there?" Claire demanded.

"Don't move! On the floor and face down." Harrison's voice went deep when three men began to move as if they were about to run. Claire had her Glock out and was pointing it to the ground, finger off the trigger, but she was ready, looking about her while keeping an eye on the woman and the tattooed man. Where did that guy disappear to?

"I want lawyer," one of the men said clearly.

"It's whatever Immigration and Customs Enforcement has to offer," Claire said.

Pandemonium broke out. The men scattered, and regardless of what either detective yelled, they disappeared between furniture and into the back. Claire grabbed Maria with one hand and kicked the legs out from under the nearest man that made to grab her gun hand. Moving fast for a guy his age, Harrison shouldered one man into another.

"Down!" Harrison shouted. One of the men didn't obey and scrambled to his feet, but Harrison coldcocked him with his fist. The man landed unconscious, sprawled out over the top of a couch, while Harrison elbowed another in the chest.

"Hands above your head and spread your legs," Claire told the two who were covered with her gun. Both complied. "Where the hell is our backup?" Claire asked angrily.

"Ouch." Harrison shook his hand out. "Did anyone point out to you that it's against the law to yell 'fire' in a crowded auditorium?"

"My mother did say that."

"Yelling 'immigration enforcement' in a room full of immigrants is damn near the same thing."

Harrison glanced up at the four uniformed police officers that arrived with guns drawn. "Check out the back, Officer Calagna," Harrison said. "One has gang tattoos. Be careful."

Calagna nodded and looked over to his partner, Officer Maenad. The two men moved into the back. Maenad had his taser drawn.

Harrison gestured to the two other uniforms. "We need these six taken in and held for ICE. She's with us."

Maria was weeping as Harrison and Claire walked her to the cruiser. Harrison had to ask the same question three times.

"Maria, where do you live?"

"My name is not Maria, it is Acela," she finally got out.

"Acela, we have to move you and your family," Harrison said. That surprised Claire, but considering all the changes around the department, she said nothing.

"I have a daughter. She is with the babysitter, on Aveneida. Where are you moving me?"

"To a safe house. Who do you owe?" Harrison asked.

"Cesar. He…" She started to cry again.

"There was no Cesar in that group," Claire said. "But if she was called Maria by that one guy, what are the chances that the names they gave us are right?"

"No Cesar there," Acela said. "He stays at Aveneida. Very mean." Her voice broke.

"He's probably heard by now that she and the others have been rounded up," Harrison said. He picked up his cell phone that had been recharging in the dash and started making calls. Claire drove to a neighborhood that once had nice cottages with well-tended yards. Now, the yards were dirt with vehicles parked wherever they could fit. She pulled up to a house where children were playing in a small fenced-in yard that had a faded playhouse and other daycare toys. Men were standing around. Claire guessed they were lookouts for a drug dealer.

"Harrison, I don't like this. Where's your child, Acela?"

"She sees me. There."

"Go get her," Harrison said. "Hanson, stay behind the wheel and be ready to roll." He got out of the car and walked across the street as if he intended to speak with the man who was standing on the porch.

"Damn, Harrison, you're pushing my buttons," Claire whispered to herself.

Harrison was at the bottom of the driveway when Acela scooped up her daughter. He waited until Acela and her daughter were in the car before starting back. He nodded to the men who stood in the shadows.

Claire could feel the sweat pool under her arms as she drove within the speed limit to the nearest freeway entrance. So far they weren't being followed, but that didn't mean someone wasn't sitting on an overpass waiting for them or would catch them in a drive-by.

"Take that off-ramp. We'll get them some clothes from the mall," Harrison said.

They stopped at four stores, one for luggage, one for adult clothes, and one for baby needs. The last was for food. Harrison was using his credit card.

Back in the car, the little girl was talking to her mother and anyone who would listen. Claire's eyes kept wandering to the rearview mirror, watching for anyone who might be following them, and catching Acela's eyes as she looked at her worriedly.

"Do you know the way to Union Train Station?" Harrison asked Claire.

"Downtown Los Angeles?"

"That's the one."

Claire looked for the off-ramp that would take her to the 101 freeway to downtown Los Angeles. The off-ramp and street signs were easy to follow to Union Station. Claire waited in the car while Harrison escorted the two into the train station. She studied every car that came into the parking lot. All her senses were active, thinking of the house they had just visited and how they had plucked out Acela's daughter without gunfire. It was a Mexican drug house with children used as hostages, she thought, though some were probably there willingly. What was Acela involved in?

Harrison slid into the car. "Let's get back to work."

"Do you have anything you wish to share?" Claire asked.

"Not at this time." He glanced at her and grinned.

"Are they going to be all right?"

"They'll be fine. There's someone on the train that'll keep an eye out for them until they arrive at their destination, and then another team will take over."

"Protective custody. That's the U.S. Marshals Service. So, you worked for the Marshals at one time? Where—"

"Don't go there, Hanson."

Did she just stumble into something? Why did she feel that with every rock she turned over there was another discovery that needed investigation?

"Take 40th Street," Harrison said. He leaned over and looked at his charging cell phone.

Claire did as he directed. "The phone charge is going to take more time, Harrison. That's why I carry more than one battery." She glanced at him. "Are you looking for something?"

"Another place appears in a lot of reports. We'll take some pictures to get a clean perspective." He pulled his digital camera from his pocket. "This one takes panoramic views. Handy to have when you visit the Grand Canyon."

"Are we going to all the crime scenes to get our own pictures?"

"Yes. In case you didn't notice, we all have new PCs. The FBI confiscated the others, so we can't read any of the previous detectives' original reports to see if they have the missing shots. It would have given us an idea of who had the software to change the photos for the reports that made it to the files. I don't think Sanborne is going to find anything in the CSI files. His PCs were the only ones the FBI didn't confiscate, but from the reports I've been reading, the detectives were at crime scenes sometimes hours before CSI got there."

They drove past gang-infested neighborhoods, slowing down when Harrison wanted a picture. Claire could feel her heart rate increase as they neared the corner where Sam was said to have been shot.

"Slow down," Harrison said.

Claire forced herself to focus on the present. A group of gang-types, all boys not old enough to enlist in the military, were standing around, looking vigilant while carrying on their conversations. Their pants hung lower than their butts, and cigarettes dangled from their lips. They flashed gang hand signs and did their gang dance for Claire and Harrison's benefit. They all looked tough, and Claire knew they could, and would, at a single word, prove it with violence against them or anyone else. It would be a badge of honor to be asked to kill a cop and accomplish it.

It would also be stupid, since police would be after them with a vengeance. Their stay in prison would be day-to-day survival with other gangs staking out their territory and dominance. There was no security in their life, in or out of prison.

"I... I can't..." Claire started to hyperventilate. She gripped the steering wheel as she turned left a block before the corner and accelerated the car. The street was not a through street, but there was an alley that would take them away from the corner. She kept on driving until Harrison's voice penetrated through her fear.

"We're fine, Claire. It's okay. Park the car. Come on, Detective Hanson," Harrison's voice coaxed. "That's it. Stop right here. Now, take a deep breath."

Claire banged her palms on the steering wheel. *Damn you, Sam!*

When she felt more in control she asked, sounding harsher than she intended, "What did you want with those kids?"

"I wanted to tell them there's an ordinance out that they can't be gathering in groups larger than one. The ordinance was passed two days ago. It's not important. We'll tackle your problem with that corner another day. Are you okay now?"

Claire nodded, embarrassed.

"Okay. Let's get back to base. We need to discuss this."

Claire was disappointed in herself that she had fallen apart in front of her new partner and captain of the detectives. Sam Thompson was a real pain, dead or alive.

The parking lot was filled, so Claire drove into the parking garage. As they were getting out of their car, she reached back in to retrieve the rifle. Harrison had the same idea and was leaning in when the first shot pinged where Claire would have been standing, sending shattered glass all over her.

"Cover!" they shouted in unison as both dropped to the ground.

The second shot was at the car, shattering the back windshield and slamming into the dash. Claire thought of exploding gas tanks and how trying to replace whatever damage the explosion would cause would bankrupt the city.

You have the strangest thoughts when someone's trying to kill you, she admonished herself. *Get out of here!*

She took off, zigzagging through the parked cars. Harrison shouted something unintelligible. Another shot hit the car she was headed for. That was a good clue she was the intended target. She stopped and looked out to where she thought the shots were coming from.

"Hanson, see that sign across the street?" Harrison yelled.

"Yes," she said. Someone dropped from the sign.

"That's our target. Call it in!" Harrison ran a zigzag pattern across the street.

Claire hit her auto-dialer. Harrison didn't have as much to worry about since he wasn't the intended target, she thought. By now the shots would have everyone inside the PD building hitting the ground.

"Petima Police Desk!" an excited voice barked.

"11-99. Hanson here. We have a sniper at the girlie ad sign one block over. I saw someone drop to the ground and run toward Wood Ave. It may be the shooter. Get us backup around that block."

"Roger that."

Claire snapped her cell shut and secured it in its holster. She climbed down the stairs at the backside of the parking structure and ran across a busy street as two black-and-whites screeched around the street farther up. She signaled them to go down one more block.

Harrison met her below the sign. There was blood everywhere, but no body. They were joined by two lieutenants whom Claire didn't recognize. She could hear gunfire in the distance, toward the station.

"Did either of you shoot this guy?" one of the men asked.

"No shots fired from our side. Three from up here," Harrison answered. "Looks like the barbed wire did some damage. Hanson, let me borrow your cell." Harrison stepped away to make a call.

The lieutenant pointed to two uniform cops. "The two of you look for a trail of the one who ran away." The name over the lieutenant's pocket read Bostitch. He was the new department manager who hadn't sent the backup Harrison had requested at the warehouse. "Hanson, climb up there and check it out."

"Hey, Hanson, watch your head," one of the uniforms snickered.

She glanced at him, annoyed. "Gee, thanks for setting me up, buddy."

"Stop jawing and get up there," Lt. Bostitch said impatiently.

Wasn't it against department policy to needlessly put a life in danger? Surely they could wait out whoever was up there.

While she mentally went through protocols and wondered if she could disobey a police lieutenant's order if he wasn't her CO, a fallen ladder was righted so she could climb up. There was a bloody print smeared on it. Didn't they realize they were messing up the crime scene? Compromising evidence?

She pulled on her gloves so as not to mess up the prints on the ladder and palmed her gun. She was halfway up when someone tapped her leg. Harrison had returned and was standing among the gathered officers, all with their weapons aiming above her head. He gestured for her to come down.

To Claire, the thought of getting caught in the middle of a shoot-out with most of the bullets coming from her brethren was downright scary.

Raising her head for a final look, she saw a face above her. Reflexively, she launched herself from the ladder. In an instant a hail of shots was fired, and Claire knew there would be no witness left. She could hear the chief shouting at the officers to stop firing. She rolled onto her back and looked up at Harrison's worried face. He offered her a hand.

"I hope they missed me," she said hoarsely.

"Yes. We already have more bodies than we can handle," he told her.

Claire's ears were ringing from the gunfire, and her legs felt like jelly. "Just as long as it's not one of the good guys." Harrison's statement about the bodies finally registered in her brain. "What bodies?"

Claire's hands were trembling in Harrison's firm grip. When he released her, he grasped her arm and steadied her.

Claire looked over at Lt. Bostitch. She wondered what his motive in sending her up the ladder had been, when it would have been more prudent to just wait the shooter out. Chief Dobbs had arrived, and Bostitch looked annoyed with whatever the chief was telling him. Bostitch's eyes met hers, and for a moment Claire thought she saw something unfriendly in his. Did they know each other?

Harrison's gaze followed hers, and he seemed to study Lt. Bostitch intently. When Claire's trembling lessened, he released her arm. "What bodies?" she asked again. They headed back toward the station.

"The guards loading the prisoners from here onto the bus to the downtown jail were distracted by our shootout," Harrison said, "and a group of prisoners broke loose. Police tried to round them up. Coincidentally, all those arrested at the furniture store are dead. The tattooed guy, Juan Rodriguez according to his booking, was hit by an SUV while he was fleeing in another direction. The driver of the SUV was questioned and let go. The prisoners were out of their cuffs and leg irons and had weapons. What are the chances something like that can happen in a prisoners' bus where everyone is shackled to their seats? Another item out of place: there was a car in the parking lot with the motor running and the trunk open."

"Rodriguez wasn't running to the car?"

"No. Apparently, no one did."

They looked at each other, weighing what that meant.

"That escape," Claire said, "took quick planning and coordination between different parties." In her mind's eye, she went over the police parking lot and thought of the logistics of having a car with a motor running without someone investigating, especially with the vandalism that had been going on. Maybe the car carried the weapons to the prisoners. The sniper was a perfect diversion.

"We need to go back to the furniture warehouse and do a top to bottom search for anything that ties them in with something illegal."

"I'll talk to the chief and get a search warrant drawn up."

"Scratch that," Chief Dobbs said behind them. "ICE is taking over that investigation. You two need to get your paperwork on this case together to hand over to them. Put it on my desk before you leave for the day."

"Why ICE, Chief?" Claire asked.

"They have history with this group. There's going to be a lot of people looking over your reports, so use spell check." He turned to leave.

"Chief, that guy we put bullets through on the sign, he wasn't one of us, was he?" There was something about the shootout that didn't feel right to Claire, and it was always a worry that an undercover agent might be killed by one of their own, by intention or by accident.

Dobbs looked at Claire and didn't answer her question. He glanced at Lt. Bostitch, who was standing at the bottom of the stairs to the station. "Do you have history with Lt. Bostitch, Detective Hanson?"

"None that I'm aware of."

The chief gave Harrison a glance then went to join Bostitch and the assistant police chief.

"You sure you don't know him?" Harrison asked in an undertone.

"He may know me, but I don't recall him. What's his story?"

"I don't know yet. But if that's an example of his leadership, he flunked. That's twice in one day."

"I had my hopes up after seeing the place all painted, new furniture, new equipment, and shiny new faces smiling instead of leering, that the department was on the road to becoming legit."

"You're doubting the change?"

"No. I just thought it was too perfect without some flaws. The trouble is, these flaws carry guns that they're not afraid to use."

"Bostitch should start looking for another job... not in police business."

Claire glanced at his face. Harrison's angry tone matched his expression. Pausing, she looked back at the sign. She could see the yellow tape around it, the coroner's wagon, and a PCSI officer taking pictures. Glancing at the police parking lot where the six prisoners were shot, she saw more yellow tape. Monica was standing next to a uniformed officer and taking notes. Claire looked for Linda, Monica's partner. She saw her leaning into a car with a PCSI officer, pointing at something. Flashes from a camera had Claire looking at Harrison's retreating back as he disappeared into the building.

Claire went inside to her desk, stripped her gloves off, and dumped them in a paper evidence bag. She labeled it and put it in an evidence tray, which she took to the PCSI side of the building. Carla Watkins, her name tag read, collected the evidence and signed for it. Another new face.

Harrison was hanging up the phone when she returned. She saw he was typing up his version of what happened.

"You know, the Feds are going to want Acela, whether she can help them or not," Claire said softly.

"They won't get her," Harrison said. "The last witness they had who was dealing with the Mexican cartel was found dead in a bathtub full of his own blood. The guy had around-the-clock protection."

"Can you do that?"

"I guess we're going to see just how far the Feds want to push it." He looked over his computer monitor and smiled. "You do what you can do at your level, and let those at the other levels do what they can. It'll work out in the end." He sounded overconfident.

"You know," Claire said, "they have the power to disappear you." Harrison shrugged and continued typing. Claire frowned at her screen. "I want to know more about this Lt. Bostitch. Where did he come from?" She began typing in his name then hit Enter. "Ah. Here's his résumé."

Harrison walked behind her to read over her shoulder. "Anything look familiar?" he asked.

"Nothing in his history brings us in contact. Harrison, did you get the feeling I was the target of the sniper?"

"Yes. Is there something you aren't telling me, such as why this feels like you have a contract out on you?"

"Like I know? For months I've been cooling my heels at a desk job while my notorious ex-partner's murder was investigated. I was the outsider, and frankly, being friends with Jackson or anyone in his group was not healthy. But then again, neither was being outside of that group. I didn't order out anything from restaurants, because I didn't know what I would be getting and if it would arrive at the station." The cold feeling in the pit of her stomach was so sudden she clutched the chair's armrests.

"When you first were a detective, what kind of cases did you handle?" Harrison asked.

Taking deep breaths, Claire forced herself to relax. "None. I was to be seen and not heard."

"Your partner got away with that?"

"We weren't partners long enough for me to find a way around his managing me to do nothing." She didn't want to deal with how many times she could have died. She'd think about that when her assignment was over.

"Harrison, the guy with tattoos, Juan Rodriguez, he felt like someone important. Do you think they were set up to be killed?"

"Everything that happens around here is suspect, including the reported death of Detective Sam Thompson."

"So, you heard the rumor that he's not dead." Feeling more in control, Claire fiddled with the pen on her desk. "I'll wait awhile before giving my opinion. With the vandalism going on here, I wouldn't put it past someone with an axe to grind to plant evidence on legitimate crime scenes."

Harrison grimaced. "That's possible. Who reported Thompson dead?"

"The coroner, Dr. Nick Lockwood, who was conveniently killed in a car accident six months later. So there's no going back to question him, unless Lockwood's death was staged."

"Did you see Thompson's body?"

"No. And the casket was closed at his viewing."

"Let's get our paperwork finished and call it a night. We'll get back to this subject tomorrow. Do you think you can handle going over Thompson's death?"

"I still have a copy of my first draft of my recollection of what led up to us stopping at that corner. But my memory is unclear, and my shock at waking up in a hospital was compounded with Jackson interrogating me as I was waking up. My doctor saved me by demanding security personnel escort him out of the hospital. From what I gathered, Jackson was feeding me phrases to say and recording them."

Harrison sighed. "What a nightmare. It makes me want to ask why you chose to remain."

"I'm asked that often. The money's good, the benefits are great, is what I say."

Claire was relieved Harrison didn't push for answers. She returned to typing up her report and e-mailed a copy to the chief.

"I'm going downstairs with this pile of reports," Claire said to Harrison, "since we're finished with them. It'll be nice to see one stack gone when we get back to work tomorrow. If you're done before I return, have a nice evening."

"Okay. Good night."

The second shift was in the staff hall getting their assignments and updates.

Claire looked around her as she headed to the basement. The atmosphere wasn't as bleak as it had been when Jackson and his group were present. At the file room, once her domain, she paused and stared hard at the closed door. Usually the door was wide open. The old wariness at finding a booby trap or something unpleasant from the Boys' Club returned. Slowly she pushed the door open. Even without the lights on, she could tell the place was a mess. The smell of catsup was strong.

She'd been "Clued In." It was a phrase the Boys' Club used when they sabotaged someone's desk or car just because they could. Flipping the light switch on revealed catsup goop everywhere, with empty packets left where they were dropped. The desk and chair were covered with it. The desk drawers were pulled open, and their contents scattered on the floor—all but her index cards. The information on the index cards was on a CD and thumb drive so she wasn't worried about the loss of information. Someone had come in here between this morning and a few moments ago. Everyone knew she was made detective before she knew about it, so they would also have known this was no longer her desk. This was probably aimed at the chief.

She took pictures with her cell phone then sent it to Harrison's cell.

A minute later Harrison joined her at the bottom of the stairs. "What's that smell?"

"Catsup. It's all over the file room. This is a typical message from the Boys' Club."

"We'll get the crime lab techs in here." He pulled out his phone and made a call. "Are you finished down here?" he asked Claire.

"I'm not waiting around for CSI to come, then maintenance to clean up, so yeah. I'm ready to go home."

They heard footsteps in the stairway, and Anthony, the second shift PCSI tech, arrived. He studied the mess. "I thought we got rid of the whole lot of them."

"We'll get out of your way," Claire said.

"Get someone to look at the back exit," Harrison said. "Whoever did it had to have come through there with all these packets of catsup. It also means someone from inside left that door unlocked." Harrison glanced at the camera that was turned away from the back door. "Probably a smoker with a dependable break time for a smoke."

"We'll get on it," Anthony said.

"Let's go, Hanson. We have another report to write before we leave."

Claire brought the files back upstairs, dropped them in the drawer, and locked it. It took fifteen minutes to type up what she found and download the pictures from her cell phone.

Harrison walked her out to her car. Claire checked her car out with a flashlight and then got in. He borrowed her flashlight and did the same to his vehicle.

"You're going to make me a real paranoid individual," Harrison told her as he handed the flashlight back.

"And your wife will thank me for it."

Tired, but pleased with her new partner, Claire hummed along with a song she played over and over on her way home. After a stop at the supermarket for cat food and a week's worth of groceries, she headed home. She spotted someone following her. To her that confirmed her ability to pick up if she was being tailed. The Feds lied about having her under investigation. If she were being staked out, there would be pictures, and her undercover team leader would have let her know. Maybe it was time for her to arrange a face-to-face meeting with Deputy Marshall Stiller. It went against her practice when undercover to make any physical contact with her team unless utterly necessary. But then, could Vanessa's similar practice have contributed to her death?

She parked two blocks away from her apartment and walked with all her senses in hyper mode. No fresh smell of cigarettes.

"Hey, guys." Cleo and Ramses were at the door when she swung it open, mewing to be fed. She followed her evening routine of feeding the cats and letting them wander around outside for a few hours while she found something to do. Tonight it was inspecting her apartment and finding new electronic devices Matt had installed where there hadn't been any before. She found fifteen. An e-mail from Matt told her there were nineteen. She had her job cut out for her.

She checked her voice scrambler and then called Gail and Margie.

"Hi, Gail, this is Claire."

"How are you doing?"

"Great. How come you didn't tell me there was a Federal cleanup at Petima PD?"

There was a slight pause on Gail's end. "We thought you knew and you didn't mention it because it was a secret."

"I didn't know anything about it. I felt pretty stupid when I walked in there and had to be told what had happened."

"Sorry about that. It's better now, isn't it?"

"Sure is, though I'm not certain they cleaned out everyone."

"Just be careful until you're sure."

"I plan to."

So how was your first day back to work?"

"Good. I'm back to detective, and I actually have a partner that gets pissed if someone intentionally tries to hurt me."

"Captain Harrison Harvard? He's a good guy."

"You knew that, too? Since you know so much, do you know who has a contract out on me?"

There was a long silence, and if Claire hadn't heard Margie's voice in the background, she would have thought she was disconnected.

"No. When they sent the box of broken pens to us with your name on it, I had one of the new guys research the archives for anything with a hit man or woman sending pens to his or her victims. We haven't come up with anything. I checked with a profiler. He finds it interesting."

"Hopefully, this doesn't end up with me or anyone I know getting murdered."

"I agree."

"Okay. I'll catch up with you later. Good night, and tell Margie good night, too."

Gail laughed. "She thinks MaryLyn was kidding her about a squirrel causing you to fall down a hill. Is it true?"

"Hey! You have to hear my side of the story. When did you talk to her?"

"You had your chance, and you didn't even mention it."

"Is MaryLyn there?"

"She's gone now. She was leaving when you called. "

"I didn't realize you all were so close."

"She was in the neighborhood and stopped by."

"I need to get going. I have to clean my clothes regularly now since I don't send them to the cleaners to be starched any more."

"Why did you starch your uniform?"

"To see if I could get it stiffer than Officer Mosley's. I wonder what that guy is doing these days since he's out of a job at PPD."

"Is he someone to worry about?"

"I like to keep people in sight who went out of their way to harass me."

"Sleep well. Now that you're back to detective work, you'll need to sleep whenever you can."

"Isn't that the truth."

Chapter 10

It seemed she had just closed her eyes when something woke her. At first she thought it was the alarm, except she was on the couch, still dressed. It was her cell phone, ringing in its charger.

Groggily, she reached for the cell phone. Cleo, who was lying on her stomach, jumped down and trotted into the kitchen.

The caller ID said it was from the PPD. "Detective Hanson," she said.

"You're on call this week, Detective Hanson," Officer Gloria Malone's apologetic voice explained. "We have a fire at the furniture warehouse. The fire department said they can smell burning bodies."

"Okay. I'm on my way. Did you reach my partner?"

"He's on his way, too."

"Okay, bye." She was tucking her badge over her waistband when her cell phone rang again. "Hanson."

"You up?" Harrison asked.

"Yes. Where are you?"

"About ten minutes from your apartment."

"I'll be ready."

She snapped her phone closed and checked to see where the cats were. Cleo was eating her dry food, and Ramses was watching her from the cat pole. Quickly she undressed and headed to the shower. She had slept five hours. That wasn't too bad.

In fresh clothes and damp hair, she ran down the stairs. A familiar SUV stopped at the curb. Claire peeked in the front seat and then in the back when she spotted movement. Ellen was in the back with Blueblood.

"Good morning. I hear the furniture store was burned down." Claire climbed up into the cab and quickly secured her seatbelt. Harrison handed her a cup of coffee and a bag with a donut.

"Coffee and sugar fix. You're going to need all the strength you can get," he said.

"Hi, Ellen. Are you and Blueblood going to make sure the SUV doesn't get stolen?"

Ellen laughed heartily. "No. Big Blue and I are here officially this time. According to my handler, we have a drug bust where the drugs disappeared."

"Linda and Monica will take the furniture store. We're being sent to another address. Remember the house we picked Acela's kid up at?"

"Heavily guarded. Not safe to visit, especially at night. That's our call?"

"That's it. We won't be alone. Feds, helicopters, uniforms— it's a real social gathering. Blue and Ellen will be working. We're there as observers."

Harrison parked in the middle of the street, the only place available. The apartment complex was lit up by the lights of the squad cars and the helicopter that was circling above. Blueblood was sniffing the air and wagging his short tail enthusiastically.

"He loves the action," Ellen said. "Sit, Blue."

Harrison assigned two uniforms to accompany and protect Ellen and Blueblood. He and Claire headed to where plainly marked ICE, DEA, and FBI agents were questioning the locals. As Claire's eyes swept the area, she was surprised to see a familiar U.S. Deputy Marshal in uniform standing with a group of agents. Their eyes didn't meet. A woman broke from the group and strode toward them.

"Agent Angie Nullar, Detective Claire Hanson," Harrison said.

"Harrison. Nice seeing you again. Detective Hanson, how are you?"

"Fine, and you?"

"Busy."

"What's going on?" Harrison asked.

"What I'm authorized to tell you is this: We've got a body with a bullet through his head. A neighbor identified him as Cesar Enriquez. If that is Cesar, we have a favored son in the Mexican cartel executed. I was informed that you two are here only as observers." She moved away to speak with someone.

"According to the intel on this property," Harrison said softly, "this residential house is used for making deals with other drug traffickers and settling turf conflicts. I got a glimpse of the house plans. It has a cellar, dug after the building was constructed, five tunnels leading to houses on this block, and one tunnel that leads to the park."

Agent Nullar came back to stand with them and watch as bags were brought out of the house and added to a growing number of them in the back of an unmarked van.

"Does our observation cover questions we might have?" Claire asked.

"You can ask what you like," Nullar said.

"Just what went on in that house?"

"Like I said, you can ask what you like. Excuse me." She joined three men, one of them the U.S. Deputy Marshal, as they went into the house.

"Acela's father was an important member of one of the drug cartels in Mexico," Harrison said. "He was assassinated at a family gathering in Mexico, along with the majority of her family, by a rival cartel. Acela was in Los Angeles with a cousin when it happened. She was fourteen. She was handed over to Cesar as a peace token by her aunt. Cesar could have sold her as part of the skin trade they're heavily invested in, but he didn't. He kept her close to him. After five years of proving she wasn't a threat, she was given the books to take care of—books for drugs, skin trade, paybacks, and soldiers. Her daughter was Cesar's guarantee she wouldn't turn on the cartel."

"If Acela's going to be a witness," Claire said, "she and her daughter will be targets for the rest of their lives, whether they're in the witness protection program or not."

"She's not a candidate for appearing as a witness. But you're right. By now the cartel has put a reward out on her and her daughter, and everyone with connections to the Hispanic community will be looking for them."

"That's a scary life. So someone wasn't happy with Cesar. You have a real nose for picking out key people, Harrison. Or did you already know who Acela was?"

"I've been around. I recognized her from a previous job."

Once they let Blueblood do his work, it took him ten minutes to find fifty-thousand dollars, bundled in twenties, and what looked like a five-million-dollar stash of pure cocaine buried under the plastic playhouse. Harrison and Claire were given a chance to see what the rock cocaine looked like, and it appeared to be a lot like what Claire found in the box that had been planted on her. This was a major bust for the Feds.

There was also a stolen bank bag with tainted money buried with the cocaine. Agent Nullar donned gloves and a breathing mask and counted the money in the bag. According to the paperwork accompanying the money, the bag should have contained twenty-thousand dollars. Five hundred dollars of the money was unaccounted for. Claire had a good idea where that money was. If she was correct, that was another possible connection with Jackson and his posse. Claire would pass that info on to Stiller.

"I'll write the report," Harrison said. Ellen dropped them off at the office after they made a coffee stop. It was mid-morning and the day shift was busy. After working the furniture warehouse fire, Linda and Monica were out questioning witnesses to a carjacking.

"Your admirer, Lt. Bostitch," Harrison said, "mentioned he was a Robbery and Burglary detective for three years. Since the detective position was filled here, he took the opening for head of the uniforms for day shift."

"That's it! That's why he's pissed at me. He wants my job."

Harrison laughed. "He wanted my job."

"Captain of the detectives? No way. You're kidding, right?"

Harrison shook his head. "I see you have a strong opinion on him."

"He's lucky I typed up my report before I thought about it. I would have added a lot more, like my ideas of how it should have been handled."

"And I would have had you rewrite it without your comments. The report is enough to show his handling wasn't senior management quality."

Harrison pushed some papers around. "Let's move on to a recurring problem—Sam Thompson. I spoke to Chief Dobbs. He says no one has actually seen the resurrected Thompson, but his DNA keeps turning up at crime scenes. There are two recent deaths under investigation in someone else's backyard. LAPD sent a detective to see what we have on Thompson, like the certificate from the coroner saying he's dead. They have DNA with his name on file. Is there anything you remember about Thompson's death?"

"No." It was amazing how calm she felt when she said that.

"According to the report, you were drugged with Rohypnol. They found traces of it in your drink in the car."

"The date rape drug of choice for frat boys and gangsters." She recited it automatically. It was as if she were far away, carrying on this conversation. She cleared her throat and focused on being present. "I'm surprised there was any evidence to investigate. Our crime scene team wasn't a sterling representative of timely arrivals."

"The chief said he authorized another city's CSI to investigate. Their patrol car heard the shooting and arrived on scene first. The crime site was part of a common city border dispute. I believe the chief has ironed that out since."

"There were a lot of disputes between PPD and our neighbors, I'll give you that," Claire said.

"What do you remember of that day?" Harrison asked.

"I remember getting out of the car to order a drink with lots of ice. It was hot, and Sam drove with the windows down. He didn't like air conditioning because it messed up his sinuses. Before my drink was delivered, Sam told me to go back to the car and call in a Code 7. I figured he wanted privacy to speak with two uniforms that showed up.

"When Sam told me to get lost, I learned to do it without asking questions. His method of breaking me in was to leave me alone in a gang-infested neighborhood. I knew from listening, that if anyone called the front desk for assistance, unless Jackson personally okayed it, it would be ignored.

"So I called in our break and waited in the car for Sam to finish his business. He surprised me and brought me my drink. I should have known not to trust anything he handed me. I remember finishing half the drink, and he was still with his cop friends. I also remember he was a lot more relaxed around them than the guys at the station. It was odd, considering."

"Do you have any idea why he drugged you?"

She shook her head. She had been helpless and unable to defend herself. A snitch had probably saved her life by shooting Sam, and the guy didn't live long enough for her to thank him. Claire swallowed a few times before continuing.

"This cigarette butt evidence is getting around. Does the DNA show it's from Thompson?"

"Yes."

"Why would someone fake Sam's death and then have him come back and leave all this evidence?"

"Money and drugs are strong agents for resurrecting dead issues," Harrison said.

"Did evidence of Sam appear before or after the Boy's Club was busted?" Claire asked.

"After."

"Maybe Sam's alive and has a reason to rattle someone's cage."

Chapter 11

"Detective Harvard, the chief said thanks for the folder."

"Put it in my in basket, right on top."

When the clerk left, Claire squinted at the new file in his stack.

"If you're that curious, take a look."

"Thank you. I will." Lifting the bulky file carefully from his stack, she glanced at the label. "It's on the fire at the furniture warehouse." After fifteen minutes of reading and looking through photos, she laid the file aside and stared at Harrison with an unreadable expression.

"What is it?" Harrison asked.

"Sam's cigarette butts were found at the site... or similar butts."

"Seems so. The guy is sure getting around." The chair creaked as he leaned back to stretch then leaned forward to pick up his water bottle.

"Sometimes I get the sense that someone is trying to wrap something up, and then I think something completely different is going down," Claire said.

"Like?"

"I think a war has been declared, and the evidence left behind is intentional."

"Who do you think it's aimed at?"

"Someone that used to work here, or still does."

"All the evidence is pointing at you."

Claire sighed. She couldn't argue with that. "It doesn't make sense, even in my dreams."

Officer Lyle rapped on the door jamb. "Hey, Hanson. The chief asked if you can move your things out of the locker before you leave tonight. Since you're not wearing a uniform anymore, he wants to make it available to one of the rookies."

Harrison waved at Claire to indicate that they would resume their conversation at another time. Claire glanced at the clock. It was late. "Harrison, it's about time for you to take your wife out to dinner."

He tapped a small clock on his desk. "I've got five more minutes. If I get home too early, I have to dress up and wait."

"Have a nice evening." She clomped down the stairs, thinking how nice it was not to have to make a daily pilgrimage down to the lockers to start her day. Though the environment had changed considerably, the walk to the lockers had a lot of unpleasant memories. Vanessa must have had a lot of bad dreams going down these stairs.

"Now this is nicer." The previous night the lockers had been painted, and each of the ones in use had a character representing the owner on the corner. One of the rookies was an artist. Claire's locker had nothing painted on it, but she no longer used it. She lifted the lock and let it rest in the palm of her hand, thinking of what character she would have had painted for her. Roadrunner, Wile E. Coyote... Daffy Duck, maybe. Spinning the lock, she heard a click from inside of her locker. She automatically dropped to the floor with her head covered. An explosion had stars flashing behind her eyes.

Chapter 12

Claire blinked a few times and felt a straw pressed to her lips. Thirstily, she sucked up the cool liquid.

"Hey there, girl." A warm hand gripped hers and squeezed.

"Sandy?"

"Yes, it's me."

"I feel like crap, but I've been a lot worse off," Claire mumbled. She felt her forehead, which had a bandage on it.

"That you have."

"How many days?"

"One. They did CT and MRI scans, and you have a concussion too soon after your last head collision with something hard. You're on a month's sick leave."

"What was it?"

"It was a gun. If you had been standing upright, the bullet would have hit you in the chest. If you were wearing a bulletproof vest, it would have knocked you over. The bump on your head is from the bench you hit when you were ducking."

"I hope with all this sick leave I have a job to return to."

"Detective Harvard and Chief Dobbs are wondering what it is about you that has someone gunning for you." She leaned in closer, "Have you told either of them about your undercover assignment?"

"No. I feel like I've been set up. While I was on vacation, the Feds cleared out most of the department and didn't even warn me."

"Don't take it personally, Claire. Ray told me that bust happened simultaneously all over the United States and Canada. It was a coordinated major bust of a slave-trade ring. It seems you weren't on the 'Need to Know' list that the good old boys like to make."

"Well, someone's pissed off with me for some reason."

"Once you get out of here, we're taking you up to the campground so you can recuperate in safety. Ray thinks someone is on to your work with the U.S. Marshals Service and that's why you're on a hit list. Sore losers, he says."

"Is someone taking care of my cats?"

"They're perfectly fine. It's you who needs watching over."

"I really feel like crap. They didn't give me morphine, did they? I get nauseous from it." Claire drifted back to sleep.

When she awoke again, she was alert and worried about her cats. She had just gotten back from a two-week vacation and hadn't been home much since. Ramses took her absences personally and sprayed things to let her know how upset he was.

"Good. You're up."

She turned her head. "Hi, Gil. What are you doing here?"

"Your presence is stressing the hospital staff worse than a SARS patient. Since I was in town, I offered to pick you up."

"Can I take a shower first and put something on that doesn't have me mooning the staff?"

"Clothes are right there. Need help?"

"No. Did anyone talk to Gail about my cats?"

"Sandy took care of that. I'll wait outside the door. Holler if you need help."

"I can wash and dress myself," she replied firmly.

"I bet if it were a female offering, you'd be quick in taking her up on it." He shut the door behind him.

"If I felt better, you'd be right," Claire muttered. She slid off the edge of the bed and held on while her legs stiffened to hold her weight. There were a lot of questions running through her mind, and the fear of not knowing who was after her had her worrying about her friends as well.

The ride to the campgrounds was quiet. Not even the radio played for background noise. Claire slept. She woke up close to their destination.

"Gil, where am I going to be staying?"

"How does a tent sound? Make you feel at home," he said.

"You're kidding. You are, right?" It was winter, it had rained, and she just got sprung from a hospital. He had to be kidding.

He laughed.

"Just don't laugh us into an accident," Claire warned him. "So?"

"You're going to be staying in a shack."

"What shack?"

"The shack near the restrooms."

"Not that stack of wood! It's got a full house. Bugs, snakes, spiders, and other things."

"There's a bomb shelter beneath it. You'll be all locked up, safe and comfy."

She didn't appreciate his sense of humor.

"Just what am I going to do besides stare at spider webs and look for their friends?"

"Ever hear of reading a book? You need rest, Hanson. Let the cops on active duty do the work." He gave her a quick glance. "Do you want to catch whoever's after you or not?"

"What makes you think they're going to come looking for me there when a bunch of retired cops are going to be waiting to take potshots at them?"

"You have something they need."

Claire shook her head. "In case you haven't noticed, they're trying to kill me."

"According to the Feebs, you've got something someone wants. Why don't you just give it up?"

"Since you know so much, tell me just what I'm supposed to have."

"I don't know." Gil's tone of voice told her he knew something, but wasn't going to say. "You heard Sam Thompson is still alive, right?" he asked.

"I'll wait for the conclusive proof. They identified his DNA at a few local crime scenes, but it could have been planted."

Suddenly, Claire released her seat belt and slid down to the floor, ignoring her protesting body. "Keep going!"

"Why?"

"Keep going!"

Gil drove around the bend.

"Gal, you're not getting paranoid on us now, are you?"

"Do you see any stopped cars or pedestrians?"

"No."

"Then stop right here," she told him from her cramped position. "I'm getting out."

When the car stopped, she waited for Gil's all clear signal.

"Don't forget your pills. Where are you going to be?"

"I'll let Ray know."

She stumbled across the two-way road, trusting that in the dark she would be able to tell when a car approached. For self-preservation, she needed to be less predictable. Making her way down the rough and uneven road, she felt every sore muscle in her body. Waves pounded not too far from her, and the wind blowing hard against her ears made it difficult to hear. Suddenly she stopped.

This was predictable. She was heading for the beach to hang around the camp. If she got knocked off, she'd be another woman camping alone and killed by an unknown assailant.

Chapter 13

Claire walked back toward the city, taking breaks when needed. Her intention was to catch a bus in one of the beach cities. Near midnight, she found two elderly women with a flat tire along Pacific Coast Highway. They were waiting for AAA to arrive. Claire didn't feel comfortable leaving them alone and waited with them. They recounted stories of their family.

When the tow truck operator arrived, she felt justified at remaining. He looked too predatory for her comfort. Claire allowed that she may well be too suspicious, but she got a lift from the sisters for her caring. The sisters left her off five blocks from her apartment.

Normally, the distance was nothing, but by the second block she was tired, her stomach was upset, her eyes hurt, and her head was pounding. Perhaps she should have stayed in the hospital a little longer. The directions on the pill bottle said she was not due for another one for two more hours. If it was lighter, she would like to see what she was taking. Maybe she needed something in her stomach before taking her next dose.

As she approached the local 7-Eleven, she realized it was too busy for this time of morning. Standing in the shadows at the apartment complex next door to the store, she glanced at her watch to be sure she was not mistaken about the time, but her watch was missing.

"So, what's your plan now?" MaryLyn's voice asked.

Claire turned to find MaryLyn's shadowed figure near her. She was wearing a watch cap, zipped up black coat, and black pants with black shoes. The only reason she knew it was MaryLyn was the voice.

"Coffee?" MaryLyn offered her a cup.

Claire shook her head. "I don't think my stomach can take any more acid. What are you doing here? And what's with the burglary getup?"

"Black is in. I stopped at the hospital, and they said you signed yourself out, so I headed for your apartment. Imagine my surprise when a police radio dispatch reported you missing. Are you accusing me of stalking you? The way you're hanging onto that fence, you should be appreciative that I'm here."

"Missing? I signed out of the hospital with Gil. Sandy said I have a month off for medical reasons." She frowned at the police car that pulled up at the store. The milling customers gathered around the car.

"What's that all about?" she asked.

"I don't know. There were a lot of people interested in me when I went to your place."

"How did you get my address?"

MaryLyn's voice sounded amused. "I'm a bounty hunter. Investigating is part of my job. You really look like crap. Do you want a place to crash? I have a car nearby."

It was a good example, to Claire, of a good deed being rewarded. "If you don't mind. I don't think I can walk another block."

MaryLyn slipped her arm through Claire's and took most of her weight as she guided her away.

"How did you know I was going to be at the 7-Eleven?" Claire asked.

"I saw you walking along the street. You didn't look well. I was thinking maybe you should have remained in the hospital for another day."

"My bodyguard recommended against it. I'm on someone's hit list."

"Where is this bodyguard of yours?"

"Gil? Back at the campground. He thought that's where I would be safe while I recover. In a small space full of bugs and other earthy things." If she had the strength, she would have shivered.

"Gil of Gil and Doris, the writer? I personally wouldn't go anywhere he says is safe. If you think your life is in danger, there are two places you shouldn't be at: the campsite and your apartment. At the rate of attacks against you, you should think about staying at a safe house."

"Good idea. I hope your car isn't much farther."

"Right here. Do you think you can climb up?"

Claire looked up at the Toyota Tacoma. "If there isn't any more climbing involved, I think I can manage."

A slight push from MaryLyn had Claire in the cab.

As MaryLyn fastened her seatbelt, she looked over at Claire with a worried expression on her face. "How are you feeling?"

"Terrible. In another hour I can take my meds and hopefully sleep this off. I liked Sandy's medication better. I got to sleep through the miserable part."

Claire remembered being wakened up to walk a short distance to a room, where she gratefully passed out on the bed.

* * *

Sensing movement, Claire reluctantly opened her eyes. She knew exactly where she was and rolled her head slowly to see a dressed MaryLyn walking out of the bathroom.

Claire closed her eyes, collecting herself. The pulse behind her eyes reminded her of what a migraine was like. In this case, however, instead of on one side of her head it was on both.

"Good morning," MaryLyn said.

"Morning? Is it the same morning I went to bed?" Claire whispered.

"Yes. I'm going to go out and get you something to eat. Do you have any requests?"

"No sugar and no coffee. My stomach and head aren't into anything actually. I don't feel too good."

"You look like you feel. I'll be back. Will you still be here?"

"Unless someone's chasing me. I'm afraid you're stuck with me."

"Okay. The only person I expect is the cleaning woman. I don't want to put out a sign just in case someone is watching this place."

"What'll she do if she finds a woman sleeping in your bed?"

"Probably the same thing if she were to find a man. Turn around and leave." She closed the door behind her.

Claire pulled the covers tightly around her and curled up into a ball. In a few minutes she would pull herself together and then look through her clothes for her pills.

It only seemed a minute after she closed her eyes that she was being shaken awake.

"You look worse," MaryLyn whispered, "but we've got to get out of here. I want you to get out of those clothes. Underwear, too. Change into these."

Claire groaned. With help, she moved her arms out of her shirt and into another.

"I need to take my pills. Maybe I'll feel better." Claire spoke with difficulty.

"Who gave you these?" MaryLyn rolled the bottle between her fingers to read the label.

"Gil picked them up at the nurse's station when I signed out." Claire put her hand to her forehead, wishing the pounding would lessen.

"Never heard of that happening," MaryLyn said. "Usually they have them waiting for you in the hospital pharmacy." She pocketed the bottle then helped Claire to her feet. "You're not going to throw up, are you?"

Claire grimaced. "I hope not," she said faintly. "It wouldn't do a thing to make me feel better."

The two stumbled down the hall and into the next section of rooms so they exited on the other side of the hotel.

A truck was waiting with the engine running. A man jumped out and quickly grabbed Claire. He laid her on the backseat and hopped into the passenger seat as MaryLyn rolled the truck out of the parking lot.

"Cuz, this place is getting crowded with suits. What's coming down?" He glanced at their passenger in the back. "She looks like she's been chewed up and spit out. You give her something?"

"No, Bo. I think my friend Claire there is taking bad meds. Do we know a doc around here?"

His eyebrows lifted as he pulled out his cell phone. "Friend? That's right. She picked you up after you let that bail-jumper Pritchett get one over on you." He chuckled heartily.

"I don't want to hear you talking about Pritchett anymore. In return, I'll not talk about Burton."

"Agreed and sealed. Warts and skin tags will grow on whoever breaks the agreement," the two chorused. "And green toads will forever stalk the liar's bedroom."

Bo hit the auto dialer. "Hey, Connie... Yeah? No. We're heading toward Hollywood. Sure. Do we know a doctor we can drop in on? No, not that guy. He gives our boss the creeps." He laughed and winked at MaryLyn, who scowled. "Okay, thanks. No, it's the woman who took our boss on her first camping trip. She's going to need blood tests to see if she's been poisoned. No, I don't think it's anything the boss cooked. Yeah, that kind. Thanks. I'll see you later." He made a kissing sound and hung up. "Doc Chaplin," he said.

"Okay. I'm going to pull in over there and get in the back with her. You drive to the doc's."

Chapter 14

Claire could hear someone playing the piano from far away. She opened her eyes and found herself in an old-fashioned, queen-sized canopy bed with pastel-colored fabric draped above the bed. A breeze from the nearby open window fluttered the curtains and brought in the scent of rain. An old tree outside the window gave her the impression she was not on the ground floor.

She heard the faint sound of a phone ringing, then someone shouted "I'll get it," and the sounds of the piano were lowered. She looked at her arm and pulled off the tape that held a wad of cotton over a needle mark. She remembered giving blood and then throwing up and having a horrendous headache. There couldn't have been anything in her stomach because she hadn't eaten anything solid for days, or so it felt.

Her headache was gone, her body was pain-free, and her thinking was clear. Her stomach growled.

She rolled to the edge of the bed and slid out, testing her legs. They held up better than when Gil had come to get her out of the hospital. She counted three doors in the bedroom, and it was easy to eliminate the double sliding doors as not opening to the bathroom. Her first choice, the door nearest the bed, was correct. Staring at her reflection in the mirror on the door, she startled herself. With the exception of a severe case of bed hair, she looked a lot better than she could have hoped for.

"You're up," a soft Southern voice said. Her eyes sought the reflection of the visitor behind her. He was a thin man with bleached-blond spiky hair. He studied her critically. "I'll let MaryLyn know. Clothes are in the closet." He pointed with a long, painted nail to the sliding doors. "They'll fit you fair enough." With that he left, closing the door firmly behind him. His clothing was color-coordinated down to the shoes. If she were typecasting, she would peg him as a queen.

The clothes in the closet were not to her taste. She turned around at the sound of a soft knock on the door. "Come in," she said.

MaryLyn stepped in. "I don't think there's anything that will suit you in there. It's Connie's old clothing. A bit too femme, don't you think?"

"Yes. That was Connie?"

"No, that's Connie's cousin, Mike. Except when she's dressed for show, then she's Janey. Mike helps out between his other jobs. Connie is our secretary, office manager, babysitter, and when need be, bail-jump chaser."

"The last I remember, you and a friend took me to a doctor."

"That friend is my cousin, Bo. The doctor is Stan Chaplin. Come on. I'll show you to some less frilly clothes. They were mine when I was in a different space."

"Why do you keep them?" It was a mystery to her why people hung onto things they knew they were not going to use again. It helped that she had so little closet space she couldn't indulge in that kind of behavior.

"Because..." MaryLyn led her two doors down into a designer room, the kind that magazines liked to put between their covers. Claire looked around, curious to see what she could learn about MaryLyn. For all the room's warmth and comfort, there was nothing personal in it, such as pictures of family and friends.

Sliding the double doors back, MaryLyn gestured to a corner of the closet. Claire stepped in and went through clothes she characterized as nondescript and genderless.

"These look like they'll fit. I'll get them back to you when I can."

"Clean clothes and a nice hot bath will make you feel better. Are you hungry? Mike is preparing tuna melt sandwiches. When you're ready, just follow the stairs down and to the left. Holler if you get lost."

"MaryLyn, where am I?"

"Think of it as a safe house. I'll show you around after you've bathed and eaten."

"Okay."

"And, Claire, don't use the phone yet, okay?"

"All right."

An hour later, Claire stood on the stairs, studying everything she could see. There was another floor above the one she was on. Climbing a dozen steps to see what was there, she found a cozy sitting room with a life-sized carved statue that could have been a griffin, three comfortable reading chairs, and a couch. Antique reading lamps were at each end of the couch and over each reading chair. It was like going back to a time when servants delivered drinks and made the beds while the genteel went about their day. Three closed doors were on one side of the sitting room, a window, a storage room, and on the third side another room. Outside one room were dirty dishes. Just like room service in a nice hotel.

Turning back, she went down the stairs. Following the sound of voices, she stopped at a spacious room with a dining table large enough to sit a dozen people. The furniture was heavy carved oak.

"Hi. You're looking a whole lot better. My name's Bo Smith." Claire turned to the voice behind her. Bo wore a wide smile that Claire found engaging. "I want to thank you for picking MaryLyn up on that back road."

He was tall and dark-haired, with muscles stretching his T-shirt just enough to give a nice outline of his upper body. He might have been the guy that she first saw MaryLyn with in the police department.

She shook hands with Bo, wanting to know more about him. It was amazing how much you could learn about a person in a handshake. Was it a hard grip, asserting dominance when it wasn't necessary? Was it too limp, which for a muscular guy like Bo would be a sure indication of incongruence? Or was it a damp hand that…

Claire mentally shook herself to stay present.

"Not a problem. Hi, Bo. I'm Claire Hanson."

His handshake was firm and not crushing. "Come on in the kitchen. Mike's going to show us how to make tuna melts the way his momma made them."

MaryLyn wasn't around.

"Everyone, this is Claire."

"Hi, Claire, I'm Connie." A beautiful woman reached over to shake her hand, not waiting for Bo to finish the introductions.

She brought her attention back to the group as Bo leaned over and gave Connie a kiss, which she returned.

"You've met Mike. The other bleached blond is Carlos, and that's Mr. Jack Brown with the shaved head. He's a part-time actor so every now and then, stare at him so he thinks he's something special."

"Hey! When are you going to drop that? Cripes almighty, but that's getting old," Jack said in a deep baritone voice, then he winked at Claire. Claire smiled reflexively, then grinned at the deep laugh he gave when Connie fluttered her eyes at him.

"He was supposed to be bodyguarding a celeb." Mike drew out "supposed" and waved his knife in Jack's direction. "A couple of preadolescent girls fluttered their lashes at him asking for his autograph, and he fell for it hook, line, and sinker. So while glittery, starry-eyed boy is being distracted, one of them slips by him and heads to his assignment with spray paint. If the boss hadn't been hovering around and hadn't stepped in front of the kid, we would have lost some money and our reputation."

Mike sliced the cheese as he tattled on Jack. He added the cheese to a plate with pickles. From there he moved to the burner where tuna was warming in a skillet. The cheese slices were placed carefully over the globs of tuna then moved to slices of bread, where tuna, cheese and slices of pickles were turned into sandwiches. He then cut each sandwich in half and placed them on plates for everyone.

"He's hot about it because Jack's supposed to be on a leash. As in a committed relationship," Bo said.

Everyone laughed and picked up their plates then sat around the kitchen bar swapping stories and jibes. By the time the dishes were cleaned and everyone broke off to go to wherever they spent their day, MaryLyn was back, dressed in a red silk suit with heels and jewelry to match. Mike perused her closely.

"Not bitch enough, but if you have to run, you have to dress with the right shoes," he said.

"Where are we going?" Claire asked, hoping the flush she felt at seeing MaryLyn dressed up wasn't too obvious.

"The library and then the courthouse. Research first, then I'll know what to ask for," she said.

Research in a library was not a skill Claire practiced in her detective work, but she realized it would be a worthwhile one to cultivate. Law enforcement databases didn't have all the information, she reminded herself.

As they stepped on the curved driveway, she turned to look at the three-story mansion MaryLyn called home and office. "Wow. It must be tough to clean all those rooms. I guess everyone's responsible for cleaning up after themselves."

MaryLyn didn't comment, but led the way to a Cadillac CTS sedan. The engine was running.

"So, what are we looking into?" Claire asked.

"I'm looking at dates, then on to the hall of records."

"Are you looking up information on Sam Thompson?"

"That man is a curse," MaryLyn said. "Why do you think I have him on the mind?"

"It's a hunch. What did you say your interest in Sam was?"

"All right, if you really want to know, the rewards on him and three others."

Claire wondered whether this could be a clue to why she seemed to have a contract out on her life.

"Big rewards," MaryLyn said, "are big incentives for finding the people who were involved in a jewel heist in New York six years ago. Remember the diamond you found in the box? Grade D. That's what all the diamonds that were stolen were. D is the highest and rarest of diamonds. I'm willing to bet my time and effort that that diamond belonged to the ones stolen."

"I'm confused here. What do Sam and the diamonds have to do with the drugs planted in my bag?"

"That is a puzzler."

MaryLyn's cell buzzed, and for the rest of the ride, Claire was just a passenger, not understanding MaryLyn's cryptic side of the conversation.

From the parking lot, they had a long walk to the public library. The library was one of the oldest buildings in their city. It had been retrofitted soon after the earthquake. It stood adjacent to an almost windowless and very exclusive private men's club, where women were not permitted, and that included cleaning staff and female law enforcement, or so its history went. Claire knew five Federal judges, a retired police chief, and a few mayors who belonged to it. It was an expensive club to belong to, and she guessed their dues came from the taxpayer.

"Hey, are you paying attention?" MaryLyn whispered.

Claire hadn't realized she had stopped to stare at the brownstone building. She turned to trot after MaryLyn.

"Don't get any ideas of following a clue in there. It's as hardcore male-only as it was when first established," MaryLyn said.

"How do you know?"

"I know quite a few of the members, and as nice as they are about women's lib, that's where they draw the line."

"Their doorstep."

"Yep."

They entered the library, passed through rows of books, and MaryLyn pointed to a chair in front of one of the computers. "I'm sure you have some of your own research you want to do."

Whatever MaryLyn was researching, she obviously didn't want Claire peeking over her shoulder. Claire busied herself with looking up information on Sam's shooting. It seemed strange that until now, she hadn't wanted to think about the shooting and what might have happened to her if he hadn't been shot. She stared at the black-and-white picture of the street corner where Sam's shooting took place. It was marked by dark stains on the sidewalk. The description underneath the photo reported it was the murdered detective's blood.

"Shot in the chest?" Claire reread the sentence in a muted voice. "I thought they said it was a head shot. None of this is what I was told. I should have read the newspaper account and not relied on what the detectives working the case told me. It doesn't say who found me."

"Two cops—Colonia and Espinoza. Ever heard of them?" MaryLyn stood next to her. Apparently, she had finished her research.

"No."

"They heard a gunshot and came to investigate. They were off duty."

"That wasn't a nice neighborhood to be in. No off-duty cop would be there unless he was dealing in something illegal." Claire looked up at MaryLyn.

"Did you find everything you needed?" MaryLyn asked.

"Yes. What dates were you checking on?"

"Dates of local robberies, and other things."

Claire logged off and stood, thinking MaryLyn was ready to go. Instead, MaryLyn pulled on Claire's arm and dragged her around one stack of books and then around another. MaryLyn gestured for Claire to remain where she was while she moved to another row of bookcases that had a better view of the computers they had just left.

Through the stacks, Claire could see someone take a seat in front of the computer she had just vacated. From the back, Claire thought it was her ex-partner, the ghost of Sam Thompson. She nearly fainted. When he turned to leave fifteen minutes later, she got a quick look at his face and it wasn't Sam. They followed him as he exited the library and walked to an underground parking lot.

"We can't lose him," whispered MaryLyn.

"Was he following us?" Claire asked.

"I don't know."

"I don't hear an engine, but he may be driving a hybrid. Stairs and elevators over there lead to the court building. Who was that?" Claire asked.

"You didn't recognize him? That's Sam Thompson with a change of face."

"How do you know? It could be a family member."

"Trust me on this. That's Sam," MaryLyn said.

Claire was stunned. MaryLyn usually knew what she was talking about, but Claire had trouble accepting this. Her mouth opened twice before she could get the words out. "But he's supposed to be dead."

"Remember his casket was closed? I'd guess that he really got shot, but they saved him and faked his death. And I—" MaryLyn stopped in the middle of the sentence and didn't finish.

The smell of cigarette smoke had Claire ducking behind a car until she located where it was coming from. Sam was a chain-smoker. Then again, a lot of people smoked.

MaryLyn took her heels off and followed behind Claire as she moved to the next level of parking.

"Near the elevator," MaryLyn whispered.

Two men were talking intensely. One of them kept looking around worriedly, as if not wanting to be seen. When the light from the elevator hit his face, Claire recognized him.

"Damn," she cursed softly. "It is Sam." Anger began to build in her because of the hell his supposed death had put her through. She pushed her emotions down.

"Do you know who he's talking to?" MaryLyn whispered.

"Jorge. He's a night supervisor of the cleaning crew in the courthouse."

When the two men finished their conversation, Jorge went up the elevator and Sam headed to a car. He tossed something into his vehicle and climbed in. When his car passed them, MaryLyn followed.

Claire wanted the cigarette butts the two men had tossed. She ran to where they were standing, picked up the butts, and dropped one in each pocket. She ran to catch up with MaryLyn, who was waiting for her, shoes back on and foot tapping impatiently. When she caught sight of Claire, she headed to the courthouse.

"Did you get the car's license?"

"Yes. I called it in. My team will pick him up and follow him."

"Why are we going to the courthouse?" Claire asked.

"Public Records. What do you know about Jorge?"

"He makes sure the cleaning staff stays busy. Why are you looking into Public Records?"

"I'm following the money," MaryLyn said.

"What else do you know about Sam?"

"He's involved with a bunch of shady stuff."

"Sam was terrible as a detective. Why was he even a cop if he didn't want to follow the law?" Claire asked in an undertone as they rode the escalator to the second floor.

"What better place to keep an eye on drug movements and gangs that are your competition?"

"You're saying that Sam is part of Jackson's gang that infiltrated the PD?"

"I'm focused on the diamonds that were stolen from the New York airport, so I'm speaking from that point of view. Thompson was part of a five-person operation that took advantage of what they thought was a gift from the gods—inside information about the delivery of diamonds from Africa. They stole them then couldn't cash in, because if any of the diamonds appeared on the market they would have been recognized. My guess is, even their criminal connections wouldn't accept the diamonds because of that. So, what are you interested in?"

"Justice."

"Still slaying dragons."

"I'm not interested in recovering stolen jewels from New York or looking for who is responsible. As far as I'm concerned, my job is with PPD and the cases I'm assigned. I have enough on my plate." It did occur to her that Detective Linda Chandler was from New York, and if Sam Thompson was suspected of being a part of the jewel heist, that could mean that Linda Chandler was here out of more than an interest in starting a new life.

"And you're on medical leave because someone apparently has a contract out on you. Don't you want to look into who it is, and why, while you have time off?"

"Yes, of course. In your research on the New York jewel heist, did you hear if Linda Chandler was involved in the investigation? She's one of the new detectives on PPD. She's from New York."

MaryLyn shook her head. "No. Describe her."

"She's so New York," Claire said in a mocking tone, "according to her partner. Five-six. Fair complexion. Dyes her hair black but has brown roots. Wears contacts. Eye coloring shows as brown. Leftie, but has learned to use her right, could be from a childhood injury or forced to not use her left hand when a child.

She's blunt and her desk doesn't have any personal stuff. She has a photographic memory so she didn't carry a notebook until Harrison said something about proper procedures." Claire paused as she thought about how little Linda gave away. "She and Monica are black and white when it comes to their approach to working on cases. But Monica is fresh out of college, and Linda learned her skills from on-the-job training."

"Monica?" Before Claire could answer, MaryLyn snapped her fingers and continued. "Monica Mendoza until she divorced and changed her name back to Norton. That Monica?"

"You're kidding? I just know her as Norton."

MaryLyn glanced back at her before stepping off the escalator. "She talks too much and tries to fit in too much." She smiled at Claire's upraised eyebrows. "I told you, I go to cop conventions and bars that cops frequent. I hear a lot."

"What was her husband's name?"

"Jorge. Coincidence?" MaryLyn asked.

"What does he do for a living?"

"She never said. She started out in parking enforcement and graduated to cop, continued her schooling to become a detective. If she has time, she'll keep going to college to become a forensic specialist. She stops at the bar on her way home from school to relax. I wonder if your Jorge and Monica's Jorge are one and the same." MaryLyn didn't give Claire a chance to comment. She stepped up to the counter.

While MaryLyn went through the steps of getting the ownership of property pulled, Claire thought about Monica and her ex.

Chapter 15

In the dining room of the three-storied house, MaryLyn spread a survey map out over the table. Carlos retrieved small tabs from one of the pockets of supplies hanging from the table legs. MaryLyn wouldn't tell Claire who she was tracking, but whoever it was owned a dozen homes and MaryLyn was marking them on a map. Claire guessed it had to do with the robberies MaryLyn had looked up.

Exhausted, Claire dropped gratefully into the comfortable reading chair in the corner. If she had more energy, she'd have joined them around the table. While MaryLyn's team talked about something that didn't fit in with her own agenda, her thoughts wandered back to Monica. She felt certain that her cover as a cleaning lady had been blown with Jackson's posse and they were looking to kill her. Did Jorge recognize her through his connection to Monica? Monica was Norton for as long as she'd known her, so unless Jorge had visited Monica at work and seen her... but Monica would have said something to Claire because Monica was like that... unless she was one of Jackson's group, and was lying low.

It was dusk outside when MaryLyn prodded Claire gently. "Hey, a nice comfortable bed is waiting for you upstairs. I'm going to be going out, but Connie will be here if you need anything."

Claire sat up groggily, stifling a cry at seeing a black-clad figure in front of her, then realizing it was MaryLyn.

A tone sounded. Footsteps and movement in other rooms started suddenly. MaryLyn grabbed Claire's arm and pulled her up.

"Change of plans," MaryLyn said. She went to the south wall of the room and pushed on a panel. The proverbial hidden door opened, and she stepped through it. She turned to an open-mouthed Claire. "Come on!"

It was not a dark corridor smelling of damp earth and urine with lots of spider webs. The floor had tiny lights running its length, that guided them around a corner, and the place smelled of wood and perfume. They took a flight of stairs down, then walked along another corridor and into a room that had a small elevator that took them into a garage. Before entering the garage, MaryLyn checked to make sure it was secured, and then gestured for Claire to get in the front passenger side of a stretch limo. MaryLyn tossed a uniform coat and cap across Claire's lap. Claire gathered she was to dress in them.

When MaryLyn joined her, she had added a black coat and a chauffeur's cap. The automatic garage door rumbled open. Before it was completely open, MaryLyn rolled onto the road that ran behind the property and out the back gates.

Claire glanced in the panoramic rearview mirror. She was startled to see a heavily made-up woman behind the glass partition, talking to someone on her cell and making dramatic gestures with her hand.

MaryLyn was also talking softly to someone on her hands-free cell. She hung up and glanced at Claire. "We're dropping Janey off at the club. She has a performance tonight."

They stopped at the back of the club. A tuxedoed man guarding the door stepped forward to assist Janey out of the limo. MaryLyn's next stop, two blocks away, was a hamburger stand. "Here's our relief."

Two people slid into the backseat.

"Toss your coat and hat into the back. We'll switch," MaryLyn directed.

"What's going on?" Claire asked.

"Our security cameras picked up some Hispanic men looking suspiciously like gang types casing our gate and fence. Since we usually don't get that type of visitor, we guessed it was you they're interested in. I don't want my neighbors upset with us."

"How are they going to know I left, and how did they know I was there?"

"When we left the house, about five cars with passengers left the estate. As for how they knew you were there… there are a lot of possibilities."

Twenty minutes later, they were dressed as street bums.

"Hunch over," MaryLyn said. "No, that's too much. Can't you remember how a street person walks?"

"How's this?"

MaryLyn laughed at Claire's exaggerated walk as if her underwear were soiled. "Haven't you role-played before? Be the street person."

MaryLyn was looking like a street person. Even her fingers were blackened with dirt.

"Where are we going?" Claire asked softly.

"To a house that's being rented out to a name on the Federal protected witness list. The renter is attractive enough to have a visit from the landlord's ex-husband."

"How did you find that out? Who is the ex-husband?"

"The owner has connections. Two of her ex-husbands were in the FBI. Now shush. I don't want anything overheard."

The house was in a run-down neighborhood. By the light of the few street lamps, Claire could see a ragged awning that had once hung above the front window, now lying in dead bushes. The porch had a weathered couch on it for three people to comfortably sit and watch others passing by. Businesses were on one side of the street, and residences were on the other. The businesses looked about as beat-up as the residences. Nothing was happening on either side of the street. MaryLyn joined a figure between two of the businesses, leaning against the wall to blend in.

"What do you have?" MaryLyn asked the shadowed figure.

"A DEA agent, Emanuel Rodriguez, is in the target residence. Our mark from the Mexican cartel joined him about an hour ago."

"Anyone else?"

He shook his head. "We've got a thermal on the house. Just those two. The woman that's usually there left early this morning and hasn't returned."

"Anyone follow her?"

"Yolanda. She checked in five minutes ago. The woman's still in the apartment where her sister lives. You would think if she's on the witness protection list she wouldn't be visiting her family. I gave Carl a break. He should be back in a few. He's parked three buildings down. The motorcycles and car are there."

"We'll take this point. Go back to Yolanda, give her a break, and find out what's going on in that apartment. When she comes back, take a break yourself."

He nodded and left through the alley, where a few minutes later a muted putter from a Vespa could be heard.

"Just how much are you getting for all this work?"

"For finding the people involved in the diamond theft, a million for each one. For the suitcase with the diamonds, if over half of them are recovered, another million. Four different groups are offering a reward. There are some very angry people out there."

Claire's eyes opened wide. "Wow!" When she got over the amount and thought about all the people-hours involved, she decided that the profit wouldn't be so dramatic.

MaryLyn's gaze was fastened on the house across the street. "You really are being stubborn with not looking at the connection between the stolen diamonds in New York, your ex-partner, and the contract that's out on you."

"I don't see where I fit in, except someone planted the diamond on me. We were partners for a very short time, and we were partners in name only. I'm happy that Jackson's posse has been eliminated. Now when we investigate a crime, we aren't planting evidence and/or eliminating witnesses."

"You think they really cleaned house?" She glanced at Claire. "You don't. You think there's still a few around. Who do you suspect?" she asked in a taunting tone.

"That guy that Sam Thompson was meeting up with, Jorge. I didn't know he and Monica were related until you told me."

MaryLyn stared at Claire for a moment then returned her gaze to the house. "If it's the same Jorge. Monica's gender is wrong for Jackson to have on his team. Nor would she connect with Thompson as his girlfriend since his type of women were the thin and druggie ones. They were easy to control."

"What does it accomplish to let everyone know Sam is alive?" Claire asked.

"To flush someone out, or to shake someone up."

"It shook me up. When Monica told me, I had to use the sink to hold me up."

"Do you think she told you to shock you?"

"She said she couldn't believe that I didn't know of the department cleanup that started, according to her, the moment I left work Friday for my vacation. What strikes me as interesting is that I left early on Friday to beat traffic. If I hadn't left early, I would have witnessed the sweep. I didn't tell anyone that I was leaving two hours early."

"Wasn't that what you wanted? A house cleaning?"

"That's what I wanted."

"It took a lot of planning to put the box of cocaine and diamond in your pack and have the DEA drop in, and they said you'd been watched for a while. My question is, if you're not a player, why are they using so much muscle to take you out?"

"I'm more open to the idea that Jackson is involved."

"The Feds planned to arrest him, so how could Jackson arrange for the Feds to drop in on you?"

"I don't understand their reasoning in associating me with drugs and diamonds. How did you get involved in this jewel thing?" Claire was still working out where people fit in the picture, and she was finding she had to keep enlarging the circle.

"It's my business... rewards and all."

"Tell me more about the heist."

"Six years ago, a suitcase arrived in New York under heavy guard. A customs officer at the airport wanted the suitcase opened. A rather interesting request, but the briefcase wasn't x-rayable and the guard stated it seemed too lightweight to be jewels. The flight was international, so on the surface, it was a valid request. They took the case to a secured room. Everyone in the room, including the customs agent, was found dead, and the suitcase of diamonds was missing."

"You sound like a treasure hunter," Claire said.

"It is a treasure. The Feds were called in, and Agent Rodriguez, who just so happens to specialize in gems, was part of the team the Bureau put together. About the time Sam was supposedly killed, Rodriguez transferred over to DEA."

"Was Sam interviewed by the FBI at the time of the theft?"

"Yes. He had a car at the airport in long-term parking that he didn't pick up. It got the FBI curious, so they questioned him. He claimed he had nothing to do with the heist and had proof he was in the Caribbean on a vacation-business trip. I think the attempted execution of Sam was evidence that someone didn't believe him."

"Six years later?"

"He had relocated to the West Coast where he joined the PPD."

"Why plant the diamond on me with drugs?"

"I don't know." MaryLyn said it so matter-of-factly, Claire glanced at her. MaryLyn looked irritated.

"I feel used and abused," Claire said.

"Ain't that the stink of a skunk? A lot of this case has me puzzled. Bo likes to stay focused on what it takes to get our reward, just like everyone else who's hunting those who are left and trying to figure out where the suitcase is. We have a dead customs agent, but no one else. Hopefully, when we find the suitcase, it's still filled with diamonds."

"For all that money, why isn't this place swarming with diamond or bounty hunters or for that matter with FBI agents?"

"Well, it's like reaching for a poisonous snake in a bag of poisonous snakes..."

"There's something more to the story of how you got involved. I don't buy that it's just for the reward. You're too emotionally involved in this," Claire said.

"You've got good instincts, Detective, when it's not about you. My one-time lover, Lenny, was the customs agent who died at the airport."

"I'm sorry."

MaryLyn didn't look bothered. "Nothing to be sorry about. Our relationship had ended long before. He was a roommate who was smart enough not to steal from me, and since I spent a lot of time away from home, it was convenient to have him showing someone lived in the apartment."

MaryLyn was quiet for a while, studying the house with binoculars. "Lenny got suckered by a large cash payment into lending a helping hand to the diamond thieves. Since he took up entertaining glamour queens, he always needed money." She glanced at Claire. "I knew Lenny before he got into glamour queens."

"How did you know he was involved in the theft?"

"He wasn't totally stupid. He left information for me about the heist that one of his boyfriends delivered two weeks after the fact. I figured Lenny was the only one to receive cash payment instead of a share of the diamonds, so one or all were interested in getting the cash back. His information led me to the bills, and I lifted fingerprints from them. They matched Sam Thompson's and one other person I still haven't placed. I traced Sam Thompson, by way of his fingerprints, to the Petima police department. Anyway, since it looked like one of the thieves headed out here, and because there were large rewards for the remaining thieves and the diamonds, I moved out here and set up house and a business."

"You own that house?"

"No. We rent it."

"Don't you think it's too coincidental about our meeting and that a diamond you may be looking for is placed in my backpack?"

"I don't believe in coincidences, but if you have a better explanation, I'd like to hear it. I'll even accept the divine intervention that Connie uses for the unexplained. When the Bobs said there was a diamond in the box and described it, I felt as happy as a tick on a fat dog. We were lacking leads on that case and busy with other business."

Claire was about to say something when she heard a car door slam, and then another, with less force. Lights came on and a car moved out from the back of the house. MaryLyn looked at the heat signatures on her thermal reader. No one was in the house, but there were two people in the car. She moved between another set of buildings, pointing the reader at the garage in the back.

"Gotcha!" MaryLyn said. "I'll bet they're using a thermal doll. They're using a lot of gadgets to throw us off the scent, so either they know they're being watched or they just aren't taking chances."

Twenty minutes later, a VW bug came rolling down the driveway with one person driving, but the heat signature read two people.

"What are we going to follow them with?" Claire asked.

"A motorcycle. Are you okay with that?"

MaryLyn ran to the alley where a motorcycle was parked near a car. She stashed her equipment in the car trunk, yanked out a hooded sweatshirt and a coat, and slammed the trunk closed. She handed Claire the sweatshirt. "Put that on. It gets cold."

There were two helmets. Claire pulled the sweatshirt over her clothes, then donned one of the helmets and tugged the chin strap tight. She swung her leg over the back of the motorcycle and settled behind MaryLyn. The takeoff was sudden and Claire hung on.

MaryLyn banked the bike around a corner, and Claire caught sight of the VW two blocks away. MaryLyn reached into her coat for her cell phone. "We're moving on the second vehicle. Blue VW bug. 2000 model," she shouted into the phone. She gave the license number and slid the cell back into her pocket, then sped up. The bike banked around another corner as she raced ahead of the VW, turning onto Santa Monica Boulevard. There were two people sitting in the car. One wore a baseball cap with the bill not pulled low enough to hide his face. It was Gil Maxwell.

"Damn! Did you see who that was?" Claire shouted in MaryLyn's ear.

"That explains who could have planted the diamond and drugs on you, but not why."

MaryLyn stopped at a used-clothing store. They went in the back, and thankfully, MaryLyn let her change into something which smelled clean and was less wretched looking.

Once they were changed, MaryLyn led them to a coffee shop, where she gestured for Claire to sit at one of the outside tables while she ordered coffee and something to eat. It was late and the bar after-theater crowds were gathering.

"Are we waiting for someone?" Claire asked.

"Yeah. Your tail. Whoever it is, they're good."

"Why?"

"Don't you want to ask your tail who sent him or her, and how they're tracking you?"

"In case you've forgotten, someone is shooting at me. This is a public place. Someone could get hurt."

"You're nervous. Let's go inside then. I could use the restroom."

"Me, too."

They were separated in the crowd as a group got up to leave. Claire continued her way to the restroom, and by the time MaryLyn got in the line, there were several women between them.

When Claire finished, she went to wait near the front entrance for MaryLyn. She spotted two familiar faces outside, scanning the customers. Jackson's posse. Turning to the women's restroom, she saw MaryLyn was just exiting. There were too many people between them. Claire panicked when one of the men reached inside his coat. She ducked out the door and ran.

Two hours later, Claire was back at her apartment. She entered via the back stairs. Both cats were meowing their dismay at her long absence. Quickly she fed them and then made her way into the bedroom, careful not to cross in front of a window. She grabbed the backpack she used for camping and added clothing. The pockets were already filled with survival tools and food. From her toy box, she added night-vision goggles and two throwaway cell phones. Finally she got a warm, all-weather jacket with many pockets from her closet.

She picked up her car keys and exited out the front door. She suspected everyone watching her apartment knew she was in. Her car had a ticket on it, which she tossed onto the car seat. At the 7-Eleven only one person was buying coffee. It was someone she recognized on his way to a part-time job. She pulled the easily-located GPS off her tailpipe and attached it to the other vehicle in the lot. While she waited for the other car's driver to get back in and take off, she chewed her sandwich. When the driver left, she followed for a block then peeled off in another direction. Her destination was Northern California.

She stopped at a friend's garage because Claire knew where she kept a spare key to her vacation vehicle. It was a pickup that had seen many trips up to the mountains and had a lot of engine replacements. After swapping vehicles, she locked up the garage and took off. She dialed Kim's number and left a voice mail that she was borrowing her truck.

Claire entertained hiding out in Kim's cabin but thought better of involving her friends. She needed somewhere quiet to sort out the characters and decide if her assignment was complete. With the arrests of Jackson's group, her job should have been finished, yet it wasn't. Someone wanted her dead. And then there was the new business of seeing Gil with someone that MaryLyn identified as mixed up in a jewel heist.

At a rest stop, she pulled over and visited the restroom. Pausing at the snack machine on the way out, she perused the selections while surreptitiously noting if any new vehicles had arrived while she was in the restroom. She returned to the truck and took a nap, feeling sleep was a good resource for sorting things out.

The sound of rain woke her. It was cold.

"Well, Claire, now what?" Thoughtfully, she sipped from the water bottle. "Do I lay low for a month and let MaryLyn and the others sort things out, or do I find out who and why someone is trying to kill me? Who sees me as a bump in their road that needs to be smoothed out?"

The truck windows were fogged. As she turned on the engine to drive closer to the restrooms, she saw taillights come on and quickly go off in the rearview mirror.

"If they're following me, I can at least give them a merry chase with an empty bladder."

With her business done, Claire headed to the freeway, intent on finding a gas station. Under a light, she planned to look the truck over. Either someone had planted a device on the truck when she wasn't looking, or they were using a crystal ball. Whoever was tailing her was always close by. MaryLyn thought it suspicious, too. The Feds had some agents who could play the surveillance game first-rate with satellite or small-plane surveillance... and tiny ID chips. Claire shook her head, not wanting to believe she was that important to someone that somehow they managed to plant a chip on her. She frowned, thinking of her five hospital stays in the last six years.

She saw a gas sign further up the freeway. Glancing in her rearview mirror, she located a vehicle that might be tailing her. As she took the off-ramp she noted it continued on, but she was sure there would be a second car that would follow her. In the parking lot of the gas station, she picked a spot far from the store. She glanced around to see if anyone had pulled in after her, then exited the truck, taking her backpack with her. She ducked behind the building, then headed to where trucks were parked on a vacant dirt area close to the freeway on-ramp. She would use them to hide her departure.

Cold and wet, huddling under the freeway bridge, she took out her NV binoculars and watched the pickup truck. After thirty minutes, it was hauled onto a tow truck. An official DEA vehicle pulled up and four people got out. They weren't there long before the two vehicles headed to the bridge, but by then she was gone.

Claire looked over the structure she was huddled in. It was an abandoned equipment shack with three standing walls and a partial roof. No bugs in sight, and she was sitting on a plastic sheet from her pack. Day was just beginning to break, and she was somewhere in San Bernardino along the I15 freeway. She could see the outline of a handful of horses as they plodded toward a barn. Her hands were tucked inside her coat under her armpits to keep them warm, and she had pulled the emergency blanket over herself.

The truck driver who had given her a ride to San Bernardino last night was an old man who listened to country western CDs and loved to sing along. He was on his way home and was barreling along when he noticed she was walking in the rain. His rig was waiting for her up the road, and she was very suspicious of him. He let her inspect the truck before she got into the cab. After singing along for two songs with him, she fell asleep. A gentle shake woke her up. She ate some food and two cans of caffeinated soft drinks that he shared, and then she was back walking, looking for a place to hole up for the night. The shack looked better in the dark.

She picked up a stick and drew meaningless lines in the dirt, trying to relax her legs and shoulders. All night her mind worked on putting puzzles together, but memories of Sam were messing with her. Though she and Sam were partnered for a short time, they had a lot of cases. She was aghast at his lack of follow-up and the few notes he took on questioning witnesses. Harrison was going through those cases. If her life was in danger for something she might know about Sam, it had to be in a case they'd shared. Or maybe it was the day he was shot. Why did he sedate her heavily?

What about the two police officers he was talking to? What was her impression of them? They had kept their backs to her most of the time, so she only saw a profile. Their body language was easy to read, though. One of them had looked awkward with his weapons belt, not knowing what to do with his hands. Was he a rookie? You could tell if a rookie was standing with veterans. The older guys had an attitude toward rookies, and there wasn't any of that among the three. Sam was more relaxed around those two than he was around Jackson's posse, that she was sure of. The three knew each other very well.

What did Gil have to do with this? He was with a Federal agent. Was he working with the Feds? MaryLyn thought this agent was dirty. Did that mean Gil was? Was he working undercover? Gil didn't strike her as the type that would do well in undercover work. Personally she didn't like him. Was that why she was so ready to believe he was a crook?

Shivering, she tugged her hood over her head, burrowed deeper in her coat, and tucked the emergency blanket closer around her. Her eyes were heavy with sleep. When she woke, the wind was blowing dark clouds across the sky. She folded up the blanket and tried to get it back into the small packet it came in. Gazing out over the road, she wondered how far she would get before it started to rain again.

In the distance, she could see a black-and-white turning onto a dirt road. It was enough to send her sprinting across the road and squeezing through the barbed wire fence not meant to keep people out. A muddy gully with a drooping tree hid her from the buildings behind her, as she made her way farther inland.

On a back road, she grabbed a lift from a trucker who had just unloaded bales of hay to a ranch. He seemed pleased to have someone to talk to, and he talked. She dozed off during his chatter and awoke to find he had not stopped where she'd asked him to. Claire waited until he stopped at a gas station. She jumped out before he could say or do anything.

A husband and wife trucking team gave her a lift back the way she had come, to the next city, where she got a motel room, showered, washed her clothes, and got a decent eight hours of sleep. When she got up, she found a pay phone and called Gail.

"You have everyone going nuts! Tell me you're okay."

"I'm not okay. Listen Gail, do you remember the diamond heist that took place at the New York airport six years ago?"

"No, not really. You found more diamonds? Give them back and get home."

"I wish, on all counts. I think, though, that someone thinks I know their whereabouts."

"Why would you know? I thought you were in the army then?"

"I was just out. MaryLyn said Sam Thompson was in on that heist. There were five people involved. One is dead. There's a million dollar reward for each of the remaining four. I think Gil Maxwell is involved."

"I don't like the way this is sounding. Is that why all these attacks on you lately?"

"I don't know why the attacks. According to MaryLyn, there's a connection. I don't know if she's telling the truth or not."

"I trust her. If you have any questions about where she stands, ask her. Your time's up. You need to change phones."

"I'll call you later. Feds are tailing me for some reason."

Gail's sigh of exasperation was the last she heard when she hung up.

Claire purchased a bus ticket and sat away from the window. It was dark when the bus arrived at the Los Angeles station. It took awhile, but she finally found an available payphone that not only worked but could be cleaned with a Handi Wipe. She called an ex-military friend, Emma, who was currently living in Long Beach, and soon after, Claire was on a tram into the city.

Emma worked for the city as one of many lowly prosecutors, and Tammy, her spouse of five years, worked part-time in the law office library. Emma was heavier than Claire remembered and seemed happier than she ever was in the army. Tammy had two young daughters. The couple gave her the girls' room, and the kids got to sleep in the front room in their sleeping bags, under a makeshift tent made with a sheet stretched over a couch. It was an exciting adventure for the girls. They squealed over each other's theft of pillows from the couch that they added to their side of the cozy den. Claire smiled at their antics.

"Claire, are you being chased by someone's significant other who caught you where you shouldn't be?" Emma teased her as she helped change the bedding on her borrowed bunk bed.

"I don't have that rich of a sexual life. I'm more the type who falls in love and then jumps into a relationship."

"That could take a long time. Do you test your batteries now and then to make sure the important things still work?" Tammy asked.

"Everything works just fine. Do you two still have that toy box—"

"Toy box!" a little voice piped up.

"You can't play with my toys," another small voice told her seriously. "You can play with Dora's. She's got more than me."

"Girls," Emma said, "if I hear that again, we're going through your toys and count out ten for each of you and whatever is left goes to children that don't have toys."

That set off two wails.

"Emma. Don't stress them like this before bedtime," Tammy said. "They're going to have nightmares."

Tammy went into the front room to calm the girls, and Emma sat on the bed and patted for Claire to sit next to her. "So what's going on? Is this another mission?"

"Remember Vanessa?"

"Oh, girl." Emma groaned dramatically. "She was a crusader who was into extremely dangerous stuff. I heard she joined the U.S. Marshals Service."

"She was killed working on a case."

Emma took a deep breath then sighed. She was quiet for a moment. "I'm so sorry to hear that. Did you two stay in touch?"

"Yes, but I was out of the country when it happened."

"So, where are you going with this?" Emma asked.

Claire shrugged uncomfortably. "When I got back, I had a message from her. She was working undercover, and she felt her days were numbered. She didn't know if her team would be able to protect her, and she was in too deep to back out. She was assigned to gather information and evidence on people involved in jury tampering, but while doing that, she uncovered evidence on an international human trafficking ring."

"Human trafficking?" Emma sounded appalled.

"Yes. Importing children and women for sex in the United States isn't new. But human trafficking in the States, with its rapid growth, has become as profitable as running drugs. Gangs are kidnapping women and children, some from the supposed safety of their own homes, and selling them like cocaine or heroine. It's become a major source of income for mobs all over the world. And it's growing larger each year."

"Oh my God. That sounds like something Vanessa would want to investigate."

"Because she was closely watched, she wasn't able to pass the information on to her team, so she left it where I could get it. I turned it in to the Marshals Service. It dealt with the human trafficking, but it didn't include any evidence of someone tampering with jurors in an L.A. court. Have you heard anything about anyone suspecting their jury delivered a surprise verdict?"

"Damn! Whose court is that?" Emma asked.

"So you have."

"Whose?" Emma asked again.

"I can't say. Not right now, because the Marshals Service is investigating it. Can you tell me what you've heard about jury tampering?"

Emma sighed. "There's a few very pissed-off lawyers who feel they had a perfect case and suddenly one or two jurors changed their minds. They felt someone threatened the jurors, because when questioned, none of the jurors would talk."

"My guess is the jurors' rooms are being bugged." Claire couldn't divulge that she knew it for a fact.

"I wonder if that's why Jenny's in town?"

"Jenny JAG?" Claire asked.

"Not JAG anymore. She's with the FBI. I saw her the other day in the law library."

Both were quiet for a few moments.

"What's your next move?" Emma asked.

"I don't know."

"How much time do you have?"

"I'm on a month's medical leave." Claire could feel her face heat up with that confession.

"Why?"

"My locker was booby-trapped. I bumped my head on a bench when I ducked. Got a concussion."

"Good heavens! Claire, are you sure this is the type of life you want?" Emma put her hand on Claire's arm and squeezed it.

"It's not always this exciting. And the time off gives me a chance to find out why I have this mark of death on me."

"You can get a lot of things done in a month without dying."

"I'll give it a try. I hope you aren't in my profile. So far, they've been right behind me, even when I used a friend's truck instead of my own."

Emma frowned. "You aren't forgetting about that tiny chip they've been implanting in special ops personnel and some of the other high-risk ops people, have you? Just like dogs, remember?"

"I never got that close to high-profile cases for them to be interested in me." But it did start Claire reconsidering. A full MRI would turn up something like that. Was this paranoia? When you knew about some of the things the government did to their own citizens and military personnel as test subjects, and the ways they influenced people to keep quiet, it paid to have your own secret resources and to hope that they had not been compromised.

Everyone was expendable to black ops, but this wasn't a black ops situation... or was it? Stolen drugs and gems had a lot to do with black ops.

Claire rubbed her eyes in weariness. "I've changed clothes, watches, backpacks, and cell phones. I can't think of anything else that tells them where I'm going, so yeah. That could be a possibility."

"Go to sleep. A fresh mind will help you figure it out. I'll leave a name and number for you with a friend at St. Mary's. They have an MRI and a tech experienced in looking for small implants. Remember Captain Burns? He's one of those guys who believes in UFOs and that aliens plant microchips in special people."

"You still know that big cheese?" Claire remembered him. He used to be a doctor in the army. His far-out ideas got him an early out. Claire had thought that was his intention. Apparently, he really did believe in what he talked about.

Chapter 16

The next morning, Claire was on Emma's PC doing research on diamond companies when an advertisement popped up. *EZ Loans for your dream diamond ring. J.M. Norton.* The seller had a store in two major shopping malls—one in L.A. and the other in New York.

Norton.

Checking the clock, Claire noted that if her special favor was going to be done, she needed to get to St. Mary's before normal hours. She had thirty minutes.

The person waiting for her wasn't anyone she recognized, but whoever it was, he knew not to ask questions. For thirty minutes, the machine banged with her inside the tunnel lying very still. When he slid her out he was excited, and ex-Captain Burns was beside him.

"You have something right there." Burns showed her a dot on her shoulder. "They're always close to the surface. So tiny you or anyone you're intimate with wouldn't notice it. Come with me."

Claire followed him to an office. She grimaced at the shot and then squeezed her eyes shut at the idea that she was being sliced open. After an hour, she was back on the street feeling much better about not as easily being found.

After two changes on public transportation, Claire was at the L.A. mall. She purchased coffee, a bagel, and a newspaper then waited for the jewelry store to open. With pencil in hand, she was marking want ads that looked interesting. Her eyes flicked toward the store where she caught sight of Agent Rodriguez and Sam Thompson's arrival. The owner was just opening up. They didn't come together. Where had they been waiting for the owner's arrival?

The three greeted each other, but not with a handshake or nod. It was a verbal acknowledgement that Claire wished she could hear.

She didn't get the feeling that they were friends, or even acquaintances.

An hour later, Thompson and Rodriguez left the diamond store through a side door. She spotted two people interested in their departure so she leaned back and continued with her reading. Two people went into the store, disappeared in the back, and then returned to stand behind the counter. They worked there.

"You're like the cat that keeps coming back, you know that?" MaryLyn's voice informed her.

"Leave me alone," Claire grumbled as she paged back to another part of the newspaper. She put the newspaper down and frowned at the young man dressed in a suit standing before her. For more than a few heartbeats, she studied the image, very aware she was attracted to this woman who was dressed as a man.

"If you were after who you said you were, why haven't you picked him up?" Claire asked.

"It's a complicated case."

"I'm not interested in your business. I'm out on worker's comp. I'm just sipping coffee and—"

"Being so much smarter. You're wearing a bulletproof vest I see... unless you gained a lot of weight in a few days," MaryLyn said sarcastically.

The shop owner chose that moment to exit through the back door, and Claire rose quickly to follow.

"I've got a car. Do you want a ride?" MaryLyn asked.

"All right," Claire said.

"Not that way. He's parked over in the lot this way. He's just making sure he's not being followed."

"I want to follow him," Claire told her.

When he stepped onto the escalator, there were four teens separating them. He entered a toy store and exited five minutes later with two stuffed animals. Then he led the two women to a fast-food hamburger joint. There he was met by a woman and her two children. He gave each child a stuffed animal. The man kissed the woman on the cheek and paid for their food. Though he sat with them while they ate breakfast, Claire noticed the lack of a family bond. Even the children seemed to have no connection with the woman.

"Maybe she's a new babysitter or nanny," Claire said to MaryLyn, who was moving quickly to an exit, probably anticipating the woman's departure.

MaryLyn used her cell. "Hey, Bo. How's your mark?"

"They know they're being followed."

"Something stinks here. Break off and come on back to the mall. Let Tommy pick it up."

"Okay."

"Meet me at the east side behind the bookstore," she said before signing off.

"Have you ever thought," Claire said, "that someone might be using you to put pressure on these people you're chasing, to flush out the real holder of the diamonds? And why didn't you tell me that Monica Norton is related to the Nortons that own part interest in the stolen jewels?" It wasn't really a wild accusation on Claire's part. She simply wasn't a believer in coincidences in her line of work.

"Monica has never lived or been to New York, and as far as I know, she's only met two of her relatives, besides the aunt who raised her. Sam is worth a million dollars, so I'm interested in him. We've waited to see if he would lead us to the diamonds, but too many people are gathering, and that means we could lose our investment if he gets turned in without proof of his involvement in the diamond heist. I don't want to lose the million and additional rewards for other information we gathered."

"Where does Monica fit in this? And Gil?"

"Monica is on the fringes. She's a cop who studied to be a detective and finally made it. Her mother's family is in the gem business."

"Wait a minute. I heard Monica say she's an orphan."

"She is. Her mother died in childbirth at the age of sixteen. The family secret is who the father is. Her lesbian aunt raised her. In that family circle that's a negative triple whammy. And depending on who she's talking to when she's drinking, it could be a bad or good thing."

"Is the Norton name supposed to be big with diamonds?"

MaryLyn glanced at her. "They have a partnership in a diamond mine. On this continent, they have one outlet in Canada, one on the East Coast, and one on the West Coast."

"What about Gil? Where does he fit in?"

"I'm working on that. I need his fingerprint or DNA. You don't happen to have a picture of him, do you?"

"No. I can do a sketch of him if you'd like."

"I would."

A Hummer came around the corner. MaryLyn was opening the door before it came to a complete stop.

"Hi, Bo," Claire said as she slid into the backseat.

"You're back, huh? You two have something going?" he asked with a grin. "Where to, boss?"

Sitting in the Hummer they had a better view of the parking lot.

"See that woman with the two kids? We're following her," MaryLyn told him, ignoring his comment. "There's two stuffed bears that may be of interest to the DEA. She's delivering something in them to one of our targets."

* * *

An hour later, they were back to Aveneida where Acela's daughter had been in childcare. The yellow crime scene tape had been removed.

"Look familiar?" MaryLyn asked.

"This was where a Mexican drug cartel boss had his headquarters," Claire said. "He was executed here. Why would they continue to use it? Did you know they have a bunch of tunnels running from that house to the park and a dozen homes?"

"So we heard," Bo said.

"How do you know so much?"

"Research," MaryLyn and Bo said simultaneously. MaryLyn glanced at Bo. He nodded at her and drove around the block.

"This is a good place, Bo. Let us off here."

As the two women walked along the sidewalk, they saw a car turn the corner and pull in front of the house. DEA agent Rodriguez and Sam Thompson stepped out of the car with what might have been bodyguards.

"Keep walking," MaryLyn said.

Claire looked around her nervously, hoping there wasn't any sniper aiming at her. "You look nice in a suit. Dress up often?"

MaryLyn turned to her startled, and then smiled while a blush crept up Claire's neck. "Whatever the job calls for."

"Would you like to go out one evening?"

"One of these evenings." MaryLyn returned her attention to the house.

The conversation took them past the house that now had four cars parked in front. "I have an invitation this Thursday night to an Eve Lauren performance. Would you like to go?" MaryLyn asked.

"Yes. I'm free for a few weeks, as a matter of fact. Shall I drive?"

"I'll drive. Come this way." MaryLyn turned left and crossed the street. She walked up the street and passed the back of the house. Claire could see her speaking to someone else and guessed it was via her cell, hands free.

"We'll watch from up there." MaryLyn pointed to the top of the slope. "My guess is that every agency involved will be here in a few moments."

They heard the distant sound of a helicopter. As they reached the top of the slope, black-and-whites and unmarked cars converged on the house.

"A raid. Did you turn them in?"

MaryLyn nodded. "I couldn't just ignore the drug connections."

"What do you think was in those stuffed animals?"

"I don't know. It's probably drugs, considering the agent is DEA, and it's big business for the cartel."

Police dogs were barking, and people were yelling from the houses below them.

"Come on. Let's go find our ride. Want to come back to the house? One of our contacts with the DEA should be calling in what happened. At the very least, they should be arresting Thompson and Rodriquez."

"No, just drop me off at my place if you don't mind."

"Okay."

A nondistinct vehicle pulled up next to them. The driver got out and sat in the back. "Leave me off at the corner, boss. I'll stay with Bo and take notes on their cleanup just to keep them honest."

"Maybe this time we'll get lucky, and Thompson can squeeze out of it," MaryLyn said. "I'd love more time to connect him with the diamonds."

* * *

Tiredly, Claire unlocked her door and looked around for the cats.

"Hey, guys, I'm home. Want dinner?" She kicked off her shoes and leaned down to pick them up to toss in the closet when her senses picked up that she wasn't alone. Whirling, she caught one man with an elbow to the side of his head, stepped into a rifle butt that was aiming for her ribs before it had much momentum behind it and dragged that man off-balance with a chop to the side of his throat. Something fell across her legs, knocking her off balance.

A fist grabbed her by the hair and pulled her up. A gun with silencer pressed against her forehead. She hoped the neighborhood watch was on patrol and help would come before she suffered irreparable harm.

"Where's the book?" her attacker demanded.

When she shook her head, she got a jab in the stomach with the rifle. As she dropped to the floor, she began to wonder if maybe she was in the wrong line of work.

"Where's the book?"

"I don't know anything about a book," she said, wheezing.

"Sam gave it to you before he was shot, so don't give me that crap."

"Nothing," she whispered.

Her attacker was one of the cops at the taco stand the day Sam was shot. It was a very brief, enlightening moment that was quickly put aside. She had survival to think about. She saw two men standing, one with a silencer pointed at her head and the other with a shotgun. She recognized the equipment. SIM, specialty impact munitions. Beanbags. At this range they could kill her. There was a third man groaning on the floor.

"I saw the list of names in the book. He showed it to me at the taco stand," the man said. "He didn't have it when the gang-banger popped him. That means you've got it."

"I don't know any—" She saw the hit coming and shifted her weight, surprising him. She twisted his wrist so his pistol was pointed at the guy with the shotgun and snapped his wrist. She fell to the ground and was rolling away from the entanglement of legs when something hit her in the chest and knocked the breath out of her. Her vision blurred, and the sounds around her were like being underwater. Helpless, she lay staring at the ceiling. When were they going to finish her off? Minutes passed, and gradually she heard normal sounds: the cat's purr and someone's steady breathing. A blurry face above her took on a familiar shape.

"Hey, how are you doing?"

Claire managed a grunt.

MaryLyn showed Claire a SIM beanbag. "Believe it or not, getting hit with this beanbag is better than a live round."

Claire struggled to her feet. Her hand went to her chest. It hurt. "I'm doing better. I'm waking up in my own apartment, and thanks to the bulletproof vest, I managed one superwoman feat. I think I'm going to start sleeping with one on."

"I hope you reconsider that when you have overnight company." MaryLyn held up an envelope. "I'm afraid your landlord is evicting you. This was under your mat. I read it, thinking your visitors left you something less bruising."

Claire took the envelope and dropped it on the couch next to her. "So, what happened to the guys who were beating me up?"

"There was only one of me, unarmed, so they got away. Two of them didn't look good. No police report, unless you want to call it in."

"I'll call it in. I found out what everyone wants."

"What's that?"

"They said Sam gave me a book the day he was shot. It has a list of names. Why would he tell them that? Why would he give it to me?" she asked tiredly.

"I don't know. After all this time, if you or anyone who used your patrol car hasn't found it, I would say Sam managed to lose it and is assuming you have it."

Claire watch two golden eyes blink at her from inside the tube on the cat perch. Cleo seldom came out of her safe place when there were visitors.

"How did you know to come back?"

"There were three cars with suspicious people guarding them not far up the block. I thought I would park around the block and check up on you. Their lookouts probably thought I also called the police."

"What does that tell us?" Claire asked.

"That they're worried about uniforms, but not about a detective," MaryLyn said.

"At this rate, I'm going to move to a castle with a moat. I hope it comes with crocs."

"The moat will attract more mosquitoes than you can ever imagine and rotten things that the crocs don't eat, and in your surrounded castle, you'll have bugs of all kinds and drafts. And then there's the housekeeping, which surely will kill you if disease and pestilence don't. Are we still on for Thursday evening?"

"You just took all the fun out of having my own castle. Yes. When is Thursday?"

"Tomorrow. You sure you're going to be up for it?" MaryLyn looked at her closely. "Close your eyes for ten seconds and then open them."

Claire did so.

"Well, your eyes are okay. You lucked out. No bruises on your face and no hard knocks to the head."

"I wouldn't have been going out in public with a shiner. I came back from one vacation recently with bruises. I can't do that again. I'll never live it down. Are you going to hang around for the police?"

"Not if I don't have to." MaryLyn sat on the couch with a sigh. Leaning back, she closed her eyes. "You know cops take hours to appear to take a report."

"Yeah. They send detectives three hours later, and CSI comes sometime within 24 hours. What did you do before you had your surgery?" Claire watched her expression closely, looking for something that would tell her she was asking a question that was too personal.

"I was an undercover agent for the FBI. When the dark ages came to the White House, we had a new boss and my assignments took on a more lethal bent. I resigned, as I was meant to. It was fine with me. I had money, an appointment in Colorado, and a great support group while I healed."

"But not your faithful boyfriend," Claire said.

"He needed me more than I needed him. I provided a nice enough apartment, paid the bills on time, and didn't nag him about staying out late at night. The only thing I missed was my team. We were like the four musketeers, but we called ourselves the Dynamite Team. Gainer, Harwich, Harrison, and me. We had code names: Gainer was Junior, Harwich was Gumbole, Harrison was the Nose, and I was Baby Cakes."

"Harrison as in…?"

"Your partner, Detective Harrison Harvard. Like me, he didn't want to wait around for the FBI to redeem itself."

"So, as Baby Cakes you were bait?"

"Yes. Junior was my pimp and the other two were Junior's henchmen. We worked in child kidnappings for prostitution. When the incoming administration took over the country, our team was broken up, and instead of focusing on the real crooks, we were spying on anyone that opposed them. What we were hearing was scary. I quit before it was too late.

"When I came back from Colorado, my neighbor told me that my roommate, Lenny, was killed at the airport. I saw it on the news on my flight back to New York, but it didn't occur to me that he was one of the dead.

"One of the queens Lenny knew got in touch with me, and I met him in an alley. He said Lenny left some papers with him that he was to turn over to me should anything happen to him. He wanted money for the envelope.

"I left him alone in the alley for five minutes, and guess who comes down the alley with bats and tasers? Christian soldiers from a corner church that made money on hate speeches. I always wondered when one of those soldiers would ask their pastor why he was driving a brand new car, looked younger than his age, wore all those diamonds and designer clothes, while they were taking the bus and living in near poverty. Anyway, I pulled out my gun and pointed it at the first guy and said, 'Please, please, please, make my day and do something stupid so I can shoot someone.' One guy raised his bat and I shot it to bits." MaryLyn laughed. "I thanked my great aunt Beth for insisting I practice shooting with her."

"So you saved the queen," Claire said.

"And I got the envelope and everything that was in it, including a cubic zirconium ring. We could all tell it wasn't real, otherwise that ass would be wearing it."

"What was in the envelope? A full confession?"

"That's exactly what it was, and I hid it in a safe place. A day later, my apartment was trashed. I went to visit Ms. Queenie, and there was crime scene tape around his apartment. According to the neighbor, someone paid him a visit and carved him up. The police took just long enough for the killers to get away. They seemed to know how long it would take for the police to get there."

"I bet you were sleeping with a gun in your hand," Claire said.

"I packed my bags and disappeared. With a whole new identity, I followed the trail to California."

"You left out a lot... like where did you pick up Bo and—"

"That's for another day."

"Thanks for sharing, MaryLyn. I think I'll leave off the police call."

"Good decision."

Chapter 17

MaryLyn picked Claire up at five thirty in a white Cadillac XLR-V convertible. The vehicle looked nice even with the top up. MaryLyn looked elegant with the right amount of makeup, jewelry, and a dress that was probably from a Rodeo Drive designer. Her coat and purse were in the backseat.

"You know, I didn't see anything on the Web that said Eve Lauren was appearing in California." Claire, still stiff from the previous day, sank slowly into the leather seat. Her chest hurt where she'd been hit, so her breathing was shallow.

"She's in town, but she's doing a private one-night appearance at a friend's place to test out her material and raise money for a charity. That's where we're going."

"Nice to have connections, huh?" Claire laid her coat across her lap and buckled her seatbelt.

"They aren't going to like you with that gun on your hip." MaryLyn pulled away from the curb and headed for the freeway.

"I'm my own bodyguard."

"I'll tell them you're with me and you're my bodyguard," MaryLyn said with a smile. "But with all that limping and leaning to the left, they may not believe it. You could have canceled until you felt better."

"No, no. I may never get another chance to see just how I'll act in front of Hollywood celebrities. In my mind I'm real cool, but I'm also playing another scenario where I make a complete fool of myself. How do you know these people?"

"They've hired my company for various things."

"Is there anything I should know so I don't make an unforgivable gaffe?"

"Don't ask for autographs, don't take pictures, and don't get in the way of a bodyguard. If I think of anything else, I'll let you know."

"Okay. Any of your people going to be there?"

"We're the security."

"Just what do you do?"

"We keep people from wandering into places they aren't supposed to be, like upstairs, and we stop guests from taking souvenirs."

"Oh. Does that mean you do body searches if someone stays too long in the bathroom?"

"That depends on who it is."

Claire studied her, wondering if she was joking.

The private showing was in the Hollywood Hills, close to MaryLyn's residence. Claire checked in her sidearm at the door, where Bo was acting as doorman. He wrapped her firearm in a sack, wrote her initials on it, and placed it in a safe next to other sacks. Claire wondered what the safe was used for when visitors didn't need to check in their weapons, and why were so many people carrying?

The attendees included faces both known and unknown to her. Claire was happy that MaryLyn didn't leave her alone except to go to the restroom.

Eve spoke with everyone, including Claire, before the show. At the intermission, Claire stepped out onto the balcony for a break from the star power.

"Too much?"

Claire turned to look at Connie, who had two drinks in her hand. She held one out to Claire. "It's nonalcoholic."

After Thompson drugging her drink, Claire was selective in accepting drinks. In some cases, however, it was easier to accept the drink and not drink from it. "Do you come to many of these?" Claire asked, taking the glass.

"These?"

"Private shows."

"Depends what you call many." Connie sipped her drink, watching the people milling around the table with snacks and drinks. "Do you like MaryLyn?" she asked too casually.

Claire looked at her startled. "I wouldn't be here if I didn't. Why?"

"Just curious."

"What do you mean by like?"

"I'm just curious why you two keep bumping into each other."

"Why don't you ask her?" Claire saw no point in explaining that she had been minding her own business and it was MaryLyn who kept popping into *her* life, which so far had been good for her health. Was that suspect?

"Hi. The second part is ready to begin," MaryLyn's voice came from behind her.

* * *

When MaryLyn stopped in front of her apartment to drop her off, Claire paused, wondering if she should ask MaryLyn the question Connie seemed to be implying.

"Thanks for the evening, MaryLyn. It was nice, if not..."

"You felt uncomfortable with the celebs."

"Yes. I'm not used to being around people with star power. I don't even know what to talk about."

"Well, you didn't say anything that ruffled any feathers, and you even managed to get out 'Hello, how are you?' without getting tongue-tied when Eve shook your hand."

"It was easy. I didn't say anything else. MaryLyn, how do you see us? You and me?" Claire asked.

"As friends."

"I... didn't want to mislead you."

"You're not putting out any vibes otherwise."

"Well, good night. And thanks again. Next one is on me."

Chapter 18

A week later Claire was in an Italian restaurant, sipping beer and holding up a tattered daily newspaper, giving the impression that she was reading the news. Her thoughts however were on the last week of failures in trying to capture one of her tails. She was going to have to ask for help.

She was expecting Gail, Margie, and MaryLyn to come over tomorrow morning and help her pack and move her furniture to her new place. MaryLyn was nice enough to volunteer Bo and Jack to help with the heavier furniture.

"Claire?" a surprised voice asked.

Claire glanced up at the familiar voice. Her heart beat faster at the incongruence of hearing that voice and accent on the West Coast.

"Herman? Hey, how's it going?" Claire had to do some mental gymnastics to associate the Herman she had known while working with the U.S. Marshals Service in New York to this Herman. The hip, street-dressed, skinny, pale-faced Herman in New York survived on the streets by renting out things that weren't his and returning them pretty much undamaged. This tanned, chubby-cheeked Herman looked like the office guy that paid his bills on time and spent weekends taking care of his mother. What was he doing on the West Coast and in Long Beach with a complete makeover? Witness protection? For what?

"Hey ya'all, this is Claire. She set me on the road to Jesus." He laughed at his joke and waved a hand as though he would have slapped Claire on the back if she were within reach.

Claire blanched at his description. They had happened to meet under a large spray-painted message that said "Saved by Jesus." The sad thing was that it was in a drug house where people lost their souls. Claire's first assignment as a Deputy Marshal was to track down a girl who didn't want anyone to find her. Her mother was in the witness protection program and threatened to surface if her daughter wasn't found. Instead, Claire ran into Herman on the wrong end of a gun held by a desperate drug addict who needed money for a fix.

"Guess you're wondering what got me out of the old neighborhood."

"I bet it's a good story," Claire said.

The men he was with looked interested in who she was, but they didn't interrupt. They all wore heavy work boots that looked comfortably broken in, jeans, and short-sleeved shirts. This was also a change in the type of people Herman used to hang out with.

"These guys are my close buds. Joe, Mike, and John. Guys, this is Claire. Want to share a pizza with us?"

Joe flinched at the offer, and the other guys laughed.

"The last time we shared, I paid," Claire said.

"That's Herman, all right," Mike said.

"I won't mind that," Joe said.

"That's no surprise there, Joe." Herman laughed. "Her paying was only fair. She was the only one with money. If any of those street slimeballs saw me with cash, I would've been a goner. I just traded things, like meals for wheels, you know?"

"You're not still hustling cars, are you?" Claire asked. Herman's biggest income earner was producing expensive vehicles for people who wanted a nice car for a few hours or for the night. When the vehicles were returned to where he appropriated them, most of the time they were so clean they looked like they were professionally detailed. All fingerprints were removed, and so was everything else that might have been left by the owner or the borrower.

"No. I'm out of that business. I have a respectable job laying line for a telco company. We're the people the big telco names outsource the dirty grunt work to."

"We took off early today," Mike said. "Joe here needed help moving his stuff out of his apartment and into a storage unit. The storage place closes at six, so we got at least one load in. Joe's paying for our labor with pizza and beer."

"What brings you to the West Coast?" Claire asked.

"What are you doing around here?" Herman asked simultaneously.

"You first," Claire said.

"Nothing much to tell."

Claire knew better. Herman's life was full of melodrama.

"I went to one of those gypsy fortune tellers," he said. "Only she looked more like a New Orleans transplant with all the bones and what-nots on her tables. She said "Go west young man, go west." When my probation was over, I thought it was a good idea. Same old neighborhood, you know? Doesn't give a nice guy like me a chance to stay good." He shrugged. "So, what are you here for?"

"I live around here, until tomorrow. I'm moving, too." Claire didn't see any reason to lie.

"No kidding? Where are you moving to?" Herman asked.

"About forty minutes from here. I'm renting a house with a backyard that has automatic sprinklers to water the yard and a once-a-month gardener."

"A yard, huh? That I can't get into. You need a truck tonight?"

"Are you hustling me, Herman?"

"Well, the fact is, we have a nice big truck, and for pizza and drinks we can be persuaded to help you move your heavy stuff." He looked at the others, and they nodded with big smiles. Claire thought either they were desperate for someone to buy them dinner or they were really nice guys. Or was Herman going to case out her new place? Claire studied Herman and couldn't see any ulterior motive other than what he offered. Why not take advantage of the opportunity? It would save Bo and Jack from having to help tomorrow.

"That's the only charge?"

"That's it. If you pay for our pizza and drinks, we'll pack up your stuff and move it for you," he said. "And Joe here doesn't have to hand over his last few twenties for buying us a pizza. He's been crying about forking out the money for our honest labor all day."

"I'll consider that a bargain. Do you want to eat first?" Claire asked.

"Do you need to ask?" Herman said.

They moved to a table out in the patio.

"Where did you get the training for this job?" she asked Herman after their orders were taken and a pitcher of beer delivered.

"It wasn't in New York." John snickered. "There you have to have family to get you in any of the union jobs."

"True enough," Herman said. "It was damn luck and some people putting in a good word for me to get the training out here. My buds here have been helping me learn the ropes since. This skill has got a future."

"It's good to hear you're staying clean," Claire said.

Herman waved expansively at the three men. "We keep each other out of trouble. We attend AA meetings together, and now we're going to share an apartment. We're like stewardesses, you know? We get sent on jobs all over the place. We just need a place to keep our change of underdrawers."

The others laughed.

"It's a nice, steady job that keeps a man out of trouble, my ma would say." Herman lifted his beer mug and saluted the others.

The pizzas arrived and conversation halted for a while.

Claire had learned long ago that it was a small world. When she least expected it and wanted it, someone from her old life would come back and mix with her new one. It was very inconvenient, but with practice she was getting flexible at handling it.

She was sure it was the influence of some dead-but-not-gone person in her past who kept throwing these wrenches in her business. One of these days, she was going to take the time to see someone who talked to the dead and get it sorted out. Claire almost snorted her beer. If word got out that she went to a séance, she knew her type of assignments would change.

She studied the men as they inhaled their pizzas and gulped down their drinks. She seriously thought they hadn't eaten for a long time. It reminded her of the first time she took Herman to a late-night diner. As Claire watched Herman interact with his new buds, she recalled a skinny lad trembling badly after she had taken the gun from the drug addict. The semi had no ammunition clip.

Claire treated Herman to a meal, where his chatty personality warmed up with each mouthful. He assured her he ate regularly, just not a feast like the one before him. It was a breakfast of pancakes smothered in butter and maple syrup, meat patties, eggs, bread, fruit, and lots of coffee. He weaved amusing stories of his life, and between laughs, they formed a friendship. He helped her find the girl she was looking for, though too late. She had OD'd on heroin. Instead of saving the girl she was assigned to, Claire saved Herman. Her consolation was that Susan didn't want to be saved and Herman did.

Claire recalled he had told her his first and last real job was at La Guardia Airport. He held the job for a week and was caught stealing suitcases, together with the person who got him the job. After he was fired, he started borrowing vehicles out of long-term parking lots in cahoots with the people who were hired to prevent things like that from happening. When he was caught and sent away for a year, it was for stealing cigarettes from a vending machine.

"Did you hear of a jewel robbery at La Guardia? It was about six or seven years ago," Claire asked Herman.

He looked at her suspiciously. "Now that's a coincidence. My cousin Walt called two weeks ago to say someone was asking about me. The someone brought up the jewel heist and mentioned a name. I told Walt that was an awful long time to remember a name and something that happened when I didn't work at the airport."

Claire blinked at him in surprise. "What?"

"Exactly—what. What would I have to do with it? Turns out one of the credit cards I stole, way back when, belonged to a name this person thinks was one of the jewel thieves. I had tried to use it, and someone remembered. I told my cousin I don't do anything illegal, and I don't want to be associated with anything illegal. I have a regular job that pays my bills and for sure I don't use credit cards. I stick to my twelve-step program, Claire. I don't want trouble."

"You've convinced me of your sincerity," was all Claire could think of to say. "Can you remember the name on the card?"

"Maxwell. I remember because of Maxwell Smart. My grandma likes that TV show. J.C. Maxwell was the name."

Claire drew a slow breath, keeping her face calm, and then asked, "Did your cousin say who was asking about you?"

"Some queen past her prime. He thought it was a friend of mine on hard times. I sure as hell won't be hanging out with old things. Besides, I stay away from those people. They're trouble, no matter what city."

Claire was surprised how irritated the comment made her and had to hold back her sharp reply. Pointing out to him that people only saw what they wanted to see would only get a blank stare from him, and days down the road, maybe, it would dawn on him what she meant by that.

"Do you remember when you acquired the card?" Claire asked.

"No. But I probably got it from one of the cars I was leasing out from a long-term parking lot. I couldn't tell you if it was there before I picked up the car or after." He thought for a few minutes. "After I hung up with Walt, I did remember that the card was maxed out."

"What did you do with it?"

"I hung onto it, waiting for the opportunity to sell it, but I was sent to the slammer before I could get rid of it. It's probably in one of the boxes I have sitting in my closet." He shrugged. "It's not like

I'm all that interested in digging through a life I've left behind." He took a gulp of his drink. "So, why are you asking about that heist?"

"Someone thinks I know something about it," Claire said.

"Six years is a long time. I had to really think what I was doing then. Do you remember what you were doing six years ago?"

Six years ago she was planning on what to do after she left the army. But it wasn't something she wanted to share. It sounded like Herman's cousin had hit a sensitive nerve. Considering Herman's lifestyle at the time, it was a wonder he had escaped without becoming a drug addict or getting shot while dealing.

"You don't think someone's mixing me up with someone else, do you?" he asked her in a worried tone.

"I think people looking for reward money are picking at the lint," Claire said.

"It's been too long past," Herman said again. "And anyone that gets involved with that treasure hunt is crazy. There are some serious people angry about losing out on a big bag of jewels."

"Why would someone looking for the people involved worry about the people offering the reward?"

Herman looked at her as if she were crazy. "Claire, it's bigger than you and me. When someone says the Russian Mafia, Mexican cartel, and everyone between are also looking, wouldn't that scare you?"

"Is that why you left New York?" she asked.

His eyes opened wide. "Hell, no! I stayed away from gang stuff. They're crazy people always wanting you to prove you're one of them with crazier and crazier stunts. One day they might ask me to kill my old grandma. She's getting kinda loose in the head but not enough to kill her to prove I'm just as crazy as those nut cases. Then I'd be looking at spending the rest of my short life in prison. NFW!"

"I didn't know the Russians or other groups were interested," Claire said.

"Everyone in a group of three or more is interested. You can't go up against the competition alone. I like my steady paycheck and not having to worry about waking up with anything more serious than an ugly hoochie mama."

"Don't you wish?" Joe laughed.

"You've got nothing more than what your hand can wrap around—" Mike stopped abruptly. He cleared his throat and, grinning at what was unsaid, stuffed his face with pizza, then rinsed it down with beer.

"You said the person asking about you mentioned a name. Why would someone who's hunting for treasure give the name of one of the supposed thieves? " Claire wondered aloud. "I hear each person involved in the theft has a million dollars on their head."

"Ha! You see?" Herman asked his friends. They all nodded. "I asked my cousin the same thing. I told him it's crazy to get involved with that stuff."

"And you guys aren't interested in the rewards?"

They all shook their heads.

"For that much money, people will kill you for a clue to that treasure," John said.

Joe snorted. "I'll stick to the lotteries. The odds are the same, and you don't have to work as hard."

"Seems to me," Herman said, "when you steal something that's traceable like diamonds, and it's going to piss a lot of important people off, you either have a buyer right away or have a long-term plan to keep yourself going until everyone who's after you dies off."

Mike nodded. "Like a retirement plan."

"Too long to keep stolen jewels," Joe said. "Where are you going to keep them stashed? What happens if a hoochie mama finds it under your mattress? Or what happens if when you need them you can't get to them?"

"Yeah. Who you going to trust with the location?"

"So you all know about the jewel heist?" Claire asked. And what was practical to steal and what wasn't.

"We've been talking about it since Herman told us," John said. He took two gulps and finished his beer. He caught the waiter's eye and asked for the pitcher to be refilled. Claire was thinking of four drunks trying to carry her heavy appliances down the stairs.

"I was pretty steamed," Herman said. "I gave Walt my number only for emergencies, and he calls me for that garbage. He accused me of sending my trashy friends to visit him. Like he's got taste in the ho's he puts out to... all the drag and drama. I wasn't evicted from my apartment because of what I brought home."

* * *

Nothing was said about the stairs they had to climb and descend half a dozen times as they moved her heavy furniture, stove, refrigerator, washer, and dryer into the truck. She hadn't removed her books from the bookcases yet, so she stacked them out of the way for later boxing so she could take advantage of the men and the truck to move the cases.

The cats had been locked in the bathroom to prevent them from getting stomped on. Every now and then, she went to the door and reassured them she hadn't left them.

The furniture was moved quickly, and by the last load, the men were looking tired. Claire added some money toward the truck's rental.

Already people were pausing in front of her new home to see who was moving in. At least when their dogs took a dump, they were courteous enough to pick up after them.

"Well, that's that," Herman said. "It was nice seeing you again. I really meant it when I said I'd like to pay you back for helping me out."

Claire handed him a business card. "If you should find that credit card, give me a call, okay? I'd like to see what fingerprints are on it, so only touch the edges. If you hear any more about that heist or anyone sniffing after you, let me know."

"Jeez. You're still a cop?" He turned the card over, but there wasn't anything on the other side.

"Detective. See there? I've moved up in the world."

Did he look disappointed that she didn't provide a private number, too? A lot must have gone on for Herman to have moved so far from his neighborhood as soon as his probation was over.

Claire drove back to her apartment, thinking about Herman. It was hard to believe the fear of prison could change a person's character that deeply. Herman was putting her disbelief to the test. His current friends didn't look gay or even interested in transvestites, but they didn't look offended or shocked when he had mentioned them. Most straight men she knew were paranoid about being associated with anything that wasn't testosterone driven.

If she hadn't packed up her computer, she would have researched Herman's story. It was too coincidental that MaryLyn was from New York, and Gil Maxwell was connected to Sam Thompson, who happened to be linked to the jewel heist. Now there was a credit card with J.C. Maxwell's name, and it was found in a vehicle that Herman stole for a night.

How did someone know J.C. Maxwell was connected to the jewel heist, if no one knew the names of the thieves? Except MaryLyn knew two of them. Sam Thompson and her ex boyfriend. Did the information he left her contain those names? She had assumed so. She would ask MaryLyn next time she spoke with her if she knew Herman and J.C. Maxwell.

Claire shook her head. She wanted to find out who ordered Vanessa's death and see that justice was done, not get mixed up in a jewel heist that took place six years ago. She flipped open her phone and called MaryLyn.

Her call went into voice mail. "Hi, MaryLyn. Does the name J.C. Maxwell mean anything to you in relation to your jewel heist? Or Herman Coleman? I had some weightlifters move out the heavy furniture and appliances, so Bo and Jack aren't needed. See you tomorrow."

Since her bed and couch were in her new house, she was left with her sleeping bag and pad to sleep in. Tired, she rolled out the bag in the front room, crawled in, and promptly fell asleep with the cats snuggling against her.

By late afternoon of the next day, her cats and most of her belongings were in their new home. She and Gail were left boxing the last of her stuff while MaryLyn and Margie went to pick up lunch. MaryLyn had said she would to talk to her about the names she mentioned, but they got busy packing. Gail and Margie wanted to get the moving going, so they wouldn't miss a radio interview a friend of theirs was giving later in the day.

"It's going to be interesting," Claire said, "to see how fast I adjust to not having stairs to run up and down for exercise."

"The high school stadium is thirty minutes away," Gail said, "if you really miss those stairs. Oh, by the way, introduce yourself to Lisa across the street in the green and orange house. Only, don't say to her that's its green and orange. It's terra cotta and hush green, or something like that. Janette's on the left of you. Both are home all day. Lisa has a business at home, and Janette's between jobs. It's handy to make nice with them. When we're alone, I'll show you the alarm system. Remember, it's a secret, so don't share it with your girlfriends."

Claire looked up from a packet of old police notebooks she had rediscovered. "I promise to show restraint in sharing with the girlfriends I'll be parading through my new digs," she said, as Gail went into the kitchen to finish packing it up. Claire continued to page through the books, wondering if she should destroy them. They were from when she had first started patrol work and continued into her short stint as a detective with Sam. Two books from her patrol days would be missing. She had turned them over to the Assistant District Attorney to be used as evidence in court cases and never got them back. The DA's office always asked for the notebooks when a case depended on what the officer or detective on the case had to say.

Her fingers paused at one book. Where did this one come from? Opening it, she quickly scanned the handwriting. She didn't recognize it. Suddenly, she remembered how she had acquired it. It was in a box of her belongings from her detective's desk before she'd been consigned to the file room. The chief had the box in his office. She didn't know who had packed her desk, but she appreciated that nothing was broken and no trash had been added to it. The chief assigned her to the desk downstairs until the investigation into Sam's death was over. Rather than unpack and repack, she just took the box home and tossed most of the contents.

At the time she hadn't looked closely at it, only added it to her collection at home since her new assignment didn't call for a notebook. But this wasn't hers. It wasn't Sam's either. She knew his handwriting.

One name, and then a few others, captured Claire's attention. They were names of the dead from PPD. Dates, that she knew were dates of death, were written alongside the names. There were a dozen other names with dates, but she didn't recognize those. The names were in one person's handwriting. The numbers in the dates looked like they'd been written by two different hands. Was she looking at a death list? Staring at it, she wondered if this was the book her assailant was looking for. But if it was, wouldn't he have called it a notebook?

At rap on the door was followed by Margie and MaryLyn entering the apartment with bags of food and drinks. Claire slid the book in her pocket, planning to look at it more closely later. She wanted to think about it.

Claire breathed the smell of coffee in deeply. "Just what I need. A java kick."

The four sat on the floor and began a hurried meal.

"When do you think we'll be finished?" MaryLyn asked when she was halfway through her sandwich.

Claire looked at her watch. "About an hour after we're done our meal. With our four vehicles, this is the last load."

"Are you going to look for a safer job while you're off?" Margie asked.

"Safer? There is no safe job. Life isn't safe. Our department is small enough that homicide, drug investigations, burglary, and robbery are handled by the same department. Good cross-training. Why do you want to see me out of it?"

"That's not how you were feeling a week ago," MaryLyn said.

"I just thought, considering why you're on medical leave, that you'd be ready for a job change," Margie said.

"Are you kidding? I can barely wait to get back to investigations. I go to the doctor for my final checkup tomorrow. I've been calling the PD daily to show I'm interested, and my position hasn't been filled by someone else, so I still have a job. If the doctor clears me, it'll be less than a month. I hope to God my desk isn't buried under case files I need to review… or maybe I do. Job security."

"What have you found out about being on someone's hit list?" MaryLyn asked.

It was amazing that since the last attack, no one had made any attempts on her life or broken into her apartment. She was still followed, but not always. Maybe her tails had real jobs. Matt had removed the security system in her old apartment and was scheduled to set up a system in her new home on Sunday.

"Is someone still tailing you?" Gail asked.

"Not all the time. I guess it was Jackson's posse, and they have something more worrisome to concern themselves with, like staying out of jail."

"You're right about that," MaryLyn said. "According to talk at the cop bar, eight cops died within three years in PPD, and they're trying to pin them on Jackson and his associates."

"Eight?" Claire asked. She knew several had been killed while on duty. But eight?

"Julie Hutton, Larse Vincent, Vanessa Slaughter, Sam Thompson, Nick Lockwood, Mike Peat, John Burns, and Andy Yorke," MaryLyn said.

Those names were among the names in the book that Claire had just looked at. It was alarming that Andy Yorke was on the list; he was Vanessa's ex-partner. No date was noted after his name. He must have been killed after the book was lost.

"Andy Yorke is dead?" Margie asked, clearly surprised.

"That's what I heard. Your PPD, Claire, has a high percentage of deaths whether they were still with the department or they left," MaryLyn said.

"How did they die?" Claire asked.

"Let's see. Julie Hutton was a parking enforcement officer and was found shot in the head in an alley in the late afternoon. No witnesses. Larse Vincent died in a motorcycle accident. He was on his way into work early in the morning. Motorists called it in. No witnesses. Vanessa Slaughter, like Hutton, was found shot in an alley but at night. Sam Thompson was shot by a drug dealer, Nick Lockwood was killed in a car accident, Mike Peat and John Burns were shot in the back of the head execution style, and Andy Yorke was killed in a car accident."

"Sam isn't dead. He survived the shooting. Why would Jackson have all of them killed? It would have all sorts of people looking at the department," Claire said.

"Right now he's convenient to blame," MaryLyn said. "You know how those poor overworked detectives look for the quick answers," she teased. "I agree, Jackson wouldn't be so stupid."

"What about Gil Maxwell?" Claire said. "Do you think he's related to J.C. Maxwell?"

"I gave Connie both names to check on," MaryLyn said.

"J.C. Maxwell?" Gail asked. She slapped her forehead. "I remember you said something about that, and Margie reminded me of a police convention I went to in Laughlin five or six years ago."

"It was the only one we didn't go to together," Margie said, "because I was sick. For Gail's presentations I do the setting up and getting the list of attendees, money, handouts, etc., unless a fan volunteers."

"J.C. Maxwell was at the Laughlin conference," Gail said. "He was on three panels, one of which I was also supposed to be on, but I didn't meet him. I withdrew because I wanted to get back home to Margie." She gave Margie a quick glance.

"It helps to be a pilot," Gail said, "because I can rent a plane and fly in and out without waiting for an available seat on a commercial airline. Anyway, we were going to go through the convention boxes, but forgot."

"We bought the van," Margie said, "*Molly Bree,* from Gil and Doris Maxwell."

Claire sat up straighter.

"You what?" MaryLyn and Claire asked simultaneously.

"We bought the van from Gil and Doris Maxwell."

"Gil Maxwell?" MaryLyn said. "I've been to a lot of those conventions, and I don't recall him on any of the panels. I would remember that guy. He gives me the creeps. Bob says since Gil's joined the card games at the campground, his stories are mostly made up. Bob calls him a compulsive liar."

"We almost didn't buy the van," Gail said, "but Doris offered to sell it to us dirt cheap because they wanted something larger. Greed took over on our part. We checked their background, and they were clean, so we didn't question our good fortune any farther."

"Wait a moment." MaryLyn pursed her lips in thought. "What if those agents who dropped in on Claire and me thought it was you and Margie? We're two women and we had your dog. They said they were watching Claire for a year, but what if it was the van they were watching?"

"I can work with that," Claire said. "I know they weren't watching me. I would have spotted them. The only tails I noticed started when I got back from vacation. Some were DEA, and one was Mosley."

"I've had Jack check on that," MaryLyn said, "and he told me there are at least four different people following you. He's traced two to the Feds, and one is Mosley with another guy."

"Do you think it's a coincidence that J.C. Maxwell and Gil share a last name?" Claire asked.

"I'm not ruling anything out," MaryLyn said. "Out of the five people we believe to have been involved, one for sure is dead. The airport security guard, Lenny Bowen. Sam Thompson is under arrest. That leaves three more," MaryLyn said, "and the diamonds. Sam isn't saying anything."

"Do you know the names of the others?" Claire asked.

"You're asking me to tell you names that are worth millions." MaryLyn smiled when she said it.

"I gave you J.C. Maxwell's name. Could he be one? That's a million dollars for you right there."

"You didn't tell me where you got that name."

"At the Pizza House yesterday, I met a guy I knew from my work in New York, Herman Coleman. He and his buds moved my heavy stuff last night. I gathered he relocated to the West Coast rather suddenly. He told me his cousin back home, Walter Coleman, had a visitor, an old queen, asking about Herman and a credit card that had come into his possession when he was in the car-rental business. Walter said the queen mentioned a jewel heist. The name on the card was J.C. Maxwell."

They all looked at MaryLyn.

"That's a coincidence," Gail said.

"Is there a reason you think I would know about old queens in New York? Do you have a name for this old queen?" MaryLyn asked.

"No. Herman just said an old queen past her prime, but I think he knew who it was. He was homeless when I knew him. You did say you acted as a bodyguard to transvestites, so maybe you'd know about—"

"It sounds like your Herman hung out with a different crowd than I did," MaryLyn said. "In the homeless youth population, 30% or more are gay. That's a lot of people to know."

Claire took a stab in the dark. "I have another coincidence. Those guys who were in my apartment the other day were asking about a book Sam had the day he was shot. One of them was one of the cops Sam was talking to that day. He said Sam had showed him the book, and after he was shot, he couldn't locate it." She pulled out the book from her pocket. "I didn't know what he was talking about, but I found this with my other notebooks just before you guys returned with lunch. Somehow it got mixed in with mine, and I wasn't aware of it."

She passed it around to them.

"Oh my God—a death list," Gail said. "I recognize a lot of these names."

"So do I," MaryLyn said. "Some of them attended police conventions regularly."

"How do you know?" Claire asked.

"We offer electronic surveillance equipment at conventions as a side business. When I give presentations, I get a list of people interested in more information."

"I do, too," Gail said, "but not to sell them anything. Since I give workshops at the conventions, I get a signup list."

"What else do they have in common besides attending police conventions?" Claire asked.

"I'm happy to say not all are dead, besides Sam," Margie said. She pointed to the third page, which had Gail's name on it.

"Do you mind if we take this with us and check the names?" Gail asked.

"I'd like a copy of that list," MaryLyn said. "Two people working on it can mine the data with different results."

"When I set up my PC, I'll send you both a copy," Claire said. "Mosley's name is there. For a while he was one of my tails. Do you think he knows he's on a list?"

"Philip Mosley. Mr. Big. He puts in an appearance at my demonstrations when they're around the L.A .area," MaryLyn said.

"He's Jackson's squeeze man," Claire said. "It's hard to believe he can set up spy equipment since he's so bulky and doesn't have a sense of his body space."

MaryLyn looked thoughtful. "I don't recall him picking up anything. He's always been early to the presentations, and I never noticed him leaving. When Bo was around, Mosley was like a peacock threatened by another male and had to fluff up his feathers. Bo wanted to get him worked up just to see what he would do, but I didn't want him to antagonize anyone in the PDs that we might have to turn over one of our bail jumpers to."

"He's not stupid, just single-minded and a real soldier. He follows orders and is faithful to Jackson."

"Do you think he would kill someone if Jackson told him to?" Gail asked.

"Yes," Claire said. In her mind she replayed the conversation she had overheard between Mosley and the man he was with. Again, she could almost, but not quite, identify the second voice.

"The connection to these people could be a police convention," MaryLyn said. She looked at Gail and Margie. "Margie's name isn't here. Does that narrow it down?"

"The one and only convention at Laughlin," Margie said.

"Five years ago, no, maybe six," Gail said with conviction. "It's the only one Margie didn't accompany me to."

"That's around when the jewel heist occurred." Claire looked at MaryLyn. "This makes it an interesting crossover," she said.

"Let's get you moved in and settled so I can start my research on the names," MaryLyn said.

"And so you can get your computer set up and send us a copy of this book," Gail said.

By the time they made it to the house and stacked the boxes, it was dark outside. Claire gave everyone thank-you hugs. When they had all gone, she let the cats out of their cages. Their favorite cat pole had been set up in the family room, which looked out into the backyard. She had dry food and water waiting for them, and the new place for their litter box was the utility room, which they found quickly.

After watching the two explore their new residence for five minutes, Claire turned to her PC. She took the book out of her pocket, scanned the pages, and encrypted the file. She sent copies to a dozen people. She knew Sam's handwriting, and it wasn't his. As far as she knew about handwriting, two wrote in the notebook. Was this really a hit list, someone's dead pool? It made sense. How was Gil Maxwell connected?

Claire looked more closely through the notebook. On the page right after the list of names and dates, she noticed some depressions, as though someone had written on a paper that lay on that sheet. She got a pencil, turned the point sideways, and very carefully shaded what looked like the first word. The word popped out of the pencil shading, and she continued shading the rest of the page. She caught her breath. This handwriting she recognized. It was Vanessa's.

I found a notebook in Sam Thompson's desk. It contains the names of police officers who attended the last convention in Laughlin. Some officers have died, and their date of death is written next to their name. I don't know the significance of the list yet. I'll keep working on it. I have to put the notebook back, but I've attached a copy of the names.

Claire rubbed her forehead. Was Vanessa killed because she discovered this list? What was its significance? Claire was certain Vanessa's name wasn't on the list when Vanessa found it. It must have been added later. Maybe after her murder. Did she ever get to send the copy to her Marshal contact? Claire decided to keep Vanessa's note to herself for a while, except for sending it to Stiller.

She scanned the shaded sheet into her PC then typed the words into a fresh file. She slid the book and the scanned sheet into a manila envelope, put a note with it, and sealed it. Then she sent a coded text message to Stiller's phony cell number and set up a meet with a team member.

She dug through her clothes boxes and hung her jeans, shirts, and coats until she found what she was looking for. With her change of clothes tucked beneath her arm, she headed to the bathroom for a shower. From one of three boxes in the bathroom, she withdrew a towel, washcloth, and soap. She would be meeting her contact in West Hollywood in an hour.

She parked on a busy street on Hollywood Boulevard, where small shops were still open for evening business. She wandered into most of them, intending to drive anyone who might be following her crazy. Because she sometimes found someone following her, she kept her driving around to a minimum. She wanted to get back to work healthy and resume her investigation into Vanessa's death. She had been through Vanessa's file many times while she was down in the file room, and now she had names to connect to a possible reason for her death.

She took a break at an Internet café that had bookshelves stuffed with reading material for visitors. She paid for a cup of coffee and, mug in hand, perused the bookshelves looking for some light reading. She chose a book full of pictures. While she sipped her coffee and looked through the book, she waited for a table to free up. A couple left and she quickly set her cup and book down on their table.

"Oh, miss!" she called. She left her coffee and book on the table and grabbed the coat left behind.

"Oh, thanks," the woman said.

Claire retook her seat. While she sipped her coffee, she paged through the pictures quickly, not really interested in reading anything. She finished her coffee, dumped her cup in the container for dirty dishes, and left.

A gift shop near her car had some figurines that caught her eye. She picked up a statue of Betty Boop on a motorcycle. Her thoughts were on MaryLyn when she purchased it. Tired, she headed back to her new home, stopping to pick up a fish burger and fried zucchini. The notebook had been delivered to her contact.

Tomorrow she would go to the doctor to get cleared for work.

Chapter 19

Claire was putting her dinner dishes in the sink the next day when her cell phone rang. She pulled it out and read the message. Smiling, she flipped it open.

"Hi, Harrison. How's business? Do you miss me?" She wondered if she should say something to him about MaryLyn mentioning that they knew each other. Would he be uncomfortable that one of his partners had undergone a sex change?

"Yeah. Business is dying for you. Where are you?"

"At home."

"Since you've been calling in almost daily, I figure you're anxious to get back to work. The chief said he received a fax from the doctor's office clearing you to return. Would you mind coming in now? We're drowning in cases."

"I'll be there as soon as I can."

"And, Claire, be careful. There's another reason I'm calling you in. A body was found in the PD parking lot."

"Who?"

"Mosley. A bullet through the head. It was made to look like he committed suicide, and he may very well have. He'd be spending time in prison if the charges against him stick."

"I'll be careful." Claire's heart beat rapidly at the news. Another name on her list.

"I'll meet you here, then. Twenty-five minutes if you want coffee. I need to get something to eat."

"You have a deal. And Harrison, I have a list of names you'll be interested in seeing." As soon as she hung up, she called Gail and left a message that Mosley was dead and she would let her know more when she found out anything. Before she left, she printed a copy of the names in the book to take with her.

* * *

She arrived at the police department minutes behind Harrison. She could smell the fresh coffee as she ran up the stairs and into their office, envisioning a cup would be sitting on her desk. A cup of coffee and a box with her name were waiting for her. The picture on the box was of a bulletproof vest.

"My very own form-fitted vest," Claire said.

Harrison was looking larger with the added bulk to his already large figure. "I'm going to have to get a bigger shirt to wear this." He took it off and laid it on his desk. "You're looking like you had a very relaxing vacation, Claire."

"I did. I exercised and kept a low profile." She laid a copy of the names on his desk, then opened her box and tried on the vest.

Harrison handed her the file on Mosley's death. "His body was found in our parking lot a few hours ago, shot in the right temple. No one heard the shot."

"Who found him?"

"Monica and Linda. They were returning from a crime scene and parked next to his vehicle."

"What has PCSI said about the head wound? Mosley is a lefty."

"Yeah. That's what Monica said. But Linda said lefties learn to use both hands."

"I think she was talking about herself," Claire said. "Mosley's the type who would stubbornly stick to his left."

"What else do you see?"

"What I don't see is blood spatter," Claire said.

"Yep. Monica and Linda also noticed the lack of."

"For someone to plant a dead ex-cop's body in a police parking lot is pretty ballsy," Claire said. She looked up at Harrison, suddenly realizing that her lack of emotion about Mosley death might sound heartless. But because he was one of Jackson's posse, and possibly involved in Vanessa's death, she couldn't care less if he was assassinated.

"Monica was the one who told me about the arrests of Jackson and his posse when I returned from vacation. My feelings were hurt that I wasn't given a heads-up. But I was just a file clerk at the time. A friend said it was an international bust."

"Would that friend happen to be MaryLyn Smith?"

"No. She's a bounty hunter. It was Gail Quimby." Claire looked up at him briefly, then returned her attention to the photos taken of Mosley's crime scene when she found close-ups of the same chewed cigarette butts they were associating with Sam.

"MaryLyn is interested in the rewards offered on a gang of jewel thieves of which Sam Thompson was a part," Claire said.

"Sam Thompson? Your partner?"

"Yep. One and the same."

Harrison pursed his lips and stared at the list she had given him.

"How many people know who the Dynamite Team was?" Claire asked him.

"MaryLyn Smith told you?" he asked.

"She has fond memories of the Dynamite Team," Claire said. "Though I don't believe she was thinking of the assignments."

"We've all moved on," Harrison said. "No one should spend too much time working in the underbelly of society, no matter how valuable your cover is. Boundaries and souls become jaded."

"So, about these cigarettes?" She shuffled the photos on her desk and thought of the scales of justice and how it seemed unfair that Vanessa was killed doing her job of cleaning up the scum she found where it shouldn't be.

"I was thinking," Claire said, "that maybe different people were responsible for dropping these butts at the various crime scenes. They could use pliers or something to make the same indentations."

"Since Sam Thompson isn't at the moment in a position to be leaving butts at crime scenes," Harrison said, "who could be leaving them?"

"When Sam didn't die," Claire asked, "why would he announce to the world he wasn't dead when there are some tough bounty hunters out there, the Russian Mafia and the Mexican drug cartel among them, looking to cash in on the million-dollar rewards associated with the jewel heist?" Claire asked.

"Well, someone is poking at someone to get a message across," Harrison said. He took the magnifying glass Claire handed him and looked at the cigarette butt.

"I'm thinking that we're going to be feeling really ridiculous if it turns out someone has pliers or something like that and is just spoofing us," Claire said.

"I've been calling the various police departments," Harrison said, "that handled the car accidents and the murders of those on the list. It seems a police convention arranger already noted a pattern in the deaths, and he's been calling various police stations sounding the alarm. Chief Dobbs said he hadn't received any inquiry. According to Chief Hampton at Las Cruzes PD, one of his detectives took such a message a month ago and passed it on to Jackson. Chief Dobbs has been talking to the other police chiefs to get more information."

"Have you pulled our files on the names of our own?"

"Not yet. I was hoping you would do that." Harrison smiled at her.

"All right. And if I'm not cross-eyed after looking over all the photos and reports, I'll see if I can find when the cigarette butts started to appear."

"Sounds like you have your night cut out for you. I'll be right back. I'm going to see if our CSI thought of pliers crimping these butts."

In three hours, she had set aside the files that didn't have the telltale cigarette butts and found that Thompson's crime scene had no cigarette butts. That in itself was unusual. He always had a cigarette going, so why no evidence of cigarettes at his own shooting site? What she wanted was an actual cigarette butt that Sam had chewed on to compare with the more recent ones.

"Claire," Harrison said, "stop by CSI before you leave. They want to show you their tests in matching up the cigarette butts."

She reshuffled the pictures of crime scenes, no longer seeing them. Her thoughts were on the death list, and the fact that it wasn't just the Petima police department that was losing members to accidents and killings. She believed that more than one person was involved in the killings. One person specialized in arranging accidents, and another liked shooting them in the head.

She called Gail to see if she'd been able to find out anything on her Laughlin convention list. The call went to voice mail. She called MaryLyn and went into her voice mail, too.

It was time to go home, but first—CSI.

Only one person was in the room. Claire had to use her card, and it sounded a ding to let anyone in the lab know someone had entered. Carla Watkins was working on a dress, blotting it with something and transferring it to a glass slide.

"Good evening, Carla," Claire said.

Carla stretched her back and smiled. "I was waiting for you. Harrison said you'd like to see how we tested for what may have made those bite marks on the cigarettes."

"I wish I'd known you were waiting for me. I would have come earlier."

"No problem. I had some catching up to do." She waved toward a table against the wall. "We tried various instruments to make similar marks. Here's what we've found."

Claire walked the length of the table, looking at each imprint an instrument left. "This one is almost like it. What is that?"

"Pliers. If we filed down the teeth here, we would get similar marks."

"So we have butts that may have been crimped by a set of pliers, not teeth. Was there any DNA on them?"

"Only on these." She handed a magnifying glass to Claire.

"Not the exact same marks."

"No, they aren't. Similar, though. But these are also teeth marks."

"Someone's sending us on a wild goose chase. The good thing is, it's someone that had been near Mosley's crime scene. Aren't there cameras out there?"

"Sprayed over. But there are cameras under the eaves of the building next door, which is locked up. The owner's on vacation. So without telling too many people, we're waiting for the owner to get back in town so we can see if the cameras are connected to anything that records."

"You need to get there ASAP. If he has his recording set to automatic rewind and tape over, you'll lose what was recorded."

"You think?" Carla asked as she went to the phone and called her supervisor.

Claire left her to her job. Someone should have thought of that possibility and gotten a court order already.

Before Claire stepped outside, she wondered whether a sniper was waiting for her and then thought it was a silly idea. It didn't stop her from checking under her car and under the hood.

At home there was a message on her answering service.

"Hi, Claire. It's MaryLyn. Call me when you get in, no matter what time it is."

"Why didn't you call my cell?" She reached for her cell and found it missing from her hip. "Damn." She looked on the kitchen counter and saw the phone sitting in the charger. It had been there since dinner, and she hadn't even missed it. Claire dialed MaryLyn's number on the landline and went into her voicemail. She left a message that she called and hung up. As she was getting in bed her phone rang.

"Hello?"

"Claire, this is MaryLyn."

"What's up?"

"I heard Mosley was found dead. We were right. All those people on that list were at the Laughlin Police Convention six years ago. The group that put it on went bankrupt, and since then, that group never attempted another convention. Something happened there that those people witnessed. All the people that had been panelists, and are dead, shared a panel with J.C. Maxwell."

"Gail never sat on a panel with him, and she's still alive," Claire said.

"Right," MaryLyn said. "My name's also on that list, but as a male. It was held after I had my surgery, and the people putting the convention on wanted me to dress as a male since that's how I originally registered, or not go. I didn't go. Did you show your list to Harrison?"

"Yes, and he's investigating it."

"I need to get some sleep. I've sent two of my people to keep an eye on Gil Maxwell, and I'll relieve them later in the morning. He's in town without Doris. I think he's the key. We're still looking up the J.C. Maxwell connection. If he's one of the five, then my suspicion is the others will be in town, too. Birds of a feather and all that."

"Good night, then. Sweet dreams."

"Good night to you, too. And, Claire, be careful."

"I will. And you, too. I hear hunting for jewel thieves is dangerous business."

Claire called Gail and Margie.

"This had better be important," a hoarse voice said.

"Who is this?" Claire asked.

"Who the hell do you think it is?" Gail's voice was clearer.

"MaryLyn thinks the names on the list and their deaths are definitely linked to that police conference in Laughlin we spoke about. Did you get a chance to find any information yet?"

"We have some news for you. I dug out the box on the Laughlin convention and went through it. There isn't as much as I usually have, but it's enough. I have my list of names that attended my presentation. Not all of them are on your death list."

Gail's yawn was loud enough to elicit one from Claire. Her jaw cracked from the stretch.

"Margie said get your butt over here. You woke us up, and now we're going to be discussing this until the wee hours of the morning."

"I'll be over."

Chapter 20

Claire hurried out the door. Another advantage of having the house was that she could lock her car in the garage to prevent someone from tampering with it and she could check the car with the garage door closed so she wouldn't scare the neighbors. However, Margie and Gail lived only four blocks away and she had too much nervous energy to burn, so Claire ran the four blocks. She wasn't breathing too heavy when she knocked on their door. Gail opened the door quickly and yanked Claire in.

"I don't want you standing out on the porch making yourself a target," Gail said.

"I'm not sure I'm the target anymore."

"There's no sense in taking chances. Sit down, and we'll tell you how we met Gil Maxwell... the one at the campsite."

Claire sat at the kitchen bar. Margie was removing condiments from the cupboards—honey, brown sugar, milk, and cinnamon sticks. She set out cups with teabags on the counter and waited for the water to boil.

"We met Gil and Doris up at El Dorado Campsite," Margie said, "which Ray's uncle, Larry, a retired fireman, ran in those days. It was already known as a place cops and firefighters hung out with their families if they wanted to leave town for the weekend without going too far and spending too much money. At the time, we had an old VW camping van that was ready to retire. We'd been going up there for three years before the Maxwells showed up. It was two years after the Laughlin convention."

The kettle started to boil so Margie turned her attention to preparing their tea. "Tell her about the first time you met Gil," Margie told Gail.

"Margie and I were up at the camp hiking the trails with Bobby. Margie and Bobby had gone ahead while I was removing a stone in my shoe. Suddenly this stranger came up behind me and cornered me along one of the turnouts. It's the one with the ocean view and the cliff drop. He scared the crap out of me. Without introducing himself, he told me he remembered seeing me at Laughlin at the police conference. I don't know what I looked like, but I felt threatened. It was like he was accusing me of something I did wrong. Margie and Bobby had doubled back to see what was keeping me. I think they saved me from him. I really thought he was a crazy nut and was going to push me over the cliff."

"When I found her on the trail with this stranger," Margie said, "the hackles on the back of my neck were standing up. I probably scared Bobby half to death when I drew my ankle revolver and told Gil to back off.

"Bobby demanded to know what was with Gil, cornering Gail where she could slip over the edge of the cliff. Gil came up with a story that he thought Gail was stalking him. Can you imagine that? Bobby didn't care for Gil and Doris, and he had been telling me about these new people who had parked their Roadtrek next to their bus.

"Then a few months later we get a call from Doris Maxwell making nice to me on the phone. They want to sell their new Roadtrek. Doris said it was too small for them, and since our VW was old, she said Larry told her we might be interested in taking it off their hands. We bought it from them for a steal... the too-good-to-be-true steal. We took the van to our mechanic who said it needed some maintenance done on it, but otherwise it was in reasonable shape. Their registration papers were in order, and their one stipulation, that we not discuss what we paid for it, was simple enough, so we purchased it."

"Since we bought the van," Gail said, "Gil's been friendly, as if the meet on the trail had never happened."

"And they're almost always at the campsite," Margie added.

"Right, because their kids and grandkids moved into their house from lack of jobs," Claire said. "We've all heard that story. Is it true?"

"I have no idea," Gail said. "Anyway, the one picture in the box that I had... we think the unfamiliar guy who looks something like Gil is J.C. Maxwell."

Margie opened a plastic container with some papers in it. "At that conference," Margie said, "someone took a picture of a number of the presenters and attendees with Gail and sent Gail a photo." She pointed at a face. "This is J.C. Maxwell."

It was a picture of an older, craggy-faced man who had his arms around two women with fake smiles on their faces.

"Who are these two women with him?"

Margie flipped the picture over. The initials SVP, MN, DLL, CL, DSS, JH, JCM, and VL were written.

"The two women are Julie Hutton and Vickie Lord," Gail said. "Julie and Vickie were conference regulars at West Coast police conventions. Julie's husband took the picture where the presenters and panelists go to pick up their schedules. Vickie I know, and she was there to walk with me to my room where I was giving my presentation. She was a convention volunteer who would let me know if I was running over the allotted time. I had flown in a few hours before I was to start and flew out right after."

"How sure are you that this is J.C. Maxwell ?" Claire asked.

"He's the only name and face of the panelists I can't place," Gail said. "I never met him before. It was his first conference. Look a little closer at the picture, though. He has some resemblance to our Gil around the eyes."

"Yeah, I see. Well it's not a father-son relationship because of the age. Maybe a brother?" Claire said. She went back to the list of names. "I don't see Vickie Lord's name on my list."

"I noticed," Gail said. "I can't imagine why Vanessa Slaughter's name is on the list, except she and Julie were close friends. They lived together for a while. Julie left her husband and didn't have anywhere to go so Vanessa offered her a couch. When Julie died, everyone was suspicious that it was her soon-to-be-ex-husband's doing, but no one could locate him. As far as I know, he's still missing."

"Who are Gil and Doris at the campground, then? Is Gil related to J.C. Maxwell?"

"I don't know," Gail said. "We have the papers from the van purchase. We can check them for fingerprints."

Claire jumped up excitedly. "He touched a pill bottle I got when I left the hospital. MaryLyn was suspicious about them, so I stopped taking them."

"Sit down," Margie said, "and don't go running to find your pills. It's still too early in the morning. We need to figure out if the Gil at the campsite is the J.C. who was at the convention, but with a face-lift or something. Match up Social Security Numbers. We have the Social he used for purchasing the van and his driver's license. We need to go farther back and compare."

"Okay." Claire turned the paper with the list over and wrote down step one.

"Next, we need to find out who Doris is," Margie said.

"And," Claire said, "we have to warn Ray, but without alerting anyone because his phone line may be bugged." She noted step two and three. "The Bobs park their motor home near Gil and Doris's. Do you think they're in danger?"

"It's more like Gil and Doris park next to the Bobs," Gail said. "The Bobs aren't on the list, so maybe they're all right. We'll let Ray take care of his territory. We need to make sure we're safe. As paranoid as it sounds, I think MaryLyn is right. Margie and I were the targets of that drug bust, and that means he's going to be planning another attack. You have my coloring and MaryLyn has Margie's. The van was verified, the dog was checked, and in the dark..." Gail looked over at Margie.

"That means they would have beaten the crap out of you, Gail," Claire said. "The guy beating me up had a ring just like Thompson's."

"Fraternities and brotherhoods have rings. Do you know what the ring looked like? We can trace it," Margie said.

"Ray has a picture of it. Why would Gil want to get rid of me? He knows the difference between me and you."

"I don't think he knew you would be borrowing the van. I made the reservations, so they were in my name," Margie said.

"Oh, crap." Claire slapped her forehead. "The other voice could have been Gil's." She then recounted tailing some people to the construction site and overhearing Mosley comment about killing a cop.

"And you did nothing?"

"I thought they meant to kill me next. How was I going to explain arresting them, or even shooting them, which is what I really wanted to do?"

"Why were you following them?"

"They were people of interest in a jury-tampering case Vanessa was working on. I didn't know who I was following until I heard Mosley's voice. But the second voice, now I'm thinking it sounded like Gil's. What does Gil have to do with Jackson's gang?"

"And Mosley's dead now," Margie said.

"Another step is to list all the panelists J.C. Maxwell shared time with," Gail said.

"MaryLyn did that," Claire said. "What if Gil is really J.C. Maxwell, one of the jewel thieves, who is using Gil Maxwell's identity to hide from the bounty hunters?"

"That sounds like a distinct possibility," Margie said.

Gail was looking at a conference bulletin and the names under the panels. "All these panelists are dead, Claire. Jeez. I knew all of them with the exception of J.C. I never suspected. I never put it together until Mark Lau said something."

"Who's Mark Lau?"

"He's one of the organizers of police conventions," Margie said.

"I think Gil is J.C., and he's eliminating the people who could expose him," Claire said. "But if he got plastic surgery and a fake ID, why wasn't that enough? This guy is a psycho who doesn't mind killing forty to fifty people. We're not the only ones who are working on this. Harrison told me that a convention planner noticed that a lot of his regular panelists are dead. That must be your Mark Lau. He's been calling around at various PDs and talking to the police chiefs or detective departments."

"Yes, that would be like Mark," Gail said. "We got an invitation to the next convention in Vegas, and I looked at the list of panelists. Most of the people I'm usually on panels with aren't listed, so I called Mark. He commented there have been a lot of sudden deaths of people who regularly attend. He had asked an FBI friend to look into it, but was told their priority is homeland security."

Claire dialed Harrison on her cell. "So, he took it to the police chiefs. Harrison should know that you confirmed it's Laughlin and we suspect Gil Maxwell." She glanced at the clock and noticed it was three in the morning. That wasn't too bad.

"Hi, Harrison, it's me. We have a theory on my hit list if you care to hear about it."

"Do you know who the next person is?" Harrison asked.

"No."

"The Feds are working on the list, too. I'll set up a meeting for eight this morning, and we'll bring the list and theories. Is that soon enough?"

"Yes. I'll see you then." Claire closed her phone. "Harrison said he gave the Feds a copy of the list. We'll get with them at eight a.m."

"Just think of all the changes at PPD," Margie said, "now that Mosley's dead and Jackson's in jail. Vanessa used to say they were as close as thieves."

"You mean thick as thieves," Claire said.

"No, she meant close as thieves. She was referring to their loyalty: strong as long as the wind was blowing the right way."

"I think Mosley knew too much. What I can't understand is the connection between Jackson and Maxwell."

"Maybe it was Maxwell and Thompson," Gail said, "and Jackson was just a tool."

Chapter 21

Claire went into work early. Her mind was working overtime to try to find where she fit in the hit list. Her name wasn't on it, but she was certain that's what was going on.

"Hey, what are you doing here so early?" Monica asked. She slung her purse on her chair and came over to Claire's desk. Before Claire could hide her list, Monica had snatched it up. When Claire tried to grab it from her, Monica backed away with it.

"Monica, give it to me. That's private."

Monica took her eyes off Claire to see what it was, and Claire snatched it out of her hands.

"What are you doing? Keeping score?" Monica said. Linda walked in at that moment.

"What's going on?" she asked. Harrison walked in behind her.

"I grabbed Claire's notes," Monica said, "and she got all hyper. I was only kidding around."

"Claire, let me see that," Harrison said. He read it and looked at Monica. "This is classified. It's part of an ongoing Federal investigation. Do you know what that means?"

Monica nodded.

"Just to be perfectly clear. You will not discuss what it is, not even hints to your partner or anyone else. Do you understand?"

Monica's face went red.

"The last management here was abusive, and it's going to take some undoing of the hurtful behaviors that were once accepted. If it seems we're going to the extreme left of political correctness, so be it. Eventually, when we trust each other and have shown respect for each other, some things will relax naturally."

Claire could tell Monica was missing his point.

Harrison gestured to the circular table that was in the center of the four cubicles.

"Let's get to the outstanding cases. Anyone need to get coffee before we start?"

Linda and Monica went to get some department coffee while Harrison set his cup on the table. They could hear Linda saying to Monica, "Next time, don't grab something from another person's desk when you know they don't wish to share it. That's what he meant. I'm buying this morning. You want hot chocolate or coffee with lots of sugar?"

Harrison spoke to Claire in an undertone. "Did you find anything else on the list that says who is the next person?"

"No. But I think the list belongs to J.C. Maxwell, one of the thieves from the New York jewel heist about six years ago." She stopped when Linda and Monica returned.

"Let's start with the overlapping cases," Harrison said.

They all pulled out their pads and compared cold cases with similar evidence that might be tied in with active cases that Linda and Monica were working on. They then went over cases that the two were stuck on.

Claire pointed out things in the crime scene photos that didn't stand up to what witnesses said happened. She was impressed with Linda's and Monica's appraisals of people they interviewed. As a team they were working well.

When Harrison called their meeting done, the Feds had arrived. The Feds, Harrison, and Claire went into the chief's office.

Chief Dobbs introduced everyone.

"Agents Epstein and Anderson are working on a New York jewel heist that occurred six years ago. They took it over from another team two years ago when it stalled," Chief Dobbs said. "Agents, do you want to brief my detectives on what you need?"

"The trail was cold until a month ago," Anderson said. "We got a tip that one of the thieves with a new face and identity was located in the L.A. area." He paused to sip his coffee while Epstein passed a picture around. It was Sam Thompson.

"How many took part in this heist?" Claire asked, her pen poised to start writing.

"According to our tipster, there were five originally. We haven't verified this yet."

"Just what did you have in your file?" Harrison asked.

Anderson and Epstein looked embarrassed. In Claire's experience, FBI agents didn't have the grace to look embarrassed.

"You didn't have anything," Harrison said.

"Someone had removed everything from the folder and deleted whatever was in the computer," Anderson admitted.

"An inside job?" Chief Dobbs asked.

"We think so, but we haven't been able to find evidence on who and when. We just know that though we were handed the case two years ago, we hadn't accessed the files until a month ago when the tip came in."

"So, whatever information your tipster is feeding you could be good or it could be a misdirection," Claire said.

"Yes," Epstein said.

"Do you know who the tipster is?" Harrison asked.

"We consider the source to be reliable," Anderson said hurriedly. "It's an ex-FBI agent."

"Who is that?" Claire asked, knowing the answer.

"MaryLyn Smith," Harrison said. "Am I right, Agent Epstein?"

"Yes."

"Why didn't you look at the case when you had been assigned it?" Claire asked.

"We have plenty of cases sitting on our desk that were higher priority, and since there were no new leads, it moved farther down our stack of files," Anderson said. "For the last month we've been collecting data on the names further supplied to us by our... Ms. Smith."

"We've interviewed Samuel Thompson," Agent Epstein added, "and he refused to speak to us without his lawyer present. With a lawyer, he answered nothing."

"We have five possible names of the thieves: Lenny Bowen, Sam Thompson, Jared Maxwell, his girlfriend Doris Hayward, and Mike O'Donnell," Anderson said. "Lenny Bowen was the airport security who showed them into a room with an unsecured exit. He was killed. An attempt was made to kill Thompson, but he survived. That leaves four still alive."

Claire looked at Harrison.

"You have something to add, Claire?" Harrison asked.

"We think Jared Maxwell and Doris Hayward have been hiding up at El Dorado Park in an RV, using the names of Gil and Doris Maxwell. We also think Gil and Doris have been killing off people that are on the so-called death list."

"You're right about it being a death list," Anderson said. "We had a chance to look into the names Detective Harvard faxed us, and most of them are dead. We also heard from a Mark Lau, about the coincidence that a large number of people who appear as panelists at his police conventions are meeting with untimely deaths." Anderson looked over at Epstein.

"So what are your plans?" Harrison asked.

From the way the two agents deferred to Harrison, Claire guessed they had history with him.

"We have agents keeping an eye on Doris Hayward. We lost Jared, but we heard he's in the city. Since there've been attempts on your life, Detective Hanson, we'd like to have an agent with you until we can find out whether you're still in danger."

"I'm going to be surrounded by my fellow officers." Claire glanced over at Harrison and could see he was remembering the sniper, too.

"She'll accept your offer," Harrison said. "I want the agent to be discreet."

"I'm bait?" Claire asked.

"Why make it easy for them?" Chief Dobbs said. "You've been someone's target often enough, and you're still here. Those odds are likely to run out."

"I have no objection, Chief. I just want to know what my role is, so I don't shoot someone on our side."

"All right then." Anderson looked smug that they had gotten what they wanted without too much stress. "We'll make the arrangements."

"Claire, you can work on cold cases. We've got plenty of them to clean up. Don't leave the building without letting me know," Harrison said.

Claire nodded. As she left, she noticed everyone seemed to be waiting until she closed the door behind her before starting another conversation.

She unlocked her desk and pulled out files she had been working on. For the next few hours, she made phone calls and arranged for people to come in for further questioning.

Harrison joined her and picked up the notes Claire made for the interviews. He took the case files and handed them to Linda. "Claire arranged for a meeting with these witnesses. You take over and see if they've changed any of their stories now that Jackson and his friends are behind bars."

"What all did you decide in there? Does Chief Dobbs know about MaryLyn?" Claire asked when Linda left.

"He does. He doesn't approve of her, gays, and lesbians. I would imagine he's having a difficult time accepting you, but he's keeping his chin above water. Sooner or later, he's going to have to decide which he's going to let run his life, his religion or being a law-abiding police officer."

"He's religious right?"

"Hard-liner. He left his last job when a gay man was appointed DA."

"That's odd. Gail Quimby sees him as a straight arrow guy and she's been living with her lesbian partner for fifteen years."

"He has been fair and evenhanded, but every now and then his prejudice shows. The DA was once a police officer he supervised. A rookie. I imagine they have history he didn't want to face."

"Harrison, how do you know so much about people?"

"Research."

Claire burst out laughing. "That's exactly what MaryLyn says."

"You've been seeing her a lot?"

"Now and then. Have you spoken with her recently?"

He nodded. "So where are we with the cold cases?"

Claire's cell vibrated against her hip. She glanced at the caller ID. "Hi, how's your skulking about going?"

"Good," MaryLyn said. "We've officially turned it over to the Feds. That means we can collect on J.C. Maxwell and Doris Hayward. Bo has a line on Mike O'Donnell. He visited Sam in prison under a different name. I wanted to see if you're interested in going to a play tonight. It's kind of a last-minute thing."

"Yeah. I'd like that… you know, I might still be in someone's sights."

"Well, it's up to you."

"I'll go. What time?"

"Four. We can eat dinner before the play starts. Dress warm."

"Okay. Bye."

She looked at Harrison. "Do you need me any longer?"

"No. You put in your time. Going out on a date?"

"Yeah," she said without thinking. It wasn't until she was in her car that she realized she was going out on a date with MaryLyn. Or was she? Did she have any romantic feelings for her?

She glanced at her watch. She had two hours before MaryLyn would come by. Why was she so damn nervous?

Once home, she removed her shoes and fell onto the bed, expecting the cats to join her. She fell asleep before noticing their arrival. The doorbell woke her.

"Who's that?" she asked Ramses, who hopped off the bed and disappeared down the hallway. Claire followed him at a slower pace. She glanced at the clock as she passed the kitchen. Peering through the peephole before opening it, she was surprised to see Herman. She pulled the door open, and Herman walked in at Claire's sweep of the hand.

"What's up?" Claire said.

Herman reached inside his windbreaker and pulled out a gun. "I'm sorry, but someone wants to see you." The gun wavered and Herman shuffled his feet.

"You need a gun for that?"

"He said you wouldn't want to come with me."

"Who is he?"

"I can't tell you that." Sweat ran down Herman's face.

Claire tilted her head and stared at him. "Is this about the notebook?"

Herman looked confused. He waved the gun toward the door. "Get going."

As soon as the gun moved away from her, Claire pounced. She chopped at Herman's wrist, and the gun clattered away. She followed through with a punch to his jaw, and he fell to the floor in front of the door. He grabbed at her foot. She kicked his hand away and ran toward the den, thinking she could go out the sliding doors.

But Joe was trying to open the sliding door, and Mike was working on the back door. She ran back into the living room. Herman was on his hands and knees, crawling toward the chair the gun had disappeared under. Claire kicked him under the chin, and this time, he lost consciousness.

She grabbed her keys on the hook. She wasn't able to pull them off smoothly. Everything on the other hooks clattered to the floor.

She flung open the front door and glanced up and down the street. A pop hit the door near her hand. She threw herself forward. Another pop hit her in the leg and knocked her sideways.

She crashed into the hedges and rolled over them. She lay behind the old brick border that the hedges overgrew. Panting, she tried to figure out how not to scream from the pain and not to panic about bleeding to death. More muffled pops sounded from hits against the bricks and house siding. Whoever was shooting must have assumed she was scooting or dragging herself along the hedges, because they weren't shooting near her.

Soon she heard helicopter blades and sirens. The house alarm was working, she thought, relieved. Claire felt the ground tremble as booted feet ran up the walkway and into the house. Too weak to call out, she fainted into darkness.

* * *

Claire became aware of hospital sounds, beeps, and a hospital code spoken over a loudspeaker. She opened one eye and worried about the other. Did she have a black eye? Sandy Hershey was standing above her with a cup of water and a straw. The straw rested against her lips, and she sucked the cool liquid.

She moistened her lips and was surprised she could feel them and they weren't bruised. "I think the bad guys have more points than me," Claire croaked.

"What is not good is me seeing more of you in hospital settings than the campground."

"Did anyone get caught this time?" Gingerly Claire touched her bandaged eye.

"Yes. According to your partner, Detective Harvard, the five involved in the diamond heist are all accounted for, the majority of the diamonds have been recovered, and with Jackson, his crew, and his spies locked up until their trials, Chief Dobbs has a working police department."

"What about the jury tampering?"

"I'll let you speak with your contact about that. Deputy Marshal Stiller's been putting in time sitting at your bedside along with a few other friends of yours. Since Ray had to come into town for some business, I thought I would, too, and visit you. Anything else you want to know?"

"When do I get out of here?"

"As soon as the doctor clears you. You do have a bullet wound to heal from, and you need to not take any more hard knocks to your head at least for a few months. You're going to be like a punch drunk, missing things, if you keep using your head for deflecting blows."

"Where is MaryLyn?"

"She sends you her regards. She had a job out of state, so she couldn't be here to visit. She advised you to not lose your health insurance. Now for some bad news. Are you ready for it?"

Sandy grinned when Claire scrunched up her face dramatically and asked in a whisper, "I'm fired from PPD?"

"Don't you wish? But that would be too easy. You have a psych eval to go through with the City of Petima. Chief Dobbs thinks you attract too much violence. You never told him you were undercover?"

"I let my contact handle that part. He was fine with you and Ray knowing, but when Gail and Margie figured it out, he decided too many were in the know. So maybe Dobbs wasn't told. How's Harrison?"

"Worried about you." Sandy pulled out a shamrock painted a bright green. "Ellen, his wife, said you need this."

Claire took the shamrock. "It would have been easier if Dobbs fired me. I could then make a graceful exit. Do I get released sometime today?"

"Probably tomorrow. The doctor's already made his rounds. By the way, Gail and Margie are buying that big motor home the Maxwell's had. It's dirt cheap."

"You're kidding, right?"

"Are you going to buy their van?"

Claire was silent, wondering where she would keep a van, or for that matter, where her next assignment would be.

"Well, you have plenty of rest time to decide what you're going to do."

"I like working for the Marshals," Claire said defensively. She looked up at Sandy with her head tilted so her one good eye could see her.

"You don't like detective work? It's a lot safer than your work for the Marshals."

Claire remembered Vanessa and their last good-bye.

"So why was the sniper shooting at me?" she asked to change the subject.

Sandy looked surprised.

"I was shot, remember?"

"The gunshot wound was from a sniper? I assumed it was one of those men who broke into your place."

Claire touched the bandage again and didn't feel anything.

"It's just stitches. Two little ones," Sandy said.

The door to the room opened and Deputy Marshal Stiller entered. He nodded to Sandy who said, "Hello, I'm just leaving." She gave Claire a kiss on her cheek. "I'll catch up with you after you're back home."

"That's a promise," Claire said as Stiller brought a chair close to the bed and sat down. Sandy left.

"Well, Hanson... Claire, glad to see you're awake. How do you feel?"

"Not too bad. Just a little soreness in my leg. Thanks for coming by."

"No problem. I'm guessing you have a lot of questions, and I think I can give you some answers." Stiller removed a folder he had tucked under his arm and opened it across his knees. He looked Claire in the eye.

"Detective Harvard said you were upset not to be told about the 'housecleaning' that went on at the start of your vacation."

Claire opened her mouth to say something, but Stiller raised his hand to forestall her. "I understand your disappointment not to be involved, but your predecessor, Deputy Marshal Vanessa Slaughter, had helped us and other Federal agencies build a solid case against Lt. Ronald Jackson and some of his men in reference to human trafficking. We wanted to stop that as soon as possible."

"Is that why Vanessa was killed?" Claire asked. "Because she got evidence on the trafficking?"

"We're not sure. That might have been part of the reason." Stiller looked down at the papers in the folder. "The information you gathered about the jury tampering was first-rate. The SD cards showed several attempts by court personnel as well as officers in the Petima PD to intimidate jurors." Stiller glanced up.

"That's good to know," Claire said. "Were judges involved, too?"

"We're still working on that. Next, that DEA raid on you at the campground wasn't approved by the higher echelons of the DEA, and some heads will roll because of it. Some already have."

Claire nodded, but kept quiet. Stiller seemed to be charging full steam down the track, and she had no intention of derailing him. At last she was getting answers from the proper authority.

Stiller shuffled the papers. "The notebook that you sent us was an invaluable piece of the puzzle about so many deaths of officers and detectives in the Petima PD and elsewhere. An FBI informant helped us connect it with a diamond robbery in New York six years ago."

That was MaryLyn, Claire said to herself. She'd never guessed that MaryLyn was still so connected to the FBI. "Did the informant fill you in on the tie-in to the Laughlin Police Convention and to J.C. Maxwell?"

"Yes. Maxwell and the other principals of that robbery are in custody, and thanks partly to you, we have the information and resources to put them away for a very long time."

"Does anyone know who's been taking potshots at me?"

Stiller grinned. "I guess that is a pretty important question you want answered. We suspect it was one or more of the people involved with the diamond theft, but we don't have proof of that yet. Harrison's people rounded them up, and he's questioning them now. He might be able to give you more information on that. Any more questions?"

"Not that I can think of at the moment."

"Feel free to contact me about any other questions that might come to mind." Stiller closed the folder and stood up. He offered his hand and Claire shook it. "You've done a great job, Claire. You're a credit to the Marshals Service."

"Thank you," Claire said, truly grateful for all the information Stiller had shared with her. She doubted that was normal procedure and suspected she might have Harrison to thank for that.

Stiller gave her a small salute and left.

* * *

The next day, Harrison taxied Claire home.

"I have questions," she said.

"I'm sure," Harrison said. "How about holding them until I get you home and comfortable?"

Claire settled back into the passenger seat and tried to relax. "I can do that." She sat quietly until they arrived at her home.

"You sure you're going to be all right alone?" Harrison looked around her house to make sure it was secured.

"I've changed battle dressings, I can grab a cab to the doctor's office, and I have lots of phone numbers to call should I need my dinner cooked, house cleaned, and DVDs delivered. I'm fine, Harrison. Thanks for caring." She held her cane up. "I can also punch someone good if they get near enough to threaten me."

"All right, then." He looked at her answering machine, which was blinking rapidly. "You have messages."

"I also have questions, remember? Stay awhile. There's water, coffee, and tea in the kitchen."

Claire pressed the button on her messages while watching Harrison walk into her kitchen as though he was familiar with the layout. Of course he would be, since he and a lot of other investigators tramped through the house terrifying the cats. It was Harrison who had helped Margie cage the cats and put them in the bathroom until everyone left.

Both cats made an appearance, and giving her one meow, hurried into the kitchen after Harrison.

The first message was from Margie and Gail, welcoming her home. She deleted it. The next was from Richard, wishing her well and certifying her PC's health. Delete. Matt left a message that he went over her place to be sure it was safe. Delete.

What was she going to do with all these people she had befriended? Some knew of her undercover work, and others took her at face value.

Harrison came back in with two bottles of water, not from the refrigerator. He didn't believe it was healthy to drink cold water. He dropped on her couch and looked around him. Cleo promptly crawled onto his lap.

"I see you made friends," she said and then stopped abruptly, both at the expression on Harrison's face and the sound of MaryLyn's voice coming over the recorder.

"Claire, I'm so sorry this was a bad experience for you, and I'm sorry I couldn't tell you everything. I would like to have coffee with you and see if we can start a friendship over again. I'll be out of town for a while. I don't want to give an exact time I'll be back, just in case it turns out longer and then... Well, you know. I'll call you or you can call my cell to keep in touch. Okay? Bye."

She turned off the messages and walked over to the chair facing the couch, which Ramses was sitting on. Gently, she lifted him to her lap as she sat.

"Have you spoken with MaryLyn since her change?" she asked.

"Briefly. She and Ellen are friends. Ellen drove her to the Colorado Clinic for her surgery."

Claire could feel her exhaustion lift. She sat up higher in her chair. "Deputy Marshal Stiller stopped by my hospital room. He answered a lot of questions for me."

Harrison cleared his throat, but didn't say anything.

Claire said, "If you had anything to do with that, thank you." She hesitated. "Do you know who the sniper was?"

"Sniper?"

"The one who shot me in the leg. The one who was outside my door."

"Maxwell. He learned you were a U.S. Deputy Marshal. Not at first, but someone tipped him later. Jackson couldn't find that in your history. He believed you were just Vanessa's detective replacement."

"I guess that's why Maxwell didn't kill me when he gave me a ride from the hospital. Or maybe he expected the pills he poisoned would do the trick. How did you find out it was Maxwell?"

"From your buddy, Herman."

"Ahh, Maxwell sent him and his pals to take me outside the house."

"Yes. He threatened their families. As soon as we got everyone into custody, Herman couldn't hang Maxwell fast enough. He said Maxwell promised he only wanted to talk to you. He had no idea Maxwell was trying to kill you."

"I have to admit I was surprised that Herman got involved in that. It's not his style." Claire hesitated. "How about the earlier attack on me at the parking garage? Was that connected?"

"We know it was a diversion so the prisoners could escape. Whether it was also a specific attempt on your life, we'll probably never know."

"Who ordered Vanessa's death?"

"A foreign partner. She had uncovered some info on their involvement in the slave trade—human trafficking—and when they learned of that, they got rid of her. Jackson probably told them about it."

"Was it the Mexican cartel?"

"Russian. Is revenge on your mind?"

Claire shook her head. "No." So the death-list notebook had nothing to do with it. The Russians got to her first. What a tangled web. "Who's the Russian?"

"Alexei Alekseev. He was picked up in one of the raids that went on while you were on vacation. He's dead. Assassinated in jail by a rival."

Harrison stroked Cleo's back. "So, what do you plan on doing after you're cleared to get back to work?" His eyes didn't waver, and she wished he could read minds so they wouldn't have to discuss it.

"I know I don't have camping in my plans." He grinned and she studied him as she contemplated what else to say to him.

"Harrison, you're a great partner, and I know you could teach me a lot..."

"But?" he said when she hesitated.

"But I don't want to be a detective in a police department. I want to continue my work with the Marshals Service."

Harrison spread his hands wide. "Can't say as I understand your choice. I left the Marshals myself. Burned out. But it's certainly your right to choose."

"The Marshals Service has a lot of heavy-duty criminal activity to fight against, all over the country, including in some police departments as we've just seen. I'd like to help make a dent in that."

Harrison lifted Cleo from his lap and set her on the arm of the couch, just where she would prefer. He knew a lot about her cats. He stood and so did Claire.

"If you ever change your mind," Harrison said, "don't forget Petima PD."

"I won't. Thanks again for picking me up." She offered her hand.

Harrison took it between both of his, shook it, and said almost wistfully, "That's what partners do."

Claire gave him a wide smile. "I'll remember that... and you."

I. Christie and Sara

About the Author

I Christie is a homegrown Southern California native. Her father's parents emigrated from the Azore Islands to Fall River, Massachusetts. Her mother was a WWII war bride from France. Her whole life, I Christie has been a reader, writer, gardener, artist, and athlete, excelling only in reading. During the course of writing a dissertation, her love of writing became an obsession. Once finished with graduate school, Christie devoted her energy to developing as a writer.

Christie lives in Long Beach, California, with Sara, a tall girl who is a golden lab/greyhound mix; Cleopatra, a white blue-green-eyed cat; and three calico sisters: Calie, Cagney, and Lacey. There are also the parakeets and finches that never cease to fascinate the three sisters.

Christie's favorite downtime activities are taking Sara for a run at the dog beach and playing catch with the three sisters. Cleo rules the house.

If you enjoyed this book, you'll be sure to enjoy I. Christies exciting science-fiction adventure, **MERKER'S OUTPOST**:

Merker's Outpost has a secret that spans galaxies. Below its hostile, barren red surface, a once-thriving research complex now lies seemingly deserted, watched over by an entity called Guardian.

Lieutenant Harriet Montran, a Collective Space Centurion officer, is betrayed by her shipmates and stranded on Merker's. She is rescued by Guardian, who enlists her aid to evict a group of smugglers who have set up base in one of the Outpost's underground cities.

Major Zohra, an undercover operative for the secret watchdogs of the galaxy, Naboth's Vine, is also on Merker's Outpost. She has infiltrated the smugglers with the intent of ending their illegal trafficking in sentient beings. Montran and Zohra join forces with Guardian to thwart the smugglers and protect Merker's Outpost. Soon, the bond that joined them when they were cadets flares anew.

Confronted by smugglers, renegade soldiers, programmed assassins, and betrayal within their own ranks, Montran and Zohra are caught in a desperate race to discover the planet's secret before it falls into the wrong hands. Can their feelings survive it? Can they?

And look for the exciting sequel to Merker's Outpost,

Available soon, only from

Check out these other exciting titles from Blue Feather Books: